For Jeff, always,
and for Troon Nicholas Harrison
and Heather J. A. Graham, with love

ACKNOWLEDGMENTS

My thanks go to Kristin Hannah,
for being the first to believe;
to William C. Hopkins, M.D., for his assistance
with the psychology of MSBP;
to Troon, Heather and Jenny Andersen, for
timely comments on short notice and unflagging
faith in me; to my parents, Dan and Carol,
for their love; and to Debbie aka Ms. Peaches,
Connie, Marti, Apples, Marge and Bernice of the
PMB, for their support and willingness to share.

SHELLEY BATES

GROUNDS TO BELIEVE

Steeple
Hill®

Published by Steeple Hill Books™

STEEPLE HILL BOOKS

Steeple
Hill®

ISBN 0-373-78512-7

GROUNDS TO BELIEVE

Visit us at www.steeplehill.com

Printed in U.S.A.

AUTHOR'S NOTE

Ever since I was a child, I've solved problems by writing them into a story. This book began as I was struggling with issues of faith: Who is God to me? How do I know whether I'm saved? If faith without works is dead, what's the point of grace? My struggles and discoveries became those of Julia, the woman at the center of this book. She has grown up in a toxic church, where worship is based on works, and the traditions of men take the place of doctrine and lead to judgment, not Jesus. The Elect of God, of course, are an entirely fictional group, as are all the characters and the town where they live. But Julia's struggles were mine, and as she found her way, I did, too. The research, the writing and then living the journey were not easy. But they were worth it. I love to hear from readers; visit me on the Web at www.shelleybates.com, or send me an e-mail at shelley@shelleybates.com.

Prologue

❧

1997

His daughter was in their hands.

Deputy Sheriff Ross Malcolm lay on a dusty hillside in central Washington State and watched the cluster of weathered buildings below. It had been a town once. The Apocalypse-focused Church of the Seventh Seal rented the few acres for cash from an absentee landlord. They'd thrown a wooden palisade around the unpainted houses, what looked like a barn or meeting hall, and half an acre of struggling vegetables.

Rocks and pieces of dead cactus dug into his belly and the worn thighs of his jeans. Ross put the binoculars down and slid his sunglasses back into place.

Kailey was only sixteen months old. With every fiber of his being, he wanted to get her away now, so she wouldn't remember these people and that...cult. He had papers in his jacket pocket to start the process, ready to serve on Anne as soon as he found her. Paperwork was all he'd been able to accomplish since Anne had walked out of the house with the baby, joined the "Sealers," and vanished. The last year was burned into his mind the way the sun was burning into his back now—focused and harsh and inescapable.

He needed a plan. Despite the heavenly promise of legions of angels fighting on their side, the Sealers were well- and illegally armed. According to the one source he'd been able to find, they had been stockpiling weapons in preparation for the end of the world since the seventies, but were too smart to do it overtly. In her last attempt to bend his beliefs to hers, Anne had told him one of the first signs of the end would be agents of the government breaking down people's doors and dragging the faithful away.

Well, his paycheck had the county seal on it, so his ex-girlfriend was right on that score. But this wasn't official business. Breaking down doors wouldn't get him what he wanted anyway. Slumped shoulders and tears in his eyes might. For Kailey, he'd try anything.

He left the pickup on the far side of the hill, out of sight of any watchers at the windows who waited for an attack that would never come. In the distance a rancher was taking off his early hay crop. The valley seemed so peaceful. Ross was the only note of desperate discord in it.

His boots scuffed the dusty surface of the road, the quarter mile stretching in front of him the way roads did in his dreams—where he walked and walked and got nowhere. The compound was silent when he reached the gate. A hot, dry breeze whistled down the long valley, and a trickle of sweat ran between his shoulder blades. Maybe he should have called for backup.

He couldn't. The local jurisdiction didn't have the man-power for a parental abduction case, and no experience in prosecuting one. This was personal. Besides, the Seal-ers were too unpredictable. They might see an ap-proaching car as the beginning of the government's attack. Look what happened at Waco, they would say, and lob a grenade over the wall.

There was no one posted at the gate, nor did anyone challenge him as he approached the first of the ram-shackle, weathered buildings. He had no doubt his movements were being carefully monitored, though. He knocked at the first door he came to, the dead sound telling him how thick the wood really was. Two minutes passed while he stood there perspiring in his T-shirt and leather jacket. He knocked again.

The door cracked open and a woman peered out, keep-ing the heavy panel between him and her body. "Yes?"

"My name is Ross Malcolm," he said, trying to look harmless and smaller than six foot three. "I'm—was—Anne DeLuca's partner. I'd like to see her, if that's possi-ble."

"What for?" the woman asked. She wore a faded cot-ton print dress, and her gray hair was pulled into a knob on top of her head. The strip of leg that showed in the crack of the door was bare and unshaven, the foot stuffed into a brown loafer that had seen too much time on that road up the hill.

Ross shrugged and spread his hands. "I haven't seen my little girl in a while. I'd just like to hold her. And visit with Annie for a few minutes."

The woman gave him a narrow glare, as if searching for a lie hidden in his words. "Outsiders aren't allowed in. I'll have to see," she said, and shut the door in his face.

Well, it was better than a grenade.

Ross looked around for somewhere to sit, but there was no comfort provided for visitors. He moved into the scant shadow of the wall as the sun slid over the shoulder of the house. Loose-limbed but alert, he leaned against the unpainted wood.

If he ever got to see Annie, it would take all his self-control not to shout recriminations at her for bringing Kailey into this. What kind of life was this for a child? There was no love for God here. From what his informant had said about the Sealers, they fostered an atmosphere of paranoia and suspicion, feeding their members the kind of ridiculous lies that only the truly brainwashed could believe. Kailey would know no stability in this environment, because the group moved every time its leader got spooked—part of the reason it had taken him so long to find them—and were so secretive they stuck to rural areas where outsiders wouldn't bother them.

Annie could stay if she wanted to. She made her own choices. But she couldn't make them for Kailey and him. Any love he might have felt for her once had been burned away in his quest to locate them over the last year. If he had to arrest his former girlfriend to get his little girl out of the Sealers' hands, he'd do it without so much as a quiver of regret for the couple they had been.

Only one good thing had come of the whole terrible experience. He had been driven back to God, grieving and desperate, and had seen that he couldn't manage the search for Kailey on his own. He needed strength from a source greater than himself, a source whose power he'd proven time and again.

He had to have faith that the loving giver of that strength wouldn't desert him now.

He shifted, and something glinted in the dust. He nudged the object with the toe of his boot.

With a quick glance around, he pulled a piece of scrap paper out of his pocket and picked up a shell casing with an odd diagonal dent in the middle. To his knowledge, only one type of gun did that to a shell on its way out of the barrel.

There were more. Two. Five. He brushed away a pile of dirt. A dozen. More, all with the distinctive dent. Someone had been standing right here and had fired an HK-93 semiautomatic rifle with an illegal thirty-round clip right off the front porch. And when he was done, instead of picking up his brass, he had just kicked dirt over it and walked away.

Ross fought to be objective, fought to keep his emotions calm as he thought about Kailey somewhere within range of such a lethal nutcase. He picked up a couple dozen casings and distributed them among his pockets, then resumed his relaxed stance against the wall.

The door cracked open a couple of minutes later, and he levered himself upright, his heart rate kicking into overdrive. Annie stepped out onto the porch, Kailey sound asleep on her shoulder.

Relief washed over him with such intensity his knees almost buckled. The long search was over. His daughter looked all right. She wore a sleeveless cotton shift that rode up over her little diapered behind, and her arms and legs seemed plump enough, so they must be feeding her. She'd also grown about a foot.

"What are you doing here, Ross? How did you find me?"

He looked at Anne for the first time. Like the woman who had answered the door, she was dressed in shapeless faded cotton, her hair scraped away from her face to satisfy somebody's aesthetic of submissive femininity. Her hands, clasped on Kailey's smooth baby skin, were roughened with outside work. Her sunburned nose had begun to peel.

He struggled to find in this stony woman the laughing, savvy blonde that he'd fallen for a month after he'd met her. What an idiot he'd been, with a very young man's naive ideas about female perfection. He knew better now. Since he'd allowed the spirit of God into his heart, he had a different slant on perfection.

"I've been looking for you both since you left," he replied, pasting on a smile, his stance loose and un-threatening. The last thing he wanted was to spook her. In a second she could disappear back through that door and unleash a squadron of the faithful to chase him off the property. "You used your credit card for the first time about a month ago, at a hospital around here. I talked to some people and narrowed it down from there."

"Kailey had an infection. Moses told me not to do it. I should have listened to him."

And if she hadn't, Kailey might be dead. He should be thankful for what was left of Anne's independent streak, even if it had led him to a place that made the hair on his neck prickle with uneasiness.

"I'm glad you didn't. Mind if I hold her?" His arms ached, his skin hungry for the comforting weight of his child against his chest.

"She's asleep," Annie said, frowning, and hitched the baby higher on her shoulder.

"I won't wake her. Please, Annie."

Her eyes narrowed as she considered him. Then, with a glance at the door and the safety behind it, she relented. Ross held out his arms and Anne put the baby into them.

Kailey murmured and he settled her against his chest, rubbing a slow, soothing hand over her back. The casings in his pocket gave a tiny clink, and he settled her more comfortably. With a sigh, the baby slid into deeper sleep. Every cell in his body focused on her, his whole being concentrated on this moment. Slowly, he cataloged the details that would sustain him. The fan of pale eyelashes against her cheek. The whorl of thick hair on the crown of her head. That baby smell that provoked immediate memories of bottle feedings late at night while Annie worked the graveyard shift at the hospital. Living the moment as intensely as he could, he willed the sweetness of it into his memory and the fear of losing her retreated. For the moment.

He had too few memories. Far too few for the sixteen months of his daughter's life. He lifted his head to meet Annie's gaze. "We need to talk."

She shrugged. "Here I am." No softness in her face indicated his emotion had touched her.

"Not here."

"It's as good as you're going to get. Outsiders aren't allowed in, and I'm certainly not going anywhere with you. Whatever you have to say, say it. I've got vegetables to weed."

He forced his arms to stay relaxed. If the tension in them woke Kailey it would just give Anne an excuse to take her away from him.

"I'd like to work out some kind of arrangement with you so I can see her."

She shook her head. "I don't see how. Unless you give up the Devil's government and join us. Allow God into your heart and learn to live for His return at the end of the world."

He hated it when she mouthed her doctrine at him. "I know you don't want to marry me and give her a conventional family. But I'm willing to overlook this last year and just go with occasional visits." If he thought she'd go for that one, he was wrong. "Come on, Annie, she's my daughter. I have a petition for custody with me. I won't allow her to grow up without knowing me."

"She'll grow up knowing her heavenly Father, which is far more important in the long run, Ross. Her relationship with Him is going to benefit her for eternity."

"But it isn't going to benefit *me*. I want to see my kid grow up. I want to be part of her life."

A mistake. He knew it instantly.

"You," she spat. "Always you. You want this, you want that. Well, for once you're going to have to accept what *I* want. And I want my daughter to grow up knowing God, in the safety of His house, away from the kind of influence that will only distract her from what's important. I don't recognize your papers or your rights. When Armageddon comes, Ross, what you want will be—quite frankly—irrelevant. What she'll have will save her."

He took a deep breath, controlling his welling frustration for Kailey's sake. "What about when she gets older? What about her education? I w— I'd like to be involved there. Even if it's only financially."

"She'll learn everything she needs here. Two of us were teachers before we came to God."

"But she—"

"Schools are the tool of an evil government, Ross. They'll rot her mind. Everything she needs to know, she'll learn here. With me and God's chosen Church."

"And that's final?" he asked. His arms trembled. His rage and fear were threatening to overcome his faith that God would give him the words to convince her. He had to try one more time. "Isn't there some kind of compromise we can work out?"

She held out her arms. "We can't compromise with the world and keep ourselves pure. Give her to me, Ross."

Involuntarily, his grip tightened, and Kailey woke. She pushed back and gaped at him. Her eyes widened, tears spurted into them, and she shrieked, her little hands pushing fearfully at his chest.

Anne snatched her away from him. "I told you. You're a total stranger to her. She stays with me, where she belongs." She wrenched the door open.

"I wouldn't *be* a stranger if you hadn't run off and— wait!" The door slammed, and he was alone in the shabby porch.

Heat shimmered around him as he ran back to the truck. Jamming it into gear, he roared into town, throwing up a plume of dust that spiraled thickly in the rearview mirror.

Lord, help me. Help me.

As he burst into the sheriff's office, Ross knew he looked like a crazed gunfighter, covered in dust and sweat, tears leaking out of the corners of his eyes.

"What happened to you?" Sheriff Cornoyer looked up from the blizzard of reports on his desk. "You get run over by a cattle drive?"

"It's not funny, Corny," he told the sheriff, who had been patient in helping a fellow officer with his quest. "I need a warrant."

Cornoyer gave him a searching look. "You have grounds to believe there's a crime somewhere in my jurisdiction?"

"My ex-girlfriend won't give me access to my daughter."

"She's a Sealer. I told you she wouldn't listen. But you had to go out there and prove it for yourself."

"Knock it off, Corny."

"Get real, Ross. You're supposedly on leave, and you're on my turf. Show me some evidence that will give me the Sealers and we'll talk."

"How about this?" Ross pulled the empty casings out of his pockets and rolled them onto Cornoyer's desk, where they scattered dirt all over his reports. "If those aren't from an HK with a thirty-round clip, you can send me home."

Corny sat back in his chair and considered. "I hope you take the detective's exam some day, son. Apply to that organized crime task force I hear they're putting together in Seattle. You're wasted on patrol. Okay. We'll go have a look around first thing tomorrow." He looked up. "But you need to calm down. Get some rest. You've been running on nerves alone since you got here."

Every instinct demanded that he pound on a judge's door and get the piece of paper that would allow him to search the compound until he found his child. But instinct had to give way to common sense. They'd go tomorrow, when his head was clear and he could think rationally instead of emotionally. And after he'd spent a good long time on his knees.

I've never been so afraid, Lord. Help me.

"Okay. I'll be here when shift changes," he said aloud.

"Good man. Don't worry, it'll all work out. With any luck, we can get 'em on a couple dozen weapons charges and seize the property."

But luck had run out. When he and Corny drove up to the compound the next day and prepared to demand entry, only the hot wind answered them. The door he'd knocked on yesterday stood partly open, swinging on rusty hinges. They ran inside, then searched the other houses and the barn in about twenty minutes, but came up with nothing more incriminating than some broken windows and another cache of bullet casings out by the field of vegetables.

The Church of the Seventh Seal had pulled up and moved out, and taken his daughter with them.

* * *

Six years later

Memorandum
Date: June 3, 2004
To: Sergeant Bruce Harmon
Organized Crime Task Force
From: Lt. Leslie Bellville
Hamilton Falls P.D.
Re: Cult
File Ref: HF04-193

Per my e-mail yesterday, attached please find Forms 17A and B outlining evidence of what is believed to be a religious cult known as the Elect of God operating in the Hamilton Falls area. We believe there is child abuse among members of this group, but are unable to investigate with uniform members due to its closed social structure.

We understand Investigator Ross Malcolm specializes in cults as part of his duties in the OCTF. We request his assistance for a period not to exceed three weeks, overtime and expenses to be charged to the Town of Hamilton Falls.

Please advise Investigator Malcolm's availability ASAP.

Chapter One

❦

Who shall lay any thing to the charge of God's elect?
It is God that justifieth.

—*Romans* 8:33

The pager beeped as Ross pulled off the freeway for gas.
He glanced at the number and frowned. What was the
matter with those guys? Couldn't they survive for two
days without yanking on his electronic leash for help?

He tilted the motorcycle onto its side stand at the deserted pump and pulled the pager off his belt. He frowned
at the number on the display and stalked over to the pay
phone next to the ice machine.

His partner picked up on the first ring. "Organized
Crime Task Force. Harper."

"This had better be good, pal." Ross leaned on the
dented metal of the bracket protecting the phone from
the weather.

"Oh, it is. How's the vacation?"

"Two days isn't a vacation. It's a weekend. I'm scheduled for five days leave, Ray. Five. You page me, you better be telling me my apartment building's burning down."

"Nope. Worse than that. They got a live one."

"Who?"

"Hamilton Falls. We just got a memo asking for your services. The lieutenant out there says their fink just blew the whistle. A near-miss this time—which adds up to two and a half kids total over the last couple of months. That's 'reasonable and probable grounds to believe,' in my book."

Ross stood silently, watching a flock of children spill out of the fast-food place next door. Shrieking, their giggles high-pitched, they tumbled into the play area.

One small town. Two deaths and a near-miss in four months.

"Ross?"

"I'm thinking."

"Think fast. Harmon knows I'm talking to you."

So much for his hard-earned five days. "Tell him I'll call him from Hamilton Falls."

"What about your vacation?"

"I guess scenic Interstate 90 was it. Look on the bright side. The woman of my dreams could be anywhere, even in Hamilton Falls."

Ray Harper snorted. "Just make sure she doesn't have kids."

Ross sipped a cup of coffee and considered the manila file folders on the blotter. The lieutenant who usually occupied this office was out at an accident scene. At the front counter, a uniformed patrolman just out of the academy took a complaint, while a telephone rang insistently at an empty desk in the bullpen. Outside the door of his borrowed office, a laser printer began to wheeze.

He had never been to Hamilton Falls before, but the familiar government-issue furniture, the beige linoleum, the numbering system on the files, and even the bad coffee combined to make him feel at home. He could have been in any law-enforcement office in the state.

Ross stretched as the caffeine hit his bloodstream. He ran his fingers through his thick brown mane. Hair. One of the perks of working on the Task Force.

He stacked the files and spread the contents of the first one on the blotter. He hated reading this stuff.

The autopsy report on the so-called SIDS baby, Andreas Wyslicki, lay on top of a transcript of a police interview with the pediatrician, Michael Archer. Ross started with the interview, reading slowly. His approach to such a witness was to absorb details not of medical procedure, but of personality, of speech patterns, of hints to the habits and preoccupations of the speaker. And Archer was definitely preoccupied.

Archer advises the baby arrived by ambulance approx. 18:40 March 12th. Parents reported that the baby alarm had gone off because he had stopped breathing. They had done CPR to no effect. Paramedics could not revive him, and he was pronounced DOA at the hospital.

Ross took another sip of tepid coffee.

Archer cannot account for victim's death. Has been victim's pediatrician since he was born two months ago. Archer requests he be allowed to view autopsy report when completed.

No doubt.

The station clerk's voice penetrated his concentration. "He's in Lieutenant Bellville's office, Harry."

A uniform leaned in the door. "Investigator Malcolm?"

Ross put his hands on both arms of the chair and levered himself to his feet. "Yes. You're Harry Everett?"

"The same. Glad you could join us."

"I'm not. I was two days into a five-day leave." The other man looked intimidated until Ross smiled. Then Everett smiled back.

"Sorry about that. But these kids...well, we needed the help."

"Yeah. I've been reading the reports. I'd like to get some background on your informant."

"No problem." He leaned out the door. "Jenny, would you bring me the fink file on Rita Ulstad?" Ross watched as the station clerk, a pretty blonde with a Meg Ryan haircut, sashayed out to the records room and returned carrying another manila folder. That short skirt did less for her than she probably imagined. "Thanks." Everett smiled absently and opened the file she handed him.

"Anything for *you*," Jenny crooned to Everett as she moved away, but her glance remained on Ross, sparkling with interest. Ross had no doubt about the message. He considered it briefly and rejected it. If there was a woman in his future, he hadn't met her yet. That was one thing he was happy to leave up to the Lord.

"So." Ross tilted back in the chair and laced his fingers behind his head. "What do you have in mind for strategy?"

Harry Everett handed him the file to give himself a moment. "I've heard about you," he said finally. "That you got broken in at Waco."

Ross frowned and moved restlessly. "You heard wrong," he said shortly. "That was long before my time."

"But you're a cult specialist, right? The only one the Task Force has. You did that bunch of Aryan wanna-bes in the hostage situation in Spokane, right?"

Ross fought against the memories that welled up out of the dark place inside him, a place he tried to keep scabbed over and undisturbed. His last sight of Annie and Kailey floated in his mind's eye for a moment, the way it did every time he busted into a run-down apartment or staked out a house, searching for evidence of the organized crime these little cults were so good at hiding. The kids were the worst. Big frightened eyes. Utter distrust. Just like Kailey, screaming at the sight of him.

Ross came back to the present with a jolt and struggled to remember what Harry Everett had been talking about. Oh, yeah. Spokane. "I was involved." He got the conversation back on track with an effort. "Tell me what you need."

Everett backed off and got to the point. "I think we need an undercover. I think you need to buddy up to one of the members and find out as much as you can. I'd suggest our informant, but she's lost their trust and doesn't interact with them anymore. There's got to be a reason for these deaths, but no one knows enough about the Elect to find out what it is. They could be into blood sacrifice, for all we know, and faking the accidents afterwards."

"What does your informant say?"

"She says they're not like that. But there's two and a half dead kids. That's evidence of something weird, in my opinion."

"Two of them were natural, weren't they?"

"You have to ask yourself. Look at the last one. A pillow and some steady pressure wouldn't be very natural."

"But to what purpose? If you're going to make a blood sacrifice, why do it that way, with no ceremonial?"

Harry shrugged. "Who knows how they think?"

"Okay. So where do I find these people?"

"Easy. Pick the most upstanding citizens in Hamilton Falls and you'll find one. The principal of the high school. A fireman. A bookshop owner." He nudged the informant's file and it slid off the stack. "We'll arrange a conference for you and our fink can give you the details."

Ross pulled his notebook out from under the folders and began jotting down notes. "All these upstanding citizens belong to a cult? Usually cult members isolate themselves, don't mix."

"They don't. You can't get them to socialize at all. They won't even let their kids play sports."

"Then why are they so successful in Hamilton Falls? Do they have something on the mayor or what?"

"That wouldn't be hard," Harry scoffed. "I didn't vote for the guy. But these people are honest, even if they're trusting to the point that it's easy to rip them off. They don't believe in lawsuits or stereos or anything."

"And this makes them a cult?"

"You tell me. You're the expert."

"I will, when I know more. So who else belongs?"

"You'll love this. The doctor on all these cases."

Ross's eyebrows lifted with interest. "Yeah? The pediatrician?"

"Couldn't find a thing on him. But maybe you can—from the inside."

Sounded like the logical place to start. "Tell me about the most recent family." Ross turned a page of his notebook.

"The Blanchard kid is the son of the high-school principal. You should see the wife. What a doll. The sister's not bad, either, if you like the wholesome type."

Ross set his teeth and ignored the bait. "How did they come to your attention?"

Everett jerked his chin at the folder. "Ulstad. She's a nurse at the hospital, and to hear her tell it, these people are knocking off their kids one by one. She used to belong and got kicked out. You've got to take her with a grain of salt because she's got a massive hate on for these people, but her information is worth looking into. Especially with the Blanchard kid. He was the near-miss."

"How soon can I talk to her?"

"I'll try to get it set up for this afternoon. After that, you're on your own as far as finding a way in. Although I have a few suggestions."

He gave Everett a long look. "Like what?"

"The sister I just mentioned."

"What about her?"

"She's single."

It took a second to sink in. "Are you suggesting I pursue one of the women?" For the first time in his career, he wondered if his obsession was going to take him where he wasn't willing to go. An angry, uneasy heaviness began to swirl in his stomach as his body recoiled at the thought.

"There's worse ways to earn a living. Let's see what we can get on her." Harry leaned out the door a second time. "Hey, Kurtz! C'mon back in here, would you?"

Jenny Kurtz smiled as she did so, perching on the edge of the desk to be sure that Ross got a good view of her legs. "What's up?" she asked.

"You've lived here all your life, right?" Harry said. "You know the folks in town pretty well."

"Sure. What do you need to know?"

"Do you know the Blanchards?"

Jenny shrugged. "Madeleine was a couple of years ahead of me in high school. I don't know her husband. But I graduated with her sister Julia."

"What can you tell us about her?"

"That stick-in-the-mud?" Jenny looked amused. "What do you want to know about her for?"

"Because she's connected to this case Investigator Malcolm's here for. Tell us about her."

"I don't see her much anymore, thank goodness." Jenny giggled with a sudden memory. "She was such a Goody Two-shoes in high school. Some of the boys thought it would be funny to write her phone number up on the bathroom wall—you know, 'for a good time, call...' A couple of the crazy ones actually did it. She wouldn't know what to do with a guy if she had one. She probably tried to save their souls."

Ross eyed her with distaste. There was nothing quite like the cruelty of the "in" crowd to the outsider, all the more amazing when he reflected that high school for Jenny had been a good many years ago. Some people matured. Some just stayed stuck at seventeen forever. "How do you think she felt about it?" he asked in spite of himself.

She shrugged. "Who knows?" And who cared, from the tone of her voice.

"Do you know where she lives?" Harry asked, bringing them back to the matter at hand.

"No, but she works at that bookshop downtown. Quill and Quinn. I never go in there. They don't stock anything good."

"What about her religion?" Ross asked. "Know anything about that?"

"Only enough to know it gives me the creeps," she said, making a face. "Nothing but black to their ankles and high-maintenance hair. I went once, for a joke, when they had some kind of meeting at the hall downtown, but—"

"Where's the hall?" Ross interrupted.

"Fourth and Birch, right next to the post office. It's easy to miss, though. No signs, no cross, no nothing. Boring."

"Thanks."

Harry glanced at him and took his cue. "Thanks for your help, Jenny. Shut the door on the way out, would you?"

She slid off the desk. At the door she looked over her shoulder. "Anything else you want to know about old Julia McNeill, you give me a call." With a toss of her hair, she swiveled around the door and closed it behind her.

"We need to talk about my cover story," Ross said. "You dragged me in here with the clothes on my back. I've got a good pair of jeans and a shirt outside on the bike. At the moment I'm not very convincing convert material."

"I don't know. I don't think they're too fussy."

"I don't want to take the chance. I need an image, and I need a good reason to join."

"Why do people usually get religion?" Harry waved his hand. "They get in a car accident, they lose a loved one. Take your pick. Have a revelation on me."

They lose a loved one. He'd gotten a revelation over that, all right. The law made a great weapon, even if he sometimes felt he was fighting alone, spurred on by his fear and his memories. He'd find Kailey some day. One assignment at a time. One prayer at a time.

First, the persona—a grieving husband escaping his loss. Talk to the informant. Then, track down Miss Goody Two-shoes.

Chapter Two

✤

The woman had called herself Miriam for so many years that she'd pretty much forgotten her real name. The only entity her real name mattered to was the government, and she didn't have anything to do with them.

Or hadn't, anyway. Until now.

She looked at the child sleeping on the orange plastic bench at the bus depot and sighed. She'd signed up to do the right thing, so she had to go through with it. Moses had told her where they were going after they'd buried Annie, and she'd just have to meet them there when she was done.

Minus the child.

She picked up the pay phone's receiver and dialed Information.

"What listing, please?"

"The sheriff. And could you put me through to the number?"

"That will be a dollar twenty-five, please."

Miriam put the quarters in the phone, and the number rang through.

"Inish County Sheriff's Department."

"I'm looking for a deputy named Ross Malcolm. Could you transfer me, please?" The formal language, the politeness, felt stilted on her tongue.

The woman rang her through, and Miriam dared to feel a little hope threaded through the mass of her built-up distrust and fear.

"Human Resources."

"I'm looking for a deputy named Ross Malcolm who works there."

A clicking sound rattled in the background. "The only person by that name who's worked here since I've been here transferred up to Seattle several years ago."

The flicker of hope died. Seattle was on the other side of the state. At the ends of the earth.

"Did he go to a sheriff's department there?" she asked faintly.

"Nope. Seattle P.D. Anything else I can help you with?"

"No." Dispensing with politeness, Miriam hung up the pay phone a little harder than she had to.

Seattle. Talk about finding a needle in a haystack. It would be less trouble to take the girl back with her. She was small, but even the little ones paid their way. She might make a good shill. God knew those eyes had made Miriam herself act completely out of character.

Had forced her to make a promise she no longer wanted to keep.

Rita Ulstad had agreed to meet Ross near a drooping Japanese maple on the hospital grounds. In front of them was the parking lot, scattered with cars. Ross turned as the petite nurse slid onto the bench beside him.

"Ms. Ulstad?"

Her face was so immaculately made up she could have passed for thirty. Fashionably mussed, her hair was tinted taffy-blond. "Call me Rita." She looked him up and down. "You're Ross Malcolm? The cop?"

He crossed his denim-clad legs, and his heavy riding boots sank into the lawn. "A lot of my work takes me undercover."

"Wow. I guess I've never met anyone in plainclothes before."

"I clean up when I have to." He smiled at her. "Harry Everett says you can tell me about Ryan Blanchard."

"Whatever you need to know. I'm past the point of professional discretion here. All I want is to see justice done and those people exposed for who they are."

"Okay...who are 'those people'?"

"The Blanchards? Or the Elect in general?"

"Start with the big picture and work in. What's your history with this group? What are they called—the Elect?"

"As in 'Who shall lay any thing to the charge of God's elect.' I don't know how much you know about the Bible, but they use that verse as a recipe for justifying just about anything, let me tell you. Anyway, to get back to your question, I grew up in it. Spent thirty years in Gathering, three to four times a week. It's mind control, plain and simple." The waving leaves of the Japanese maple flicked shadows across the baby-fine wrinkles in her skin. "They're a cult. They tossed me out because I fell in love with someone they thought was unsuitable. It was that or give him up and spend the rest of my life in my correct but miserable marriage. There is no freedom of choice in the Elect, Ross. No second chances. You follow the rules or lose everything."

"What do you mean by everything?"

"Friends, family, community support, everything that's important."

"Did they abuse you?"

She gave him a look hardened by resentment into implacability. "The worst kind of abuse is to deny another person their freedom."

Ross thought about that for a moment, about the haunted eyes of all those little kids. The real root of all evil. "How well do you know the Blanchards?"

"Ryan's dad, Owen, is an Elder so he's well educated in mind control. The famous Blanchard charm is just a front. The whole town thinks Jesus has already come back, and is alive and well at Hamilton High." Bitterness crackled in her tone.

"He's the principal there, isn't he?"

"Yes."

"Don't the Outsider parents have a problem with that?"

"Oh, I'm not saying he's a bad administrator. He's too smart to bring his beliefs to work in an obvious way. But he's not the one I came to talk to you about. His son is."

"What about him?"

"That child is four years old. He's been admitted no fewer than twenty-five times. Had three major surgeries. Doesn't that strike you as odd?"

"It strikes me as hard on him and his family." Ross tried to imagine sitting in a hospital waiting room twenty-five times, wondering over and over if your child would survive. A chill ran over his skin. The maple leaves rustled behind him. "What's the matter with him?"

"That's the problem. Nothing conclusive. He has seizures where he chucks up everything in his stomach. Sometimes he's lethargic and unresponsive afterwards, sometimes not. There's no rhyme or reason to it. We've thought it was some kind of massive gastric infection, but it can't be pinned down with tests. Whatever he's got, it won't be diagnosed." She paused for breath, and the angry color faded from her cheeks. "And now here he is again, back on the ward. Something isn't right. I've tried to talk to Michael Archer but he's one of them. His loyalty is to Blanchard and no one else. I took it to the head of my department here and got the door closed in my face. As soon as you bring religion in, no one will touch it. They think I'm nuts and Archer is in the right. So now I'm taking it to you."

The hospital brass thought Rita Ulstad's concerns were nothing but sour grapes and a desire for attention. Well, Harry had warned him. Her attitude toward the Elect colored her information—maybe even twisted it. Where did that leave his investigation? Or the well-being of the little kid?

A group of people emerged from the cafeteria door and walked toward the parking lot.

"Oh, no." Rita Ulstad swung to face him, bracing an elbow on the back of the bench to put a hand to her face as a shield. "It's them. The Blanchards, visiting the boy. They're going to walk right behind us. Don't let them see my face."

All he needed was for the targets to see him with someone they didn't trust. He should have anticipated that they'd be visiting the kid and insisted on a meeting away from the hospital. Ross slid over and put an arm along the back of the bench, bending close to give the appearance of a tête-à-tête. He peered cautiously over Rita's shoulder.

Two young women bracketed a tall blond man. An older couple, the woman as well-upholstered as a pouter pigeon and the man so conservatively dressed he practically disappeared, followed them. The redhead on the blond man's left was likely the mother. She was crying, holding a tissue to her face with both hands. All of the women were dressed in unrelieved black, right down to their stockings and shoes, as though they had just come from a funeral. The men's shirts, at least, were white, but their ties were black, and devoid of anything so frivolous as a pattern.

"Julia, not so loud," the pigeon said, tapping the redhead on the shoulder with two stiffly curled fingers. "Showing so much emotion in public is like saying you don't accept God's will. Look at Madeleine. Her resignation shows a lovely spirit."

"Resignation, my foot," Rita hissed in his ear, her lips brushing his skin. "She doesn't deserve those kids."

"The brunette is the mother?" he whispered. "Not the redhead?"

"Yes. And the harpy is Elizabeth McNeill, their mother. Isn't she a terror?" Ross and his informant watched the family climb into separate four-door sedans and pull out onto the street. "All that rot about not showing emotion in public." Rita sounded disgusted. "It's unnatural."

"I don't get it," Ross admitted. "Crying over a sick kid is reasonable."

"That's because you're a rational man. It shows you how twisted their thinking is. To show her acceptance of God's will in putting her kid in the hospital, Madeleine never drops a tear. That's our Madeleine. Always the perfect example of godliness in public. Who knows what she's like in private? If I had to live with someone that perfect, I'd choke. Poor Julia."

"The sister?" The one Harry Everett wanted him to cultivate?

"Yes. She hasn't got much of a life. Imagine having Madeleine thrown in your face every time you didn't measure up."

"She's having a little trouble accepting God's will."

"She's the most human of the whole bunch. I used to like Julia, even though she never has a word to say for herself. The self-confidence of a rabbit and no wonder."

Would she make a good informant? Ross asked himself. Did she have the spine to talk to an Outsider, or would she scurry for cover before he could convince her he meant no harm? More important, would she make a good advocate for him with the church?

There was only one way to find out. He thanked Rita for her time and swung himself onto the bike.

On an assignment like this a guy needed a book to read. And if Jenny the clerk was right, he knew just where to look for one.

Miriam gritted her teeth and tried to remember Moses' sermons on patience. But waiting patiently for the end of the world was a whole different kettle of fish than trying to deal patiently with the minions of bureaucracy.

On the whole, she was better equipped for Armageddon.

"I'm sorry, ma'am, but we can't give out that information," the very young woman who answered the phone for Seattle P.D. said for the second time.

"Please. I'm his aunt. I've been out of the country for years and I'm trying to make contact with my nieces and nephews. Now, the sheriff's department in Inish County had no problem telling me he'd signed on with you folks. Don't you think Ross would want to know his aunt is looking for him?"

"I don't doubt that at all, ma'am. But I still can't give out information about present or former members of this department."

"Former? You mean he isn't with Seattle P.D. after all? Why, those girls in Inish County, they've made me waste all this money in long-distance charges for nothing."

"Ma'am, I didn't mean—"

Miriam gave a theatrical sigh. "I guess I'm just going to have to reconcile my differences with that boy's mama. Much as I hate to do it, since she was the one who started it all, but if it means not being able to see my favorite nephew after all these years in Africa, why..."

The girl on the other end of the phone was beginning to get flustered. "I'm sorry to be so much trouble, ma'am. It's just that the OCTF...well, we try to help them keep a low profile, if you know what I mean."

Who or what was the OCTF? "Oh, I do indeed, young lady. Well, thank you for your time. I'm going to call my sister and give her the shock of her life. Goodbye."

Miriam hung up the phone with a mixture of anger and glee. So the child's father had moved on from the police department, too. What kind of a fly-by-night was he, anyway?

Now she had to find out what in the world's end the OCTF was.

Chapter Three

❧

Julia McNeill crouched in the display window of the bookshop, draping blue muslin to form an artistic backdrop for a collection of children's books—a display designed to catch the eye of a tired parent with a car full of antsy children.

She heard the throaty rumble of a big motorcycle coming down Main Street, and glanced out in time to see the biker ride past—the one who had been cuddling in such a disgraceful way with the nurse on the hospital lawn. Dark hair was almost completely covered by a helmet shaped like a chamber pot. His hands gripped brake and clutch with careless control, his boots riding at an insolent angle on the foot pegs. Everything about him shouted testosterone. The set of those broad shoulders and long legs proclaimed that he couldn't care less what people thought of him.

Unlike herself. What people thought shaped her behavior, her choice of words, sometimes even her own thoughts. When you were one of the God's own Elect, you had to be responsible for your example every minute of the day. You never knew who might be watching— and be saved because of it.

"Where are the police when you need them?" she complained, looking over her shoulder into the interior of the shop. Rebecca was checking inventory in her big ledger behind the till. Quill and Quinn was no dusty hole-in-the-wall bookshop. Bars of sunlight from the skylights picked out the creamy paint, and the green trim accented the living green of ficus trees and fat, healthy plants on every flat surface not piled with books.

"What's that, dear?" Rebecca frowned at the ledger.

Julia's admiration for her boss ran deep. Rebecca was a wizard at math, her pencil flying down the columns of figures. There was no doubt she could have taken a degree and been a teacher. But showing off her brains was neither womanly nor humble. Instead, Rebecca's talent had found its outlet in taking over the bookshop after her brother Lawrence passed away, rest his soul. It was a good thing the Shepherds had decided computers were the tools of the Devil, along with radio and television. If she had a machine to do her figures for her, her talent would probably atrophy. God certainly knew best.

"It's that biker," Julia said. "I don't know why they don't arrest him for belonging to a gang. I saw him when I was at the hospital. It makes you wonder if Hamilton Falls is safe anymore."

Rebecca looked up. "Maybe he was visiting someone," she replied gently. "Even bikers have families." She made a note in one of the columns. "Look at this, will you? They've shorted me again, by six copies. You'd think a distributor as big as they are could get an order right. If you're done with that window, dear, you might try and make some sense of the back room. Aurelia Mills had her coffee group in here yesterday and the place is a shambles."

Julia finished up her window display and stepped out the front door to have a look at it from the sidewalk. The cheerful, eye-catching covers of the books contrasted well with the blue backdrop. A few more copies on the right side to balance the whole thing, and she'd defy any passing parent not to break stride and have a look.

Main Street had been created to convince the traveler to stop driving and spend some money, and it looked its best in summer. White tables with umbrellas were scattered outside the door of the ice-cream shop next door, and across the street at the coffee bar, where Aurelia Mills's women's group got their lattes every Thursday, people lounged on benches and strolled past slowly. The air smelled of the petunias and moss in the baskets hanging from the lampposts above Julia's head.

She gave a halfhearted wave to Dinah Traynell, who was across the street looking at some dresses hanging outside on a rack, although why she bothered was beyond Julia. Everyone knew Dinah made her own clothes because store-bought things weren't good enough.

The poor girl. Despite the fact that she was from a family as high-ranking as the McNeills themselves, she was so standoffish she hadn't a hope of attracting a husband.

"Hey, there," a voice said behind her. "What are you up to?"

Julia turned and stretched her mouth wide in a smile. Speaking of husbands...Derrick Wilkinson smiled back. Looking neat and dependable in his white dress shirt, black trousers, and sober tie, he joined her in front of the window.

"I just finished a display." She bumped shoulders with him in a companionable way. They might be a proposal away from getting engaged, but still, PDAs—public displays of affection—were out of the question. Julia rolled her neck, enjoying the warm weight of the sun. It seemed as though she hadn't seen it in weeks. "I feel horrible for enjoying the sunshine," she confessed. "Madeleine and Owen have been with Ryan from dawn till dark."

"I'm sure you do your part, too," Derrick said loyally.

"The Elect are wonderful. There's a constant stream of casseroles on the front porch, and people must be cleaning out the fruit stands on their behalf. Everyone is looking after them, but still...Michael says it will be some time before Ryan can come home."

"No wonder I haven't seen you lately."

Another prickle of guilt crept through her. Derrick was everything an Elect girl could want in a man. He was nice-looking, employed, responsible and drove a car that was neither too small to take elderly people to Gathering nor so big that it would be considered flashy. He was fifth-generation Elect. He was perfect husband material, and everyone in the congregation, including Derrick himself, expected that the next time he proposed, she would say "yes." Their future would be secure—and because she was the daughter of an Elder, Derrick would be named Deacon automatically. He would be given spiritual responsibility and social privilege second only to Owen's and her father's, who themselves were one step down from Melchizedek, the Shepherd of their souls and the final authority in the district.

Derrick's shoulder bumped hers again and she realized she hadn't replied to his gentle hint. "I'm sorry," she apologized. "I'll call you, okay?"

"No hurry. You know where to find me. I've got to get back to work." Dinah was still watching them from the store window, no doubt making sure they didn't misbehave on the sidewalk. He gave her a cheery wave as he walked back up the street to the lawyer's office where he worked.

Julia watched him go. So why hadn't she said "yes" the last time? His proposals were starting to become a family joke. There was no reason to hesitate, and yet when he did something as innocent and expected as sitting with her family in Gathering, she got annoyed and put him off again. Was it that she wasn't quite ready to give up her freedom for a life that focused on home and children? Every girl wanted that. She certainly didn't want to end up like Dinah, pushing thirty and haunting the edges of everyone else's lives.

But she still didn't want to say yes. Not yet.

With a sigh, Julia turned and went back inside to deal with the used books. Her mother said she was stubborn and unwilling, and she was probably right.

Rebecca kept a large selection in the back room. She hadn't been kidding about the coffee club's depredations. Children's stories were shoved on top of literature with callous disregard for Julia's careful, genre-specific filing system. Someone had made off with a Jane Austen that had come in last week. Rats. Julia had been hoping to read it during slow midafternoons. She had to remember her example even in her choice of reading material— she'd heard once that a Shepherd in a neighboring district had pulled a sexy romance out of one of the Elect's bookshelves and had spent the whole summer preaching about the dreadful things the lady of the house had allowed into her home and her mind—and by extension, into the Kingdom of God. After that, Julia had knelt by her bed and put the desire to read romances on the altar of sacrifice. She didn't want Melchizedek preaching about *her.*

She pulled over one of the straight-backed wooden chairs that Rebecca kept for the benefit of customers—a surface to sit on, but not comfortable enough to read a whole book—and began stacking the misfiled books on it. Inconsiderate New Age hippies, she thought. Swirling through here in their scarves and India cottons, talking about freeing their inner woman and doing nothing but making extra work for other people.

Rebecca stocked only literature, wholesome contemporary fiction, and lots of nonfiction, as well as the used books that the coffee club loved. She put her foot down at romances, murder mysteries or books about worldly religions. The Shepherds might raise an eyebrow over a woman in such a public career, but Rebecca had been the instrument of salvation to so many people that the Shepherd had to admit that perhaps God used the bookstore as part of His mysterious plan. Her benevolent influence was probably the only reason Julia had been allowed to work here instead of at something more womanly, such as Linda Bell's day care.

Julia sometimes wondered if God would ever get around to using her. Here she was, sister to the Elder's wife, daughter of an Elder and practically engaged to the next Deacon, and no matter how hard she tried to keep her example shining, no one had ever come to God through her. What kind of a Deacon's wife would she make?

Without actually taking the plunge and marrying Derrick, she had no way to know. Books, products of the world though they might be, were easier to deal with all the way around, she thought ruefully, and that in itself smacked of sin. She had reached the lower shelves containing the classics and was down on her knees when she became aware she was no longer alone. A customer stood in the doorway. Gathering the books that lay on the floor, she looked up with a "can I help you?" smile.

The biker smiled back.

Julia's heart gave a panicked kick and she froze, clutching the paperbacks to her chest as though they would protect her. She had a sudden vision of herself and Rebecca being attacked by this Hell's Angel. Things like that happened in the world all the time.

The blood drained out of Julia's face and she scrambled to her feet. The spines of someone's unwanted books dug into her back.

He wore a black leather jacket with the finish rubbed off one shoulder, as if it had scraped over the road. Faded jeans hugged long legs, and the toes of his boots were coated in dust. His hair was mussed and tamped down from the black helmet he held under his arm. A reddish brown lock fell over his right eyebrow. Pale gray eyes regarded her steadily—a killer's eyes, ruthless and devoid of emotion.

His lips parted, and Julia tensed, her eyes going wide with fear.

"Sorry if I startled you," the biker said in a soft bass voice that penetrated the roaring in her ears. "The owner said you'd be able to help me."

"The owner?" Julia whispered. The one who could be lying unconscious in the other room at this very moment?

"I told him you'd know where it was, Julia," Rebecca called from the front. "It's that young man you saw a moment ago."

Rebecca wasn't unconscious. She was alive and well, and so, for the moment, was Julia. "Where what was?" she asked. Her mouth was dry.

"Are you all right?" the biker queried, looking at her strangely. "You look a little green."

She took a deep breath. He wanted a book. That was all.

"I'm fine," she said. Her arms relaxed around the stack of books and began to tremble. Gently, she placed the pile on the chair and gripped her hands to hide their shaking. "Sorry. What is it you're looking for?" She tried to arrange her face in a polite, businesslike expression.

"Do you have anything by Donne?"

"Dunne. As in Dominick? I'm afraid we—"

"No. Donne. As in John."

John Donne? This filthy biker had come in here looking for *poetry?* Julia wished she hadn't put the books on the chair. She needed to sit down.

He was still standing there, waiting for an answer. "I th-think we have a used copy of the complete works," she stammered finally. "If it's still here, it would be under Poetry and Essays."

She got her feet moving and brushed past him. He was taller than either Owen or Derrick, although the boots were probably good for an inch of it. He was also big. Julia was used to standing next to people like Madeleine and her best friend, Claire, and feeling like a haystack. Now she felt small and feminine and vulnerable. It must be the jacket. It added to his bulk and made him threatening.

Poetry and Essays comprised half a shelf. "He's not very fashionable these days," Julia offered hesitantly, pulling Donne out of his place next to Boswell and a beat-up college edition of *The Norton Anthology.* "Here."

He leafed through the compact volume, holding it reverently. His hands were clean, she noted. Nicely shaped. Long, supple fingers turned the pages. The cuffs of his jacket pulled back briefly, revealing a dusting of dark hair on the backs of his wrists. "Maybe not. But he lost his wife, too," he said softly, almost absently.

Julia smiled weakly in the direction of his collar in lieu of a reply, and withdrew to the other side of the room. He stood quietly, stopping to read a page here and there, as she collected the abandoned books and began to shelve them.

"So where did you see me?" he asked, disturbing the silence. Her hands were still shaking, and she fumbled. A paperback fell to the floor with a slap.

"You—you just drove past, didn't you?"

"I did. Anywhere else?"

"At the hospital," she said reluctantly. She must be crazy, making small talk with a biker. Drat Rebecca anyway, for giving him the opportunity.

"Oh yeah? Were you visiting a friend?"

How nosy and callous could he get? But he was still a customer. Ingrained politeness and years of strictures against causing offense overcame her distaste. "My nephew." Maybe if she kept it brief he'd drop it. Ryan's life was far too important for small talk.

"I'm sorry," he said in a tone that was both soft and compelling. His boots made hollow thuds on the oak planks of the floor.

She concentrated fiercely on fitting the books precisely in their places, her back to him. When he spoke again, his voice came from directly above her. Instinctively, she tensed.

"I hope he'll be all right."

She didn't want to accept anything from him, polite hopes included. Now he was so close she could smell dust and sun-baked cotton. She stood up and moved away, putting the chair between them. "Are you looking for anything else this afternoon?" she asked in her most impersonal sales voice.

He cocked an eyebrow at her, and one corner of his mouth quirked up in a half grin. A dimple dented his left cheek. *How about you?* She heard the unspoken words as clearly as if he'd said them.

Her skin prickled with discomfort, and the walls of the back room suddenly seemed too close together, squeezing the air out. Women of the Elect did not strike up casual conversations with worldly men, and certainly not men like this. By seventh grade she'd learned that talking to worldly boys at school only brought shame and ridicule. Being the sister of Madeleine McNeill Blanchard had made her shy and diffident anyway, uncertain of what others expected of her in comparison with her dazzling sibling. Julia had become used to losing even a godly man's attention the minute Madeleine walked into the room.

But Madeleine was at the hospital, hovering over her son, and this man's attention was total. His eyes held hers with a magnetic intensity that narrowed her consciousness to an intimate circle that contained only him.

The street door bumped closed and, startled, she broke eye contact. "Miss Quinn can ring you up out front," she said breathlessly, and bolted into the sun-bright, welcoming safety of the front of the shop.

She made sure she was nowhere within speaking distance as Rebecca slid Donne into a green paper bag. She was well within hearing range, however, blocked from the biker's view by the shelves.

"'Never send to know for whom the bell tolls,'" quoted Rebecca whimsically. She had years of practice in small talk with customers, walking the fine line between keeping her business successful and keeping herself separate.

The Shepherds were firm about where that line was, and Julia was thankful for it. Beauty and safety lay inside the line. Chaos and sin prowled outside it.

"'It tolls for thee,'" the biker responded. "Beautiful words. He wrote a lot of them."

"That he did," Rebecca agreed, handing him the parcel. "And some straightforward ones. 'Hold your tongue, and let me love.' One of my favorites." Rebecca gracefully omitted the first words of the sonnet to avoid taking the Lord's name in vain.

The biker didn't seem to notice. "Your assistant's pretty good at holding her tongue," he said, neatly changing the subject and freezing Julia where she stood. "Not much on small talk."

"Julia? Oh, I've never noticed *that*. But you need to understand, her family is under a lot of strain at the moment."

Rebecca, for heaven's sake. Stop giving out personal details. Julia stepped out from behind the shelving. "Miss Quinn, could you give me a hand in the back when it's convenient?" she asked.

"Certainly, dear. I'll be right there. Have a pleasant afternoon," she said to the biker with a smile.

"Same to you," he answered, the dimple appearing in his cheek. To hurry Rebecca along, Julia strode back to the used books, her sensible shoes unnecessarily loud on the wood floor. "And to you as well, Julia," he added loudly as he pushed open the door.

Chapter Four

❧

By nine o'clock, the day had softened into the lavender-edged twilight of a northern summer. Julia closed the front door of the bookshop and paused to turn the key in the lock. She liked working Friday evenings after Rebecca went home. The tourists were in a holiday mood, and the warm, welcoming light of the bookshop and its open door often tempted restaurant goers in after dinner. People killed time there while waiting for the movie to start down the street. Sometimes the young people of the Elect dropped in to gossip about one another, and once in a great while one of them even bought a book. The only time late shift bothered her was when there was a young people's meeting or a hymn sing scheduled on a Friday night. Often she could talk Rebecca into calling on Jeremy Black, their part-time help, but sometimes she would just have to miss out and arrive late, after the singing was over and the hungry crowd had demolished most of the food.

The air currents moving down off the mountains cooled her skin after the warmth inside. The modestly long skirt of her dress—black, to signify the death of one's wicked human nature—brushed her calves as she walked toward the lot where she'd left her car. Black stockings covered her legs, a symbol of a godly woman's sacrifice of her vanity on the altar of obedience.

God's peaceful spirit might lie in the quiet of the evening as she passed under the striped awning of the ice-cream shop, but Julia's mind was full of worry and noise.

Ryan had been in her thoughts all day. Ryan and that biker. No, she thought hastily, just Ryan, lying weak and inert in the sterile hospital bed, his sock monkey the only spot of color beside him. It was no wonder she'd left the hospital crying on Wednesday. She'd dashed into the tiny waiting room a few steps down from the nurses' station, after an urgent call had summoned her away from work.

She'd found her parents and Owen waiting anxiously on the uncomfortable vinyl couches. They weren't the only ones keeping vigil for their loved ones. Madeleine had been sitting beside a young woman, her arm around the woman's shoulder, saying something soft and low to her.

Owen got up and touched Julia on the wrist. "You made record time," he said.

"I was scared. The message was that Ryan was in surgery. What happened? Who's that?" Julia asked him, indicating Madeleine and the stranger with a lift of her chin. "What's going on?"

"Her strength amazes me," Owen said, looking at his wife. "There's nothing any of us can do right now for Ryan while he's in the operating room, but instead of going to pieces, what does she do? She heard that woman's little boy was admitted with a growth on his

neck, and she's over there giving her crisis counseling."
Owen's face was illuminated with love for Madeleine,
rising like a warm tide behind his grief and apprehension.

"Do we know anything?" Julia whispered, her voice
colorless. "What happened to Ryan?" If only she could
do something besides stand here asking useless questions!

Owen sat, pulling Julia down next to him. "He had a
relapse. Lina went to get a cup of coffee and the nurse
called her back. He was passing blood."

"What did they do? What—?" The fear was like a
smothering blanket, cutting off her ability to put a co-
herent sentence together. "Is he—?"

"We knew they would have to operate eventually to
find out what's going on." Owen's gaze was locked on
his wife, as if he could draw strength from her the way
the young mother did. "But they're doing it right now instead of waiting. The poor little guy. I'm never going to
forget his scared little face as long as I live."

Madeleine gave the woman across the room a hug and
came over to her husband. Julia expected fear, the traces
of tears on her face, but she was wrong. Madeleine was
never so beautiful as she was in a crisis.

"The poor thing is deathly afraid of hospitals," she said
softly, winding her husband's fingers in her own. "She
can't be there for her son until she gets past that. I hope
I helped a little."

"If experience is the best teacher, she couldn't have a
better one," Owen replied, touching her cheek. "But what
about you?"

"I'm all right. I just wish we knew something. I'm
tempted to go find that sweet R.N. and get her to tell me
if they found what caused the bleeding in his G.I. tract."

Elizabeth squeezed her. "Now, now, dear. Have faith
that he'll be all right. God knows best."

Some time later the swinging doors leading to the operating rooms had opened wide enough to let Michael Archer through. His scrubs were wrinkled and stained. Owen straightened, alert as an animal scenting danger, and dislodged Madeleine, who was dozing, exhausted, on his shoulder. She murmured, and as her husband's alarm communicated itself to her, came fully awake.

"Michael!" Madeleine whispered. She got up and took a step toward him. Her shoe caught in the edge of the pastel carpet and she stumbled. Owen reached for her, but she pushed his arms away as though they were branches blocking her path. "Michael, what have you found? What caused the bleeding? Is Ryan all right?"

Dr. Archer had the kind of spirit and gentle demeanor that had made Julia trust him even as a little girl, coming to him for colds and bumps. His face, usually grave with a twinkle of humor behind it, was still and drawn as he looked into the white cameo of Madeleine's. His eyes seemed to have sunk a little way into his skull, as though withdrawing from the pain he was going to have to inflict on her.

Apprehension tingled through Julia's stomach. She gripped the rolled edges of the couch, her blunt, unpolished fingernails sinking into the worn vinyl.

Dr. Archer took both Madeleine's hands and looked into her eyes. Owen hovered at her shoulder. "Madeleine, Owen," the doctor said softly, "you need to be strong. We might not understand God's will, but we know it's always right in the end."

"No," she said.

"I'm so sorry I—"

"No," Madeleine said, louder, as though he were arguing with her. Her eyes were bright with challenge, her head thrown back.

"—have no good news to tell you, but—"

"I don't believe you! It was a simple investigative procedure. I never meant—it's impossible!" She covered her ears with both hands. Owen pulled them away, holding his wife's wrists, staring at the doctor in horror.

"Madeleine! No, it's not that. He's alive...barely. Alain Duboce can pull him through if anyone can. He's just completed the surgery. If he makes it through the night, the prognosis is good. But I wanted to prepare you. He's not out of the woods yet."

Julia's nails pierced the vinyl once, twice. *Help me, Lord,* she had begged an unseen spirit. *I'll do anything You ask me to. Just save Ryan's life.*

With a sigh, Julia drew the cool, moist night air into her lungs and shook away the vivid memory. Ryan had made it through the night, but no one seemed able to tell them when he'd be well enough to come home. What she needed to do was pray more. That was her problem. Worrying constantly about Ryan was selfish—as if God paid any attention to worrywarts. Prayer was a different thing. Prayer could—

Twenty feet away, a man slowed his approach, the sound of his booted feet carrying in the sweet, heavy air. "'Batter my heart, three-person'd God, for you as yet but knock,'" he said.

Julia froze. That voice. A smooth bass with music in it. The bottom dropped out of her stomach, and she wished she'd been paying more attention to where she was walking. How far away was the car?

"Pretty violent for a preacher, wasn't he?" he said. He stopped just inside the shadow of the shop's awning, a slim-hipped, broad-shouldered silhouette. "I've always thought they should make a movie of his life."

Donne had been a preacher? She'd have to tell Rebecca, who had a real thing about selling the literature of worldly religions. "I don't go to movies," she said in a tone devoid of expression. She pivoted and moved into the cold radiance of the streetlights, balancing on the edge of the curb. Out in the open, she realized how deserted the downtown area was. There were people in the coffee bar, but would they hear her if she cried out for help?

"Don't go to movies? Even one about the Dean of St. Paul's?"

"He was a worldly man. Leave me alone, please." She was almost past him now, walking fast, heading for the parking lot and the safety of her car. Her heart bumped inside her chest, almost making her sick. This was more than shyness. This was the fear of a small animal locked in a predator's gaze.

He followed her, his boots heavy on the asphalt. "Julia, please? I'm not going to hurt you. I just want to talk."

"I don't even know you. Go away!" She didn't like him using her name. It was personal. Presumptuous. Her cheeks burned, but the area between her shoulder blades felt cold.

"I'm trying to fix that. Hey, slow down."

She swung around to face him. "I said, leave me alone!"

He stopped dead, the painted lines of two empty parking spaces between them. Lifting empty hands, he moved them apart, palms up, in a gesture of appeal. His leather jacket opened to reveal a clean white T-shirt under it. "I'm sorry," he said, his voice soft. His eyes were hollows filled with pain. "I didn't mean to frighten you. I just wanted to have a cup of coffee and..." He shrugged and let the sentence trail away. "I...I lost my wife last year and I'm a little out of practice at this. Sorry."

Julia bit her lip. Her conditioning against talking to outsiders warred with compunction that she had hurt the feelings of another—one who seemed to have been deeply hurt already. The needs of others always came before your own. She had jumped to conclusions about his character because of the way he was dressed, and had let those assumptions guide her behavior—just like a worldly person. Outsiders had done the same to her often enough.

"I'm sorry," she apologized in her turn, her voice quieter but still edged with caution. "But I can't. I'm...I'm expected somewhere." She'd run over to Madeleine's and see if Owen was home with news, thereby turning her little fib into the truth.

The biker looked down at the asphalt, and shoved one hand into the pocket of his jeans. "At least let me introduce myself properly, as one lover of books to another." He took a step toward her and held out the other hand. Automatically hers came up. "I'm Ross Malcolm. And you're Julia...?" His big hand, warm and callused, engulfed hers in a firm grip. As she pulled away, his fingers slid along hers as though he didn't want to let go.

Her hand tingled and she jerked it back. "McNeill," she said reluctantly. Her upbringing wouldn't even allow her the safety of a lie.

"It's a pleasure to meet you, Julia McNeill," he said, a smile flavoring his voice with warmth. The streetlight lit his face from the side, leaving it half silver and half black. Shadows filled the hollow curve between eyebrow and cheekbone. He looked like Satan himself. Satan after God had barred him from paradise. She circled past him, edging toward her car. A truck turned the corner, coming toward them, its headlights sweeping away the dark.

"Sure I can't change your mind about that coffee?" he asked with a smile, shrugging one shoulder toward the warmly lit windows.

For half a second she actually wondered what it might be like. Then her good sense returned. *Choose as a date one who'd make a good mate.* The aphorism was printed on a fridge magnet in her mother's kitchen, handmade by Linda Bell ten years ago. She'd seen it so many times it was photographically reproduced on her brain cells, ready for moments like this.

She longed suddenly for Derrick's arms. Safe, reliable Derrick, who was both date and mate material. Bikers in leather jackets were not, great smiles notwithstanding. "I'm sorry, I can't," she repeated a little desperately. She dashed to her car and locked herself in. As she accelerated out of the parking lot and down the street, she passed his motorcycle. It was parked at the curb, its front wheel facing out.

Choose as a date one who'd make a good mate.

"Organized Crime Task Force."

The no-nonsense male voice told Miriam the folksy aunt persona wouldn't work this time. She was about at the end of her tether, chasing the wretched man all over the countryside. It was only by sheer dumb luck that she'd thought to ask the bus driver if he knew what OCTF stood for as they'd roared into Seattle the night before. She'd already found out that he had a daughter in the police department, and at the time it had seemed like a shot in the dark.

A shot whose aim had surprised her. God surely worked in mysterious ways.

"Ross Malcolm, please." There. That was a pretty good imitation of a lawyer in a hurry.

He put her through without further comment.

"O-Crime, Harper."

End it all. It was never easy. Of course Malcolm wouldn't pick up the phone. He'd probably moved to Alaska. In which case she and the girl would pack up their things and get out of this homeless shelter on the first available bus back to the meeting point.

"Ross Malcolm, please," she repeated.

"He's not here. Can I take a message?"

"But he works there, correct?"

"Correct. He's out of town. Can I help you?"

She sighed. One step forward, two steps back. "No. Can you give me a number where I can reach him?"

"Who is this?"

She hesitated. Best to go with the truth, now that she'd finally found someone who seemed to know something.

"I'm a friend of the family. I'm trying to get in touch with him."

There was a pause. "If you give me your number I'll have him call you," the man called Harper said with equal parts cordiality and caution.

"If you would just tell me where he is, I've got news for him. About his daughter."

"Daughter?"

The man sounded so flummoxed that Miriam gave up. "Yes, daughter. Condemn that man, I've tracked him all over the state and I'm done trying. You tell Ross Malcolm that Annie's dead, and if he cares about the girl, he'd better get himself back here."

She banged the receiver down on yet another pay phone, this one in the hallway of the shelter, and resisted the urge to shriek with frustration. Moses was so right. The government were all about hiding and obfuscation and preventing honest people from doing the right thing.

It wasn't until she'd returned to the cots assigned to her and the girl that she realized she'd hung up before telling the Harper man where or who she was.

Just as well. Let Ross Malcolm try and find her for a change.

Chapter Five

❧

"He asked you *out?*" Claire breathed in fascinated horror. "A real biker?"

Julia bent at the waist and began to brush her hair. "As real as they get." The image of Ross Malcolm riding that machine past the bookshop was etched on her mind as permanently as the rhyme on Linda Bell's fridge magnet. "How many bikers can there be in Hamilton Falls?"

"Not very many. This is a four-wheel-drive town if ever I saw one. So what did you do?"

"Do?" Julia straightened and flipped her hair down her back. Claire, standing at the mirror, tucked a few wayward strands into her own neatly braided bun. "I said no, of course. What do you think?"

"Well, of course you said no," Claire said, lifting her chin to adjust the bow of her black silk blouse. "What I meant was, did he give you any trouble?"

"No. Just tried to talk me out of it. Good grief, Claire, there must be a thousand worldly girls in this town. Why couldn't he pick on one of them instead of bothering me?" She took up a combat position in front of the bath-room mirror and tried to surprise her unruly red curls into a roll like Madeleine's. She never stopped hoping that a few obedient hair genes might have been distributed to her as well. A modest, godly hair style—or the lack thereof—was the biggest cross she had to bear.

Claire met Julia's eyes in the mirror. "Maybe he's searching. Maybe he sees something in you that he wouldn't find in a worldly girl."

"Oh, my," Julia murmured weakly. The roll sprang out from under her fingers and unwound itself down her back. He'd said he'd lost his wife. His eyes had confirmed it. Had she really been so self-centered that she'd mis-taken a cry for help for interest in herself? She closed her eyes in shame.

"I've had total strangers walk up to me in the street and ask what I stood for," Claire went on, pretending not to notice. "Don't you think you should give him a chance?"

Nobody ever asked her things like that, but when she did get the chance, she'd blown it. "You think I should have gone out with him. What would the Shepherd say?" She gave up on the roll and began the same old boring French braid.

"Julia, for goodness' sake, it was only coffee. It wasn't like he asked you to something that would jeopardize your soul, like a movie or a dance."

"But still...Elder's Sister-in-law Spotted in Café with Biker. Try explaining that one to dear Alma Woods. She'd think I was condemned for sure. Not that she doesn't think that now."

"I know. I wore heels last Sunday and you should have heard her. But really, you wouldn't need to explain a thing if it meant he came to Mission."

This conversation was getting completely out of hand. "Speaking of which," Julia said, snapping a covered elastic around the tail end of the braid with a sound of finality, "we'd better get going. Mission starts in twenty minutes."

On Sunday evenings, Melchizedek presided at the hall, spreading the word of God to Stranger and Elect alike. As they walked in, Julia spotted Owen and Madeleine already in the front row.

"Madeleine is such an example," Claire whispered to her. "Her service to God always comes first, doesn't it?" The first Sunday after Ryan had been admitted to hospital, Julia had been prepared to take her sister's place at the old upright piano for the hymns, thinking that Madeleine would be unable to do it. She'd even gone so far as to sit in the front row, closest to the instrument. But Madeleine, putting her own emotion aside for the sake of service to her Lord, had walked to the front and played as flawlessly as ever, even on "Suffer the Little Children." And Julia's gesture of help to her grieving sister had gone unnoticed. Which was just as well, Julia reminded herself. The sacrifices God valued most were performed in secret, anyway.

She and Claire seated themselves three-quarters of the way back with the young people. Julia barely had time to put her purse under her seat when Derrick sidled into the row from the other side and took the empty seat beside her. As Melchizedek announced the first hymn, she quietly put her hymnbook on the floor next to her purse and allowed Derrick to hold his for her.

No wonder everyone thought they were going to announce their engagement any day. Couples who were going together might sit side by side in Mission, but only the ones who were "serious" actually shared a hymnbook. If she wasn't serious about him, she should never have allowed him to do it the first time. If she was, she should stop being so difficult and tell him so.

Unbidden, the image of Ross Malcolm rose up before her, all silver and shadow and pain. She couldn't imagine a greater contrast to the man beside her. Derrick, his clean, gentle hands holding the hymnbook, was a true sheep, obedient and innocent. Ross? He was like a wolf, slipping from light into darkness and back again, stalking her for who knew what reason.

Or maybe she did know the reason. Julia bowed her head, convicted in her heart of her own guilt. She hadn't opened her heart to the promptings of the Spirit when Ross Malcolm spoke to her. She had ignored his pain and thought only of herself.

Well, she was listening now. When you heard God's voice through the medium of His Shepherd, you didn't question it. You obeyed.

When the service was over, Melchizedek walked solemnly to the back door to greet everyone as they left. As they filed toward the door, Owen and Madeleine joined them. "Four Strangers tonight," Madeleine said with a gentle smile. "Melchizedek's influence is increasing."

Julia nodded and squeezed her sister's hand. Four? She scanned the crowd. You could pick a Stranger out right away. Beside a man who must be her husband, the lady from Jim Bell's office was wearing slacks, for goodness' sake, and even a necklace. Several of the Elect women were trying hard not to stare. She glanced at the couple from Alma's apartment building, now shaking hands with Melchizedek. The man's hair was too long and his wife's too short, and their faces had a closed, uncomfortable look that the faces of the Elect lacked. However, the Spirit worked miracles. With God's help they would see their need to conform to the image of Christ, and begin dressing to fit in.

Julia struggled against an upswell of guilt and inadequacy. She had never brought anyone to Mission in her life. Madeleine brought lots of them. Even Derrick and Claire had brought friends from school. It was an unspoken measure of your worthiness when you brought people, so what did that say about her?

Maybe she could disappear gracefully, she thought as she emerged onto the sidewalk outside. Not that anyone would notice, with all the new lambs to—

The streetlights glinted off chrome and Julia stopped as though she had run into a plate-glass window. The man behind her ran into her back and let out a surprised breath. "Sorry, Julia," he murmured, stepping around her. She was too dismayed to answer.

Ross Malcolm was sitting on his motorcycle at the far end of the parking lot. Cold streaks of light gleamed on the straight lines of the machine's exhaust pipes, curved into infinity on the front wheel and the headlights. No one could possibly miss him.

Oh, no. Please tell me he's not waiting for me. Please don't let him see me.

The parking lot was brightly lit. Julia wished she could melt back into the safety of the hall, but the stream of departing people edged her farther out into his line of sight. "The biker at the Mission" would be fodder for the gossip lines for days. It would rate a paragraph at least in people's letters to their friends. Madeleine brought visitors to God. But what did Julia do? Caused a scandal with a biker.

She dodged between two cars, her head down, clutching her Bible case as she had clutched the paperbacks in the bookstore.

"Julia," he called.

The flock of old ladies spilled out the front door, chattering. Derrick was right behind them, craning his neck, looking for her. Behind him she caught a glimpse of Owen's red-gold hair. What would they say if they caught her speaking to him? The evening air felt chilled and clammy on her cheeks.

You're thinking of yourself again. She stopped, gripping her Bible, as the thought came to her, almost as if a voice had spoken in her head. She was. She was reacting in exactly the same way she had before—with human instinct instead of godly compassion. Well, the still small voice had spoken. Cost what it may, she had to listen.

Ross rose from his lazy position on the seat of the bike, and crossed the parking lot with the loose-hipped, rocking swagger that boots gave a cowboy. She leaned weakly on the rear fender of her car. He ought to know better than to walk like that. He ought to know that she couldn't speak to an Outsider at Mission, in front of everybody. No matter what the Spirit told her, she was never going to live this down. Never.

The old ladies had caught sight of them now. Alma Woods's eyes were so big that a rim of white showed around her muddy irises. Her mouth opened to give the alarm as she grabbed Rebecca Quinn's elbow.

Ross closed the last few steps between them. "Hey. What's the matter?" His leather jacket creaked.

"Nothing," she replied, her mouth dry. Blue jeans *never* looked like that on Derrick. "Wh—what are you doing here?"

Alma had the attention of three of the others, now. Even Rebecca looked horrified as she tried to steer the fizzing little group away from Julia and over to their cars. Rebecca's eyebrows lifted in a stark question: Are you all right? The whole crowd was looking their way now, people gawking over their shoulders as they hesitated beside their cars.

"I just came over to say hello," he said, leaning a hand on the roof of her car and cocking one hip as though he were prepared to stand there and discuss it for the rest of the night. "Is there something wrong with that?"

"No, of course not, it's just that—"

"Julia, is there a problem?" Melchizedek called from the doorway.

Ross braced a hip on the side of her car and crossed his arms. Beyond him, Melchizedek made his way over to her, followed by Derrick and Owen. Expressions of serious concern fought with disbelief. No one had ever made such a scene at Mission. Owen's gaze searched hers, telegraphing the same message as Rebecca: *Are you all right?*

"No," she answered Melchizedek reluctantly. To the outside observer, Ross Malcolm hadn't done anything wrong—just walked across a public parking lot to speak to her. To an insider, it was the most scandalous thing to happen in Hamilton Falls since Rita Ulstad had deserted her husband for the man renting their downstairs bedroom seven years before. How on earth was she to think about his pain and his soul when he could cause so much agitation with so little effort?

Melchizedek lifted his chin and regarded Ross Malcolm, caution mingling with his sense of duty. He extended a hand. "Melchizedek," he said, infusing the name with the authority of the law and the prophets.

Owen moved forward to ally himself with the Shepherd, and shook Ross's hand as well. The contrast between their conservatively cut suits and Ross's denim and leather was so extreme that Julia felt the hysterical urge to giggle. She bit her lip and let Melchizedek take control of the situation.

"Are you a...friend of Julia's?" Melchizedek asked. His voice was calm, but his eyes conveyed his doubt.

Ross leaned on Julia's car, his big body separating Julia from her protectors, his casual stance somehow conveying possessiveness. "We've met."

Melchizedek and Owen glanced at each other, and Julia could practically see the uncertainty telegraphed between them. Where did they meet? How does he know her? What does he want?

Mark McNeill joined them, lifting an inquiring eyebrow at Owen, who shook his head. Behind her father, Julia could see Elizabeth surrounded by her best friends, watching them with sympathetic horror. She could just imagine what her mother was thinking.

"You came too late," Melchizedek went on. "If you'd come a little earlier, you could have joined us inside."

"I was here," Ross replied easily. "But I made a bad guess on the time. I heard you singing and figured the service was over."

Melchizedek seized on his last words. "Next time, don't wait out in the parking lot. Come in. We start at seven."

"Thanks for the invitation," Ross said. "I'll take you up on it." He glanced over his shoulder. "Good night, Julia," he said in a soft voice, as if they were intimate in some way, and sauntered off across the parking lot.

The Devil tempted her to stare. And she lost.

The Elect scattered for their cars. Not for worlds would they embarrass Mark and Elizabeth with a flurry of questions, thus betraying their own lurid interest in the scene. The details would be common knowledge by tomorrow. They could wait.

Elizabeth advanced toward the little knot of men standing around her daughter.

"Julia, why don't you and Melchizedek come to the house for coffee and cake?" she asked in a cordial tone that only the most foolish person would fail to recognize as an order. Ten yards away, Ross fired up the motorcycle and its throaty roar drowned out her next sentence. Every head in the parking lot turned as he rode the gleaming machine out the driveway, paused to check for traffic, and accelerated loudly up the street.

"What did you say, Elizabeth?" Melchizedek asked, staring after him.

"I said, I think we could all use a little calming down."

Chapter Six

❧

Julia had never been in a courtroom in her life—she'd never even received a traffic ticket—but sitting in the defendant's chair must be something like this. She had tried to escape attention by helping her mother pass her treasured bone china teacups filled with decaffeinated coffee to their guests, but Owen and Melchizedek had isolated her in a corner of the living room so neatly and politely she didn't realize they'd done it until it was too late. Julia sat in the upholstered corner chair, Owen on the sofa next to her and Melchizedek on a dining-room chair he'd pulled up on her other side.

"This Ross Malcolm looks like an interesting man," Melchizedek said in a friendly, noncommittal tone, selecting a slice of cake from the china tray Elizabeth offered at his shoulder.

"Yes," Julia said, sipping hot coffee, hiding behind the teacup. Her mother never served coffee to the Shepherd of her soul in an everyday mug. The Shepherd deserved every family's best in return for the sacrifice of his life for their souls.

"Do you know anything about him?"

"No."

"He said you'd met," Melchizedek persisted, his face intent. "Where was that?"

"At the bookshop."

Melchizedek and Owen exchanged a glance. She'd made a mistake. Both Shepherd and Elder were used to the Elect telling them everything—usually far more than any human being had a right to know about another. The Shepherd was marriage counselor, psychiatrist and social worker all in one, his only training the guidance of the Spirit of God. At any other time Julia would talk to Melchizedek with loving respect, as if he were an uncle. He expected her to have nothing to hide. Anything held back from the scrutiny of the representative of God must by definition be something wrong.

She cleared her throat and put her teacup down with a tiny clink. "He came in last Friday to buy a book and talked awhile with Rebecca about poetry. I saw him once after work, too. He wanted to have a cup of coffee."

"Did he?" Melchizedek said, his eyes on her above the rim of his cup. The delicate piece of porcelain looked ridiculous in his big hands, hands that held their salvation. "With you?" Melchizedek exchanged another glance with Owen. "But he came to Mission. Has it struck you that it's what you have in your life that might attract him, not you yourself?"

Only a self-centered person would think the question insulting. She really had to learn to conquer this fault. It seemed to be cropping up all the time lately. She needed to focus less on herself and more on others, as the Spirit had told her. "Claire seemed to think so," she ventured.

Melchizedek looked past her with a faraway expression. "I wonder."

Owen spoke up. "Do you think you might see him again?"

Julia floundered for an answer. She was sure of it—for some reason she couldn't explain, Ross Malcolm wanted to spend time with her. She could see where Melchizedek's questions were leading, though. She felt like a kayaker in a swift river, backpaddling frantically to avoid committing herself to the waterfall up ahead. "I—I don't know," she stammered finally. Melchizedek was frowning at her long hesitation. "He just turns up."

"Do you feel comfortable with him? Safe?"

Julia choked down a mouthful of tepid coffee. Safe? Who could feel safe around someone who wore jeans to make women look at him instead of to work, like any sensible man? "I...don't think he would assault me, if that's what you mean," she replied cautiously. "But I don't know anything about him." She paused, remembering. "Well, he did say he'd lost his wife recently."

Melchizedek looked pleased. "I knew it! He *is* seeking spiritual comfort. Julia, if you see him again, and he asks you for coffee or something, would you go? Think what it would mean to him to hear about the Lord's work."

Anyone else would say yes without hesitation. There must be something wrong with her. "I...I don't...."

"This is serious, Julia," Owen put in. He put his cup and saucer down and leaned toward her. "If he misses his chance of salvation, it could be on your head for all eternity."

"It looks like you have a heavy responsibility in this," Melchizedek agreed. "God has chosen you for this work out of all the Elect in Hamilton Falls. It's a tremendous privilege. Are you able for it?"

The coffee had dried out the inside of her mouth. Though the room was warm, a chill crept into her hands and feet. "I don't know," she whispered. A piece of applesauce spice cake sat on the side of her saucer. The thought of taking a bite, of feeling it stick to the roof of her mouth, made her ill.

"I feel it in my heart," Melchizedek said. "Think of the service you can render to the poor man. And to the Elect. A man who drives a motorcycle as expensive as that one may feel moved to make sacrifices for God's work in gratitude for comfort in his loss. Remember, Saint Paul commended the liberality of the Corinthians because it meant furthering his efforts in the mission field."

Julia nodded wordlessly. Satisfied, Melchizedek and Owen finished up their coffee and cake, and turned their chairs to include the rest of the room in general conversation. As soon as she decently could, Julia slipped out of the living room and took refuge in her old bedroom down the hall.

Her mother had cleaned out any evidence of the teenager who had left it, and turned the room into a second guest room. Julia sank into the easy chair next to the window and covered her eyes with one hand. She'd only have a few minutes of blessed solitude to regroup and regain her composure before someone came to find her.

Every one of the Elect wanted to be used by the Spirit to bring someone to Melchizedek. They were brought up to it practically from birth. But her salvation depended upon bringing this particular man to the fold. What would happen to her if she failed? Would he ride away on his motorcycle, leaving her doomed to hell for eternity? Would God ever forgive her? Would Melchizedek? He lived with this kind of responsibility every day, but he had been called and equipped by God for it.

She was still contemplating the terrifying prospect when Madeleine pushed the door open. It scraped on the carpet just as it had for years, providing an early warning system. Julia looked up, resting her head on the back of the chair.

"Here you are." Madeleine pushed the door shut and sat on the edge of the bed. "What are you doing, hiding behind closed doors?"

"Just, um, meditating," Julia said. It was an answer that could cover a multitude of other reasons. Should she confide in Madeleine? No. Her sister had never failed at anything. She would just tell her that God's grace was sufficient for her, and secretly pity Julia for her lack of faith.

"You should be praying," Madeleine said firmly. "I really wonder about you sometimes."

"What do you mean?"

"You know what I mean. Your Shepherd and Elder have more important things to do than talk to you about your choice of company."

Julia stared at her. "It wasn't like that at all. Ross wanted to come to the service. When he saw he was late, he just waited in the parking lot to talk to me."

Madeleine tucked in her chin and looked at Julia over a pair of imaginary eyeglasses, as if trying to see in her younger sister a reason for a worldly man to do such a thing. Easy for Madeleine. Men had been trying to get her to talk to them from the age of twelve.

"He wanted to come to the service? Dressed like that? Hmph." She paused, but when Julia said nothing, her curiosity got the better of her. "What did Melchizedek say, then, if he wasn't giving you a talking-to? It was too quiet for any of us to hear."

Julia bit back a caustic remark about her sister's own lack of faith. She was going to need her—the Elder's wife—to go to bat for her reputation, the way things were heading. "If Ross is searching for God, Melchizedek thinks I could be useful."

"Really." Taken aback, Madeleine allowed her spine to relax. This was obviously not the conversation she had expected.

Julia's mouth twisted. Had the whole family thought she'd been getting a lecture on her bad taste in men? If they only knew. She stood up. "Well, I should be going. I have to work tomorrow."

"You poor thing. If you'd said yes to Derrick last year, you'd be married by now and wouldn't have to worry about things like this." Her sister hugged her, and Julia made an effort to hug her back.

When she got out of the car at home she stood for a moment in the driveway, breathing in the scent of damp soil and Rebecca's Peace roses. She must have been out here with the hose in the cool of the evening. Rebecca lived on the main floor of the tall Victorian at 1204 Gates Place, and rented the top suite to single Elect girls, of whom Julia was the latest in a long line.

She felt restless and uneasy. All she wanted was to get away from people, from speculation, from impossible spiritual burdens laid upon her by people who were supposed to love her. Besides, if Rebecca heard her going up the stairs, she might want to talk about the biker too. She just couldn't face a third interrogation.

She still had on the running shoes she used for driving, a habit she'd developed to save wear on her pumps. Locking her purse and Bible case in the car, she slipped her keys in the pocket of her dress and walked briskly down the street.

The lakeshore was nearly deserted. A few late strollers moved slowly past the darkened refreshment stand next to the public washrooms. Julia took a shortcut through the trees and came out on the beach, a narrow strip of silver washed by moonlight and the ripples of the lake.

Alone at last.

The air revived her, the silence soothed her ruffled spirits. Out here she could think. Or at the very least, feel.

Let's face the ugly truth, she thought. You're just not up to this. But somehow she had to be. Resisting the will of the Shepherd was the same thing as resisting the will of God, and that was unthinkable. That would send her to hell for sure. They wanted her to be a sort of spiritual funnel, making it easier for Ross to enter the Kingdom of God. But after that, what? Go on her way rejoicing? Marry Derrick and sit in the same Gathering with Ross Malcolm every week, trying to ignore the prickly feeling she got every time she laid eyes on him? She tried to define what it was about him that put her on edge. His masculinity, for one thing. Oh, yes. Confident, unfettered, don't-care-what-you-think maleness. With her limited experience in that department, Ross Malcolm scared her to death. And yet something about the unhappy look in his eyes in the parking lot behind the bookstore had caught at her heart even as she'd pushed him away and run. The buried pain of loss called out for comfort. Could she be the one that could give it to him? Could she approach and tame the wolf without losing her own salvation?

That was even more frightening. The future Mrs. Derrick Wilkinson, who would be the Deacon's wife some day with all the rights and privileges pertaining thereto, had no business thinking such things. But on the other hand, she didn't want to be responsible for a man missing the way to heaven. What was she going to do?

She looked up and saw she'd arrived at the worn granite steps that led up the cliff face, where the Hamilton

River leaped over timeworn ledges of stone on its way into the lake. There was a small park at the top. She'd go up to the overlook and then head home.

Deep in thought, she kept her head down until she rounded the semicircular rock wall that formed the overlook. She didn't see the big motorcycle parked in the shadows until it was too late.

Ross had seen the woman approaching since she'd emerged from the trees, and had wondered why anyone would go beachcombing in a dress. She gesticulated toward the sand, as if she were having an argument with someone in her head. It wasn't until she was climbing the steps that he'd seen her face clearly, and recognized the hair that was always trying to escape its confinement.

A ripple of dismay ran through him at the thought of sharing his solitude with a cult-conditioned woman, of getting close to her in any way. But it was his job to get close to her. Kids were dying, and he had less than three weeks to find out why.

Controlling his face, he spoke in what he hoped was a light, bantering tone. "'Once, and but once found in thy company, all thy supposed escapes are laid on me.'" A sound halfway between a gasp and a moan issued out of the shadows close to the shrubbery, where he'd parked the bike. "Except I'm the one who escaped," he added conversationally. "Didn't look like you made it."

"Who's that?" Her voice was strangled practically to a whisper.

"You know more than one guy who likes John Donne and rides a bike?" he inquired. "Come on out of the bushes, Julia. It's too late to hide, and I don't bite."

For a moment there was no sound, and he wondered if he'd scared her so badly she'd sprinted for the road. But with a flicker of movement at the edge of the moonlight, she sidled out from behind the motorcycle, clutching her elbows and looking at him as if he were singed and smelling of sulphur.

He hated that. "You cold?" He shrugged out of his jacket and held it out to her.

Her gaze ran down his body and skittered back up to his face. "No. Thank you."

He shrugged back into the jacket. Just as well. "So. We meet again."

"I'm sorry."

He noted that her gaze dropped to his mouth for half a second before centering on the bridge of his nose. Interesting. "You're sorry we're meeting again?"

"No. For intruding."

"You're not intruding. Hey, um, I meant that about escaping. Did I get you in trouble?"

She sighed, and walked over to the waist-high parapet. "Not exactly." She still gripped her elbows. If he joined her she'd probably jump over the edge, dress and all.

He slid his hands into the pockets of his jacket. "Then what, exactly? Your friends seemed pretty welcoming. I was sorry I'd messed up on the time."

She shook her head. "It's hard to explain."

Aha. No Outsiders allowed. "Okay. We can stand here and make small talk, if that'll make you feel better. When I finish Donne can I trade him for *The Norton Anthology?*"

The corner of her mouth twitched in a smile. A good sign. She was a little harder to talk to than he'd expected, but he couldn't just give up and walk away, much as he'd like to. He needed her.

"What are you doing out here?" she asked the top of the wall. The words came out reluctantly, as if she were making conversation against her will.

"I like to ride at night. I saw the turnoff for the park and thought I'd cruise down and have a look."

"Do you normally ride on the sidewalk?" she said, turning to look down the path at the way he'd come.

"There weren't any signs."

Her smile was real this time, although its primness told him what she thought of people who didn't respect the law. A big dimple dented her cheek at the corner of her mouth, and he looked away. His woman of choice was a smart brunette who knew her own mind and used it to glorify God. Despite what Harry Everett thought, staying professional on this job was the least of his problems.

"How did you know I was going to be at the hall earlier?" she asked abruptly. She released her grip on her elbows and touched the river stones of the parapet with one finger, tracing their circular shape.

She was relaxing. He could risk moving a little closer. He kept his attention on the lake, his stance casual, his hands in the pockets of his jacket. "I didn't know the hall belonged to your group. Someone told me I could catch a service there. Like I said, I was sorry I was late. I didn't know the protocol, that's all."

He spun his story with the smoothness of long practice. He moved closer until he stood about four feet from her. It bugged her if he looked her in the eye, so he leaned both elbows on the parapet and gazed into the distance, as if sharing the view with her.

"So what kind of service did I miss?"

She hesitated, which surprised him. Usually they couldn't wait to get started on drawing him into their control. "It's a mission service."

Was he going to have to pull it out of her sentence by sentence? "What happens?"

"We sing. The Shep—um, minister preaches. You know."

"No, I don't."

"Not a religious man?" She ducked her head, embarrassed that a personal question had escaped her.

He smiled. He had a B.A. in criminal justice, a master's in theology, and God had given him more peace in his heart than he could express. The first two, at least, he could keep to himself.

"Sorry," she said. "I didn't mean to be nosy." She had a nice voice. Contralto. The kind of voice suited to intimate talks in the dark.

"It's okay. I'm a believer."

"In what?"

Had she never heard that expression before? "In God. And His Son."

She looked at him briefly, as if he had said something puzzling. "You're very forthcoming about it."

And she wasn't. This was definitely not by the book.

"What does it say? 'Every spirit that confesses Jesus Christ has come in the flesh is of God.'"

"It also says to try the spirits, so you won't be deceived."

"Do you think I'm deceived?"

She sighed. "Most of the world is. It's not easy to find the true path of God. Or His will."

He had the feeling her meaning was a little more personal than she intended. He also had the feeling that he had been lumped in with a deceived world. That, at least, he recognized. Most closed groups kept the "us against them" philosophy alive as a protective measure.

She was looking at the passenger seat and the fringed saddle bags. He had a sudden brilliant idea, something that would counteract her attempt to separate them in her mind.

"Did you drive down?"

"I walked. I just live up the hill." She gestured vaguely to the east.

"Want to go for a spin? I'll drop you off at home."

With a whirl of skirts, she twisted away from him and wound up with her back against the screen of bushes. "I can't do that."

He could hardly see her in the shadows, but he could hear her agitated breathing in the silence. "Why not? I promise I won't kidnap you. You can tell Melchizedek my intentions are completely honorable."

Humor didn't have the least effect on her instant denial. "I can't. It's not... Thank you, but I can't."

"It's not what? Not proper? What?"

He could sense her misery from where he stood. "Something like that," she said at last, very reluctantly.

"At least you're honest." A rare quality, in his experience. She belongs to a cult, he reminded himself. You can't trust anything she says. "But I'll tell you straight, I'm not going to let you walk all the way home by yourself. It's—" he checked the luminous dial of his watch "—almost ten-thirty. And I'm not going to leave the bike here to get stolen while I go with you. So you're going to have to stay here and make meaningless conversation with me until you let me take you home."

She stepped out of the dark and looked at him uncertainly, obviously weakening. He held his jacket out again. "Put it on. You'll need it. The temperature is always lower when you're moving."

"I don't know...."

She wanted to go, and they both knew it. He released the spare helmet from the locking ring on the back of the bike and handed it to her. She fitted it awkwardly over her hair. When she held the chin strap, obviously at a loss as to what to do with it, he took it out of her hand. The skin of her throat felt soft and warm against the backs of his fingers, a delicate pulse fluttering beneath it.

"Okay?" She nodded, like a little girl having her buttons done up. Her face was tilted toward his, her lips parted slightly. His hands felt heavy as they fell away from her skin.

He turned the key and touched the starter switch. The motorcycle fired up with a smooth roar, and he put his own helmet on. Swinging his leg over the seat, he braced his feet on the ground and pushed the kickstand up with one heel.

He looked at her over his shoulder and gently revved the engine. "Hop on."

Chapter Seven

❦

His jacket still held his body heat. Julia pushed her arms into the sleeves, and the heavy leather settled onto her shoulders. The faint scent of his cologne drifted out of the lining and past her nostrils. She still felt the brush of his fingers on her throat.

She must be out of her mind.

"What do I do?" she asked, her voice nearly a shout over the engine. The helmet felt strange, thick, damping her hearing.

"Ever mounted a horse?"

"Yes."

"Same way. Put your foot on this peg. You can brace a hand on my shoulder if you want."

At least the saddle on a motorcycle was closer to the ground. She set her left foot on the peg, and her left hand on his shoulder. His warmth burned her fingers right through his cotton T-shirt. Rattled, she swung her right leg over, felt the other peg under her instep more by luck than aim, and fell into the seat behind him.

"Whoa. You okay?"

No, she wasn't okay. She wanted to wriggle backward and close her legs. The machine vibrated under her. Ross's body was warm and solid. She didn't know what to do with her hands.

"Next time wear jeans," he suggested over his shoulder.

She didn't even own a pair of jeans. Women didn't wear men's clothing. And there wasn't going to be a next time. Her dress bunched up between them in what seemed like a huge wad of fabric. If she pulled it loose, it might get caught in the wheels.

"What do I do with my dress?"

"Pull it up and wrap it under your legs."

Pull it up? She did the best she could, tucking the cotton knit under her. Where was she supposed to put her hands? On her own legs? In front of her? On him? She had no idea that riding a motorcycle could be this complicated.

Ross reached behind him and took both her wrists, pulling both arms snugly around his waist. A sudden sizzle shot through her, and she fought her instinct to retreat.

This is a mistake, a mistake, a mistake....

Ross kicked the motorcycle into gear and they rolled forward, picking up speed and sweeping along the moonlit path. When they emerged from the parking lot and accelerated onto the highway, Julia gasped and realized why he'd made her hold on to his waist. There was absolutely nothing to stop her tumbling off the back every time he hit the gas. The seat tilted forward just enough to force her into his body, no matter how hard she tried to put a few inches of space between them. The wind buffeted her face, and the dotted line in the center of the road whipped past in a yellow blur, inches from the soles of her feet. She tried not to think about what would happen if a deer leaped out in front of them.

"Okay?" he shouted over his left shoulder.

"Yes!" she hollered back.

His ribs were rock solid, his control over the machine complete as they cornered. "Stay with me," he instructed. "Don't fight it. Keep your body at the same angle as mine."

On the next corner she concentrated on his broad back and muscled shoulders under the flapping cotton T-shirt. It was easier to lean with him. The motorcycle growled as he accelerated to highway speed.

The roar of the engine and the rush of the wind parting around them enclosed her with him in a cell of sound and sensation. Her body moved with his, with the bike, one being fueled on the exhilaration of speed and the night. Julia was blown out of herself by sound and wind, and at the same time anchored by Ross's heat and strength.

Five miles out of town, she came back to herself and the road winding between the tree-covered hills resolved once more into something she recognized.

"Where are we going?" she called. She eased her grip on his waist.

"Where do you live?" He turned his head enough to give her one-quarter of a grin before he returned his attention to the road.

"Gates Place. We passed it way back there."

"I'll take you back, don't worry. It's a great night for a ride."

Julia gave in and let the wind blow her inhibitions away along with the motorcycle's exhaust. It *was* a great night for a ride. A great night to make a wicked memory she would never tell a living soul, and add another sin to a list that was lengthening by the minute.

At the intersection with the cutoff that led north to the interstate, Ross maneuvered the bike in a sweeping U-turn that made the pegs scrape the asphalt. No matter how she tried to hang on to every minute, to savor the changing scent of the wind and the texture of cotton under her fingers, the heat of his body seeping through her hands, they passed the sign that welcomed visitors to Hamilton Falls far too soon.

"Gates Place, you said?" The bike roared as he kicked it into a lower gear.

"Would you mind dropping me at the corner?" Even at a respectable twenty miles an hour, the sound of the engine was enough to wake the dead. It would have no problem waking Rebecca.

"Why?" He brought the bike to a halt next to the street sign for Gates Place. Tilting it onto the kickstand, he turned the front wheel and shut off the engine. The sudden silence roared in her ears.

"I don't want to wake my landlady."

"You don't have to shout. I shut it off."

"How do I get off this thing?"

"Same way you got on."

She dismounted awkwardly, caught her running shoe in the hem of her dress and would have fallen if he hadn't swung his leg over and caught her.

"Careful." One hand steadied her at the waist, the other gripped her forearm.

"Sorry." Her skin heated where his hand rested on it. He was too tall. Too close. And he smelled too good. She dragged in a breath and stepped away. "Th-thank you for the ride."

"I enjoyed it. I hope you did, too."

"Yes. I did."

Uncertain silence stretched between them. She slid out of his jacket and held it out to him. "Thanks," she repeated. "Good night."

As he took it, he let his gaze linger on her face until she raised her eyes to meet his. "Good night." His voice was low, husky. He smiled. Her heart hitched in her chest and she moistened suddenly dry lips. What a beautiful mouth he had—with the kind of full lower lip that made you think about kissing whether you wanted to or not. For the first time in an hour, she remembered she was supposed to be helping him work out his salvation. Accepting an offer of a cup of coffee and talking about his soul. Not riding behind him and secretly enjoying her sin.

She took a step back, and then another. When she reached the edge of the cone of harsh light cast by the streetlight, his voice stopped her.

"I'll see you."

Possibilities whirled through her—hope and denial mixed with the racing adrenaline of attraction. "I don't think so," she gasped, and fled into the concealing dark.

Ross stretched out on the hard queen-size bed in his motel room, and dialed Harry Everett's pager number from memory. Time for a progress report. When the phone rang, he hooked the receiver up with two fingers and drawled, "I'm in."

"Yeah? That didn't take long. Who is it?"

"The sister. Julia McNeill. I've got an invitation to their missionary meeting. She told me she wouldn't be seeing me again, but I'm going to work on that. I can probably get into the principal's house by the end of the week."

He'd bet a hundred dollars Julia's family would invite him to dinner if he showed up at the mission a second time. There was something quaintly old-fashioned about this group. Behaviors that had slipped out of the mainstream years ago were still real here.

"Nice work." Everett's voice brought him back.

"I'll keep you posted."

Ross dropped the phone in the cradle and lay back, following his previous train of thought. The Elect were living in a time warp. A Victorian time warp, complete with mourning clothes. And the hair. No hasty wraps around those fabric scrunch things—these women used real pins. Nothing else would hold up those swirls and braided loops. How many pins did Julia have to use to keep her hair from escaping all the time?

He compared the rigid conformity in appearance with the spontaneous joy of his Sunday-morning services, where kids turned up in shorts and young mothers had never even seen a hairpin. There, the focus was on worship, on singing, on learning about Jesus. He hadn't heard Julia mention the Lord's name once, which, the more he thought about it, was pretty strange.

Their good-night had been hard on her, probably for a couple of reasons. Fear that he was going to try something physical? Maybe. Fear of discovery? Definitely. She was almost phobic about that. Not surprising if she'd been brought up in a closed culture. Outsiders were bad until they became Insiders.

He tipped his head back against the headboard. It was going to take a little more work to gain her confidence than he'd anticipated, which would mean investing more time with her. His mouth twisted. And he was going to have to adjust his image. The outlaw biker part of his persona wouldn't work here. He sighed. It would never occur to his pastor at home to say anything about his hair. But it mattered here.

Oh, well. At least he'd made a start. If she trusted him enough to ride a bike for the first time, he was doing okay. Once trust was established, he could really get to work.

He thanked God for his instincts and the movement of the Spirit, and breathed a prayer for guidance. He hadn't run into such an odd group before.

Julia stumbled through Monday and Tuesday in a state where flashes of longing were immediately followed by thunderclaps of guilt. She'd calmed Rebecca's concern about the scene Sunday night by telling her that their Shepherd knew all about it and had the situation well in hand. She wished she could say the same for herself.

Sunday night was all she could think about. Ross's knuckles brushing her skin. The wind rushing in their faces. Ross saying, "It was fun," and "See you," and looking at her. Oh, the way he looked at her, with such intensity that she blushed just thinking about it. Not even Derrick looked at her like that, as though he not only saw her, but what lay behind her eyes as well.

No doubt about it, the girl who shared Derrick's hymnbook was in trouble. She had to find a way to conquer this infatuation for a complete stranger, and focus on his conversion. She had to stop thinking she was free to spend time with him, period.

Wednesday night after prayer meeting, Madeleine called. "Melchizedek is coming for dinner Friday. Have you seen your...friend lately?"

Julia was tempted to say, What friend is that, Lina? just to have the pleasure of hearing Ross's name. The big bad biker. The unmentionable. Worldly and desirable and completely unsuitable.

"Not since Sunday," she said instead. It never did any good to get sarcastic with Madeleine; she would just sound mystified and slightly hurt, and Julia would feel terrible. Madeleine had been hurt enough to last a lifetime; Julia couldn't bear to deal even the smallest poke to her right now.

"Do you think you might see him before Friday?" Madeleine asked.

"I don't know. I don't think so." Not if she could help it.

"Julia, for heaven's sake, stop being so evasive."

"I wasn't being evasive, I—"

"Melchizedek thought it might be nice if we invited you and your—Mr. Malcolm as well. I'm not sure I'm ready to entertain quite yet, but for the work of God of course we'll put our own concerns aside. Could you phone him and ask?"

All at once Julia realized that she had absolutely no way to contact Ross Malcolm. She didn't know where he lived, what his phone number was, or anything about him. Just that he rode a big, rumbling motorcycle, liked John Donne, and had a voice that sent shivers up her back.

She could just imagine what Madeleine would say to that.

"Um, sure. I'll ask him the next time I see him." Whenever that might be. Maybe he'd had second thoughts and was feeling the wind on his face—as he headed east for Idaho and out of her life. Which would definitely be the best thing for all of them.

"All right," Madeleine said. "Let me know by Friday morning if you can. We'll see you about six-thirty."

"Okay." She rang off and leaned her forehead against the cool plaster of the wall. She couldn't do this. She could read a Keep Out sign as well as anyone—and the words were plainly written all over Ross Malcolm. The problem was, everyone kept pushing her toward him. Even Madeleine, who, while she might disapprove of the man, still welcomed the lost sheep. Besides, why would Ross Malcolm accept such an invitation? It probably wasn't like his usual Friday-night dates. What did a man like that do for amusement? She couldn't imagine. Maybe they could go for a ride again, and she could hold him the way she'd done Sunday night.

She collapsed on her secondhand couch and stared glumly out into the oak tree whose leaves brushed her living-room window. On a night like this she could almost wish the Elect believed in owning televisions. It would be a lot less sinful than the pictures in her head.

Chapter Eight

❧

Ross walked into the bookshop the next evening at ten minutes to closing time.

"It occurred to me," he said, leaning over the counter and looking down at the top of her head as she sorted wrapping paper and green bags, "that even if you wanted to call and ask me out, you couldn't, because I didn't give you my phone number."

Julia banged her head on the underside of the counter. "Ow!" Clutching her skull, she stood up slowly.

"Are you okay? Why am I always scaring you to death?"

"I'm fine. Really. My bun took most of the impact." She was babbling with relief and a sort of delirium as she took in the sight of him. The jeans were the same, but instead of the white T-shirt, he had on a tropical shirt in cobalt blue that turned his eyes a smoky slate. She pulled herself together and made herself stop staring.

"Nice flamingoes," she said with just the right casual touch, and bent to slide the rest of the wrapping under the counter.

"Aren't they great?" He put his hands on his hips so she could get the full effect. She got it, all right. Between the flamingoes and the smile she was down for the count. "So do you want it?" he went on.

She was standing here with her mouth open and her knees weak and he was asking? Maybe she'd better make sure. "Want what?"

"My pager number," he said very slowly. "Write it down. 555-1287. Put your number in, and I'll call you back."

Oh. She got a pencil out of the cup next to the register and wrote the numbers down. The bump on the head must have scattered her brain cells more than she realized.

"What makes you think I'm going to page you?" she asked, flashing him a look up through her lashes.

"I don't. But I'll never know unless I give you the number, will I?" He paused. "That offer of coffee is still open."

"When, now?"

"You close in—" he checked his watch "—three minutes and forty seconds. The coffee bar doesn't. Ergo, now."

It's God's will, Julia. Melchizedek said you should go out for coffee with him, and now he's asking you. God is making the way clear, pointing out your path with neon-pink flamingoes.

She was out of her mind to even think about it. "Okay," she said. "Just let me cash out. It'll only take a few minutes."

At the café he ordered a fancy African espresso and she ordered a tall decaf mocha.

"I—I didn't hear the motorcycle," Julia said hastily, to fill the silence. "Did you walk downtown?"

He shook his head. "Nope. It's parked in front of that planter thing, where I can keep an eye on it." He changed the subject abruptly. "So let's get the small talk out of the way. My middle name is Alexander. I was born in Seattle, marital status, widower. I like motorcycles, Renaissance poetry and the blues. I hate turnips, bullies and getting speeding tickets. I have two younger sisters and I'm a temporarily unemployed mechanic. What about you?"

Julia laughed. How refreshing it was not to waste any time on preliminaries. "My middle name is Rose. I was born right here at Valley General; marital status—" she hesitated "—single. I like flowers, cats and strawberry pie. I also hate turnips, and I have one perfect older sister who tells me that my job in the bookshop is far too public and I should work for her best friend in her day care. How's that?"

"Do I detect a little sibling rivalry here?" he asked with a grin that made her feel that it wouldn't be a sin if he did. It was a novelty. Anyone else she knew would have given her some gentle but pointed encouragement on over-coming the evils of jealousy.

"What's it to her as long as you like what you do? And why is it too public?"

"Madeleine likes to organize everybody and she's good at it. She was born to be the Elder's wife. But some-times..." She stopped. How could she discuss her most private feelings and hurts with this stranger? She took a sip of coffee instead and focused on his second question. "Selling things to people is too public a job for women."

He looked puzzled. "But the woman at the till who likes Donne...?"

"Rebecca. My boss. She has been very useful to God in that position, so the Shepherd looks the other way.

I'm...not quite so useful. Women aren't supposed to put themselves forward. Their place is in the home."

He swallowed and looked at her doubtfully. "What year did you say this was?"

Julia thought of Linda Bell and her day care. All those yelling children. It had been enough to make her willing to risk the Shepherd's disapproval when she'd explained that a single person had to make a living in this day and age. She couldn't wait to leave home. Her mother had been so upset and offended when she'd moved out that the second spare room had become a standing reminder of it.

When she didn't answer, he asked a real question. "What's an Elder?"

Julia took a deep breath. Here it was. The reason she was here. "The man who leads our services Sunday mornings in the house church. In our case, my brother-in-law, Owen Blanchard. On Sunday nights the Shepherd takes the mission service. Melchizedek is the actual preacher. He lives behind the hall."

"You don't have a church?"

She shook her head. "The Bible says God isn't found in temples made with hands. So we don't make them. Each town has a hall or a rental or even somebody's basement set aside for that purpose, and we gather every Sunday."

"Makes it kind of hard for your brother-in-law to get away for the weekend if he's got to be home every Sunday morning."

"The theory is that you put God first." She smiled. "But if he's sick or he and Madeleine go away, there's a Deacon to back him up." She took a breath to tell him about Derrick, but he spoke first.

"Why doesn't your sister back him up when he's sick?"

Julia looked startled. "A woman can't be an Elder."

"Why not?"

She floundered for an answer. "Because women are supposed to keep silent in the church."

"Don't you participate at all in the service?"

"Well, no, not exactly." There were ways to get around the fact that only men actually spoke in public. Most of the married men would stand up during revelation time and share both their thoughts and their wives' on a given piece of Scripture. The women's voices were heard, even if it was secondhand.

Of course, if you were single you had to go about it differently. That was why the young people's meetings were so popular. Since it wasn't a formal Gathering, the girls and single women were free to speak.

Ross's gaze was thoughtful. "So you take St. Paul pretty seriously."

"The Bible doesn't change, no matter what people do."

"So obeying the Bible is more important than people?"

"Obeying God's word is far more important than what people think."

"That's not what I said."

"What *did* you say?" she asked crossly. "There's an order in the universe, and if we take our own way and step out of it, chaos results. Look around you."

Obligingly, he glanced around the coffee bar and returned his intent gaze to her. Was there humor glinting in his eyes, or interest? How come she felt like she was losing an argument, here? She should be used to it. People didn't usually react very well to the tenets of her faith, but given time and the working of the Spirit, they would see how reasonable it was.

"I get it. God at the top, then man, then women and slaves, then animals, vegetables, minerals. Is that really God's plan for us?"

"Don't patronize me. Human thinking gets us into trouble." This was not going very well. Slaves, indeed! How could she convince him of the truth the Elect saw when she couldn't even convince him of the basics? No wonder God didn't use her. She was terrible at this.

"Human thinking has produced some beautiful things, too. Art, poetry, architecture."

"Those will disappear at the end of the world. God won't."

He went very still. "Do you believe in the end of the world?"

"Of course. The Bible says it's going to happen. We just don't know when."

"I mean, literally. As a possibility. Now."

"You mean, do I think it's going to happen before the end of my lifetime? I don't know. It could. The Elect believe you're supposed to be prepared for it, no matter when it comes."

"How prepared?" His gaze was intense, frighteningly focused. Julia swallowed her coffee with a gulp.

"That means obeying what Melchizedek tells us. God speaks through him."

He sat back, and she saw him draw a deep breath. "He does, does he? Some people believe the government is going to start a war that will bring on the end of the world. They hide out in the hills with guns."

Julia couldn't help herself. She laughed. "I can just see my mother with a rifle." She sobered. The dangerous look still hadn't left his eyes. "I don't know what you've heard about the Elect, Ross, but believe me, hiding out in the hills waiting for the end of the world isn't on the top of the list."

He smiled at last, that look of frightening concentration fading from his face as the vertical lines between his brows smoothed out. "Glad to hear it. So what do you think about all this stuff? What's your opinion?"

Julia frowned. "What do you mean? I just finished giving you my opinion."

He waved that away as if it were a fly buzzing his face. "That was what the church thinks. Not what Julia thinks."

She sat and stared at him, her mouth partly open as she ran back through their conversation. Then she closed her mouth. It was true. Every time he questioned her or her behavior, she responded in terms of what a woman of the Elect would think or do. Not what she would think or do.

But weren't they the same?

Shouldn't they be?

Of course they should. It was blasphemous to think anything else. Hastily she rejected the awful possibility of allowing her human thinking to interfere with the doctrine she had obeyed all her life.

He tilted his head and peered into her face. "Houston, do you read? Did I hit a nerve?"

She blinked, still trying to back away from the abyss. "No, I—I don't know." Who was Houston? She gave him a mock frown. "I don't like talking to you." Bad enough she had lost her grip on her faith enough to let doubts come wriggling in. Worse that he should be sitting there confirming them all out loud, leaving her on the brink of—of something. A choice that wasn't even possible.

"Why? Because I make you think?"

"You make me sound like...like that book that was so popular in the seventies. You know, the Something Wives."

"The Stepford Wives?"

"Yes."

"That was a movie."

"I don't go to movies. I read the book."

"I didn't know there was a book."

"Of course there's a book. There's always a book. If there isn't one before, they publish one after. For people like me, so we can talk about them intelligently in cafés." She barely stopped herself from clapping a hand to her mouth. She'd never told that to a single soul. Bad enough she had had two worldly girlfriends at school, flatly disobeying the command to "come out from among them and be ye separate. " Worse that she had allowed herself to be drawn in to their interests. If Madeleine or her parents had found out, the Shepherd would have been at her door for a Visit within the hour. Too late now. She'd better confess before he got the wrong impression. "I used to do it once in a while. Not now. It's deceitful."

"Not necessarily. Call it protective coloration." Evidently he meant to be reassuring.

"That doesn't change what it is." There was no reassurance for sin. Once she'd left school, she had never contacted those girls again. It was too dangerous.

"I don't think you're a Stepford wife," he said, returning to the previous discussion. "Although you kind of look that way."

"Look what way?" She glanced down at her black cotton.

"I noticed it the other night. You women all have a certain—look."

She tilted her head and lifted an inquiring brow. "Could it be—godly?"

"I don't think basic black is all that godly. Must get hot in the summer."

Her smile flattened. "If it does, it just means we're mortifying our flesh."

Between one breath and the next, that frightening look was back.

"Is mortifying the flesh a habit with the Elect? For instance, is it required? Say, part of a child's upbringing?"

Oh, dear. She needed to remember she was talking to a Stranger, not someone who knew his biblical terms. "No, no. That's just an expression. I meant that we sacrifice our own comfort to be a good example."

A brief silence fell while he thought this over. He didn't seem impressed. "Okay. No rifles. No colors. And no movies, really?"

"Really." Maybe she should just get up right now. Maybe he wasn't interested in coming to God. Maybe he was just a bored worldly man who wanted amusement, and she happened to be handy.

"Not even *Star Wars?*" he persisted.

"No. And no, I didn't read the book." She'd wanted to. But in the end she'd sacrificed the worldly desire on the altar of prayer, and had emerged the stronger for it. She was still tempted to sacrifice him on the same altar. She would, if it weren't for Melchizedek and the fact that her eternal destiny might hang in the balance.

"I can't believe it. You must be the only person on the planet who hasn't seen it."

"Along with the rest of the Elect."

He ignored her sarcasm. "I've gotta fix this. You can't go through your whole life without seeing *Star Wars.*"

"Why not? Movies just take up time we need for more important things."

"Like what?"

"Like—oh, I don't know...visiting the sick, being with your family, helping your friends."

"Oh. Well, I suppose you've got a point. So how about we skip the movie I was going to ask you to on Friday and we'll go visit your family?"

Julia sat back and squashed her rebellious thoughts once and for all. This was ordained. There was no doubt the Spirit was working in this man's heart, so she'd better calm down, swallow her indignation, and do what she had been commanded to do. "As a matter of fact, my sister called last night and asked if I'd come for dinner Friday. She—they—they'd love to meet you."

"Would they now?" he said, considering this with a doubtful lift of the eyebrow. "Even if I drove right up to the door on my big bad bike?"

"Sure," she said stoutly, hoping it was true.

"What time?"

"Six-thirty."

"Okay. I'll pick you up at six and we'll take a ride first."

"A ride—oh, no, I couldn't do that, I—"

"Julia."

"What?"

"What are you afraid of?"

"Nothing. I'm not afraid of anything." The love of God cast out fear. At least, it always had before.

"Are you ashamed to be seen with me?"

"Not at all." Why did she have to be such a failure at this? Madeleine brought people to God as easily as some people went to the supermarket. The only thing Julia was good at was making herself invisible in times of stress.

Gently, Ross broke into her thoughts. "It's okay. I understand. Just give me their address and I'll meet you there."

"I'm not ashamed to be seen with you." Certainly not. Melchizedek would be thrilled. The rest of Hamilton Falls would have a field day. "It's just that...nobody rides a motorcycle. Particularly not a woman."

She didn't want anyone to know she'd ridden that machine with him. It had something to do with keeping those forbidden feelings a secret. It had a lot to do with riding into Madeleine and Owen's driveway and trying to explain her behavior to them. And what would she say to Derrick once he found out about it?

Wordlessly, she dug a pen and paper out of her purse and wrote the Blanchards' address down. She pushed it across the tabletop. "I've got to go now. Thanks for the coffee."

He folded the paper and tucked it in the pocket of his jeans. "Good night. See you Friday."

She pushed open the glass door onto Main Street. As it closed behind her, she saw him get up and drop some coins into the pay phone at the end of the counter. Disillusionment crashed down. He was probably calling a woman. Someone who wore black because it was fashionable instead of a symbol. Someone who could be with Ross as a woman, not as an emissary of God, who could ride behind him without worrying about who was watching.

Whoever she was, deep in her heart Julia envied her.

Ray picked up on the first ring. "O-Crime—"

"It's me. Just checking in."

"Do you have ESP or what?"

Ross frowned at the pay phone, keeping his back to the coffee bar. "What do you mean?"

"There is major weirdness around here, my friend, with your name all over it. I've been sitting here for two days trying to decide if I should page you or not."

"Ray," he said with studied patience.

"So, do you have any family matters you neglected to tell me about during the last, oh, four years we've known each other?"

"Ray, would you knock off the cryptic questions and just spit it out?"

"Don't say I didn't try to prepare you. I got a phone call day before yesterday from some woman who said to tell you that Annie's dead and she's got your daughter."

The bottom fell out of Ross's stomach and he sat down suddenly and heavily on one of the spindly chairs next to the coffee bar.

"Say that again."

"Actually what she said was that Annie's dead and you'd better get yourself back to Seattle if you wanted to see your daughter. I didn't even know you had a daughter. Which is why I took so long to let you know. Nutcases call here all the time. For all I know, she's another one." He paused. "Or is she?"

"Annie's dead? How? When? Where?" Nausea boiled in his gut. Dead. Annie dead? How had this woman found him? Could it really be Kailey? Oh, God. Maybe it was a ransom demand. Ross dragged one hand over his mouth to stop the groan of agony.

"Don't know. Who's Annie?"

Ross clutched the receiver and tried to control himself. "A woman I lived with a long time ago."

"Yeah? I didn't think you were that kind of guy."

"Before I came back to God. She left with our baby when Kailey was eight months old, and joined a religious cult called the Church of the Seventh Seal."

"Never heard of them."

"They're underground. Took me almost a year to find them, then they disappeared again. Did this woman say Kailey was all right?"

"Didn't say. She sounded annoyed that you were out of town, because that meant you couldn't come and get her, but she hung up before telling me practical things, like where she was."

"That shouldn't take too long to find out."

"About ten seconds, thanks to Caller I.D. and the cross-directory. She was calling from that shelter downtown by the bus station."

"Two days ago. She could be anywhere by now."

"Want me to mosey down there and find out? Or are you going to come back and do it?"

Ross fought a feeling of suffocation. It could just be a nutcase—a renegade Sealer playing with his head. But he couldn't just ignore the woman's request, either. He hadn't dedicated his life to cult investigations for the fun of it. He'd done so for Kailey's sake. There was no way he could let this lie. The problem was, he couldn't leave Hamilton Falls with no explanation, not when he was so close to reaching his goal of infiltrating the group.

"Can you go and talk to her?" he asked. "I'm almost in with this group and if I left now I don't know what the repercussions would be."

"Okay," Ray agreed easily. "She might not be there, anyway, and you'd've driven across the state for nothing."

"If you do find her..." Ross's voice trailed away. What? Arrest her? Take Kailey?

"I'll find her, don't worry." Ray's voice had lost its usual flippancy. "Even if she is a nutcase, I'll find her."

Slowly, Ross hung up the phone.

Annie was dead.

Kailey was in the hands of a woman whose motives he was unsure of.

And once again, he had no control over any of it.

As he drove back to the motel, he realized he had never had any control. But there was One who did.

When he let himself into his room, he fell to his knees by the bed, and long hours passed before he got up again.

Chapter Nine

✤

It might be better to leave Ross out of it when she asked Rebecca for Friday evening off.

"Madeleine's having Melchizedek over tonight, and they've invited me along." Julia unlocked the front door and propped it open, allowing the soft June breeze to flirt with the bookmarks on the stand next to the register. "Will you be all right on your own?"

Rebecca pulled the blinds up, and early-morning sunshine poured into the shop. Outside, the streets were clean and quiet, with only a few working people and the perpetual crowd of cyclists lining up at the coffee bar.

"Madeleine's entertaining again," Rebecca said with satisfaction. "Ryan must be recovering." She tugged on a nine-pocket dump of paperbacks, moving it into place on the aisle.

"Slowly. The doctors are thinking of letting him come home as soon as he gets to fifty pounds. But it isn't really entertaining, you know. Just the Shepherd and the family."

"That's not what I heard."

Julia swallowed. Uh-oh. "What did you hear?"

"Your mother and I have known each other for thirty years, dear. We do talk."

Didn't she know it. Everybody talked. It was enough to make you want to move to another state. When the Shepherd talked about the closeness of the fellowship, Julia was sure this was not what he meant.

"I understand you're working a mission," Rebecca went on delicately. "With that young man who likes John Donne."

"Melchizedek and Owen are working the mission." Julia concentrated on moving the display closer to the door. "I'm just the contact."

"He was a nice-looking young man. For a—a motorcycle enthusiast."

"In other words, anyone who likes poetry can't be all bad?" Julia teased. "Even if he rides a motorcycle? And by the way, did you know Donne was a worldly preacher?"

Rebecca's smile faded, but her concern did not. "Yes, dear. But I sold him, didn't I? He's out of the shop now." She returned to the subject at hand. "I just wouldn't want you to become...more involved than you might intend. After all, this is his first contact with God's Elect. There's no guarantee he'll accept the Word, and Julia, I wouldn't want to see you...or anyone else...hurt."

"Does Mom see that happening, too?" She squared the stand with precision.

It would never occur to Elizabeth that a daughter of hers would ever look at a man from the outside. As far as her mother was concerned, Julia was fulfilling the purpose she was put on this earth for and pointing the way for a lost sheep to find the fold. Nothing more.

"Your mother, dear as she is to me, sees only what she wants to. She didn't get a look at your face Sunday night. I did." Rebecca paused, but Julia didn't reply. "Be careful, dear. Oh my, there's UPS."

She turned away and went into the back to sign for the delivery.

The day seemed interminable. Every time a vehicle with a loud motor went past, Julia jumped and ran to the window. Each time the door opened, she popped up like a jack-in-the-box to get a look at the customer. At three Rebecca took pity on her and sent her home.

"Good heavens, child, you're wound up like a spring. Take a hot bath or something."

It didn't help. Julia climbed out of the water after fifteen restless minutes and dried off vigorously, then wrapped the towel modestly around herself as she stood in front of her closet. Not for the first time, she regretted the hair and skin that made her look dead in black. Which was completely appropriate from a heavenly viewpoint, but her human vanity still cringed.

At least it was slimming. Julia pulled on a summer-weight cotton, braided her hair and drove over to Madeleine's.

As she rounded the corner, every cell in her body went on red alert. *Is he here yet? Will he come at all? Where's the bike?*

Her anxious gaze raked the road for any evidence of a motorcycle. She pulled in behind the extra car the Blanchards kept for Melchizedek, since Shepherds didn't own worldly possessions.

Nothing. Not here. He hadn't come. It's okay. It's only just six-thirty.

Madeleine met her at the door. "Your friend isn't here yet."

"So I see." Julia leaned over and kissed her. Madeleine smelled of clean linen and a faint dusting of talcum powder. She stepped back and touched Julia's sleeve.

"This is new."

"Not really. I got it a couple of months ago."

"Why haven't I seen it before?" Madeleine walked around her. "Never mind, I see why. Julia, it has a *slit* in the back."

"It would be hard to walk in if it didn't."

"Why did you buy something you couldn't walk in? For pity's sake, I can see the backs of your knees—and more! I'm surprised at you. What will Melchizedek think?"

What will Melchizedek think? What would so-and-so say? Julia sighed. There was always someone whose opinion mattered more than her choices. "I'll try not to move much." She changed the subject. "Lina, I'm scared. What if I mess this up?"

Madeleine lifted her eyes as if imploring patience from the heavens. "You are the most self-centered girl. Bad enough you're wearing a dress that draws the wrong kind of attention. Now you're convinced that this man's salvation all hangs on you." With jerky movements, Madeleine tried to improve the hang of the cotton. "God is in charge here," she said firmly. "If you behave the way you're supposed to, His will will be done. Now, come inside. And for heaven's sake, if you have to stand up, keep your back to a wall."

Ross set the kickstand down and tilted the bike onto it as he watched Julia come flying out of the house, wiping her hands with a dish towel. She held a paring knife in one hand.

She stopped when he removed his helmet, and he could see her struggle not to stare.

He hoped it wasn't because of his washed-out face from lack of sleep. "How do you like it?"

"You cut your hair," she said, as if she couldn't believe her eyes.

He ran a hand through his new crop. He hadn't got used to it either. "I noticed the other night that all the men had short hair. I didn't want to stand out."

A blush of pure pleasure rose in her cheeks. "It's—it would be hard for you not to stand out. It's, um—it's very nice." She gestured toward the doorway. "Come on in."

"You didn't tell me half the congregation would be here. What's the deal?"

The blush faded at the irritation in his voice, and he realized he needed to get a grip. To focus on what he could control—the investigation—and not on what he couldn't. Ray would do as good a job at locating the mystery woman as he could himself. They were partners, after all.

"It isn't half the congregation. Only Melchizedek and us."

"The what-do-you-call-it?" Focus. Oh, yeah. "Shepherd?"

"Yes."

"I thought it was just the family. Your sister, right?"

Julia looked uncomfortable. Almost guilty. "I hope that's okay."

Ross shrugged, hiding his emotions. This was good. He could ask a few discreet questions of the group's leader without having to chase all over town looking for him. He followed Julia up the stairs and let her take his leather jacket away down the hall while he shook hands with the two men in the living room. Julia reappeared at his elbow.

"And this is my sister, Madeleine."

Ross looked into the eyes of the stunning brunette he'd seen at the hospital. If ever a woman was exactly his type, this was it—slender but curvy, with cheekbones to die for. The only problem was, she knew it. The attention of every man there was riveted on her, and she accepted it the way a queen does the tribute of her people: as if she were entitled to it. On the heels of this insight came the realization that Julia had disappeared. Not physically; she was still standing in the kitchen doorway. But she had diminished somehow...washed out...as if Madeleine had taken all her vitality and self-confidence and appropriated it for herself.

His instinct was to drop Madeleine's slender hand and drag Julia off for a ride or something to put the sparkle back into her. But that wouldn't get him what he wanted out of this little house party. He had to concentrate on the case. Not on his informant's feelings or his own distraction. That would only take his focus off his goal and lead to bad decisions.

"I'm very happy to meet you, Mrs. Blanchard," he said in the intimate voice he kept for pretty women. Julia turned away and he heard some vegetable die under a knife on the cutting board.

"Thank you for coming," she said. Her smile was sincere but distant. He was still an Outsider, after all. "Dinner will be ready in a few minutes."

"Won't you sit down?" Owen asked, and Ross found himself segregated into the living room while the women worked in the kitchen. Well, not all the women. A little blond girl sat tucked under Owen's arm.

"Hullo," he said, tilting his head to meet her curious gaze. "I'm Ross."

"This is Hannah," Owen said with a fond smile. "Shake hands with Mr. Malcolm, sweetie."

Her warm little fingers wrapped around a couple of his, and Ross found himself bending over like a courtier. Her eyes were huge and blue.

Kailey had had big blue eyes, too. A ball of grief and anxiety wedged itself in his throat, and he struggled to force it down. To keep himself from breaking, right here in this pristine living room.

"Are you the angel from hell?" she asked.

Owen blushed and Melchizedek looked uncomfortable. Ross smiled at the child, grateful that she'd deflected everyone's attention away from him. Little pitchers had big ears.

"No," he answered her solemnly. "I'm from Seattle. They don't make many angels there. But the ones they have ride motorcycles like mine."

"What's a motorcycle?"

"I'll show you after dinner if your mom will let me."

Madeleine called them to the table, saving Owen the embarrassment of explaining where his daughter got her ideas. Ross sat on Madeleine's left, Julia on his other side, facing the Shepherd.

"Melchizedek, will you give thanks?" Owen asked quietly, and everyone, even pint-size Hannah, bowed their heads as though a breeze had swept over them.

"Father, we thank Thee for this table spread, and for Thy goodness to us. We thank Thee for this home that has been set aside and sanctified to Thy service. We thank Thee for seed sown in even the most unlikely ground—" Ross felt Julia flinch "—and for those who carry it. Bless this food to our bodies' use and ourselves to Thy service. In His Name, amen."

During dinner the talk was general, but as they settled over dessert, a preparatory silence fell, as though everyone in the dining room knew that the preliminaries were over and the service was about to begin.

He'd been refining his game plan with every conversation he'd had with Julia. This was the acid test. Either they'd accept him as a real convert and he could really start digging, or they wouldn't, and he'd have to go back to Harry Everett and admit failure. Then he'd revert to plan B. Whatever that was.

Melchizedek cleared his throat. "So, Ross, do you think you might join us this Sunday? The invitation still stands."

Ross lifted an interested eyebrow and let it fall. He kept his expression ingenuous and open. "I'd like to. What should I expect?"

"The word of God," Melchizedek assured him, "given by a true minister."

Ross noted how his speech patterns changed when he got down to the subject of religion. Most cults had a unique vocabulary and syntax. Maybe there were clues in their language that would help him discover what kind of ritual the words were hiding.

"How do you define *true?*"

"We try the spirits," Owen put in. "God speaks through his chosen servant, so we know his words are true."

"The chosen servant being Melchizedek." Ross glanced at him, and the other man nodded.

"You seem to be pretty autonomous." He scraped up the last of his carrot cake with his fork. "Not much outside contact. Any reason for that?"

"'Come out from among them and be ye separate,'" Melchizedek quoted. "God's Elect have as much contact with the outside world as anyone. We are in this world but not of it."

"Could you be a little more specific?"

Ross heard Julia suck in a breath. Oops, he had to watch it. The Shepherd seemed to be the ultimate authority. Question him and you question God.

Melchizedek was speaking and he'd missed half of it. "—truth as it is in Christ. The Spirit in us makes us different. You've seen it in Julia. You've probably even seen it in the children."

Now they were getting somewhere.

Hannah chose this moment to reach out and take another piece of carrot cake from the plate. Madeleine took it from her with a soft murmur of correction. With a mutinous lower lip, Hannah sat back, but where any other kid would have cried, argued or at least whined to get the second piece, she merely blinked back tears and kept her baby lips firmly closed.

What kind of discipline did they use to silence a three-year-old? A cold finger of unease touched the newly bare nape of Ross's neck.

"What part do the kids play in your church?" he asked. "Do you have a Sunday school?"

"Sunday school is a worldly invention. But yes, in God's eyes, children are very important," Owen replied. "We believe they belong in Gathering on Sundays right from birth, so they grow up used to being with His Elect—and used to sitting still for an hour. In fact, many of the kids play at Gathering, don't you, sweetheart?"

Hannah, still miffed about the cake, turned her face into her mother's shoulder.

"Any special parts of the service reserved for them?" Ross asked carefully.

"Not really," Owen said. "Ryan and Hannah—I mean, Hannah..." He cleared his throat, paused for a moment to gain control of his unstable voice, and went on. "I'm sorry, Ross. We nearly lost our son recently and I'm afraid I still get a little emotional over his empty chair, even if it's temporary."

"If you'd rather not talk about it, I'll understand."

Owen gripped his wife's hand under the tablecloth as he spoke. "No, this is important. Ryan and even Hannah pass the Body of Christ to the person sitting next to them, but it will be a few years yet before they can manage His Blood."

Ross smiled warmly at Owen. "Will I be able to meet Ryan?"

Madeleine swallowed and spoke directly to Ross for the first time. "He's still in the hospital, Mr. Malcolm, but we have every hope that he'll be able to come home soon. He needs to reach a certain weight before the specialist will release him."

"I'll look forward to that." Melchizedek and Owen exchanged a glance. He'd made the comment purposely, to imply a continuing interest. Almost a promise for the future.

"What about you, Ross?" Melchizedek said. "What's been your experience with God?"

"My experience?" He couldn't tell the truth—they would lump him in with what they called *worldly churches*. Time for the cover story. "Who was that guy whose wife told him to curse God, and die?"

"That would be Job."

"Right. Job. That's how it's been for me. My wife—" Emotion welled up out of nowhere and he gave an all-too-convincing impression of a man who was about to break down. He cleared his throat and tried again. "My wife and daughter were killed a year ago. A drunk driver."

Madeleine reached across the corner of the table and touched his sleeve, tears of compassion and sympathy welling in her eyes. In that moment, he knew he'd won the Elder's wife. He dropped his gaze to her slender fingertips to hide the moisture in his own.

"Have you been able to find forgiveness in your heart for that person, Ross?" Melchizedek asked softly.

He took a moment to separate the story he had to deliver from the emotion behind it. "It's easier to forgive a drunk than it is to forgive God. I got to the point where nothing was worth the effort anymore. So I hopped on the bike and hit the road, trying to find…something…and I stopped in this town for gas. Had a bite to eat. Walked into a bookshop out of sheer boredom and saw—"

"And saw?" Madeleine said breathlessly.

He turned and looked into Julia's eyes. "And saw—" What was the matter with her? Her face was white and she looked like a rabbit caught in a trap. This was supposed to be his big moment—the moment where they'd usher him into the church.

He plowed on. "A woman who personified warmth, happiness, those things that had been taken away from me that night. There was something about her that made me think maybe God could still do good work on the earth. So I stayed. And here I am."

Madeleine's tears had dried and she was looking at Julia with a wrinkle between her lovely, winglike brows. Ross looked from one sister to the other. A moment ago Madeleine had been all melting sympathy. Ross had included the loss of a child on purpose—and he hadn't had to fake it. He'd lost his daughter as irretrievably as if she really had been killed by a drunk driver, and only God knew if he'd ever see her again, despite Ray's determination. But as soon as he'd introduced Julia into the conversation, the sympathy had evaporated. What was going on here?

"Warmth and happiness." Madeleine turned to her husband with a smile. "That does describe Rebecca Quinn, doesn't it, darling?"

"It certainly does. She's a real mother in Israel, despite being a spinster lady. Ross, I can't tell you how many people have come into the bookshop and been pointed to God, just like you."

"Rebecca?"

Julia leaned over. "'Hold your tongue, and let me love,'" she whispered.

Hey, this wasn't fair. "Actually, I was talking about Julia, not the lady who owns the shop."

Gracefully, Madeleine rose and began clearing dessert plates. "Julia has every right to be happy, Mr. Malcolm. She's a very lucky girl."

"That's right," Melchizedek said with a jocular smile. "I have it on the best authority that Derrick will be named Deacon by the time fall Mission begins. Then we'll have two big announcements, right, Julia?"

"And by that time, Ryan will be well enough to be ring bearer, won't he?" Madeleine's smile was luminous with hope and beauty.

Ring bearer? Was Julia engaged? This couldn't be happening. Time was too short to dig up another unattached female.

"Well, this has been very interesting," he said abruptly, and pushed his chair back. "Congratulations, Julia. I'll look forward to your service on Sunday night...and to meeting the lucky man."

Melchizedek smiled brilliantly at Ross. "We'll be very happy to see you. And perhaps I might come and visit you sometime? I'm sure you have more questions, and I'd like to get to know you better."

Ross nodded and strolled down the hall to find his jacket, locating it draped over what was obviously Hannah's bed.

His job in Hamilton Falls was to forge bonds with the targets, to insinuate himself into their lives so seamlessly he could operate from within until he found evidence someone was hurting the kids. He was already emotional about having to stay when he wanted to be back in Seattle. Now he was seriously annoyed with Julia for telling him she was single. This was going to blow his mode of operation to bits.

But while he was in the house, he could still work. He listened carefully. Madeleine was in the bathroom with Hannah. He heard Owen say something out in the kitchen, and Julia's reply as she ran water into the sink to do the dishes. With one finger, Ross quietly swung the bedroom door shut and did a silent, thorough search of the room. He didn't know what he was looking for yet. Ruffled ankle socks with bloodstains? Manacles in the toy box? A nice, springy switch standing by the door?

He found nothing but an ordinary three-year-old's clothes and toys. Not quite ordinary, he amended, pulling on his jacket and taking a last look around. There wasn't a single Disney character in the room, for one thing. No Little Mermaid sheets or Belle dress-up kits. No Barbie vanity strewn with mom's twenty-year-old jewelry. Just a hand-carved Ark on an antique school desk, with a wooden Noah and his animals scattered all around it.

Thoughtfully, he stood a giraffe on its feet. No doubt about it, the Blanchards were behind the pop culture curve. He could only imagine what Kailey had spent her childhood playing with. Live rounds, possibly. Certainly not something as harmless as this.

He dragged his thoughts back to Julia, and unwilling sympathy stirred. She had endured her sister's sabotage with no more than that first telling glance into his eyes. No wonder she faded from sight whenever Madeleine stepped into a room. She'd probably learned it was safer that way.

Jacket over his arm, he stepped into the hall and pushed open another bedroom door. A little boy's this time. He went through the room quickly. The only unusual thing was some kind of medical setup by the bed, bristling with plastic tubing. Out in the hall, the bathroom door opened and he pulled the boy's bedroom door shut, shifting his jacket over the other arm to cover the motion. Madeleine smiled and led him down the stairs.

Julia had her car keys in hand and was unlocking her door as he finished his goodbyes to Madeleine and Owen and loped down the steps to the driveway.

"Don't I rate a goodbye?" he asked.

She leaned an arm on the open driver's window. "Good night. Thanks for coming."

He leaned one hand on the window, his thumb brushing her elbow. "Julia." He still had a job to do.

"What?"

"This wasn't a religious service. This was a date, if you can call it that. We're supposed to leave together and go enjoy the rest of the evening, remember?"

"We are?"

"Sure. The night is young. What's wrong?"

She glanced anxiously toward the front door. Madeleine turned to go in. Owen was still standing there, good host that he was, waiting to wave his guests out of sight.

"Not now, Ross," she said. "Please."

Right. The fiancée of this Derrick character wasn't supposed to be running around with the converts. Far be it from him to criticize someone's phobias, but Rita had only told him the half of it. But if he wanted to stay on this case he had to stick to Julia like rubber on hot asphalt, and that meant playing along.

"Good night," he said just loudly enough for Owen to hear. "See you on Sunday."

She backed out of the driveway. He took his time starting up the motorcycle. When her car turned the corner, he waved once more to Owen and pulled noisily away.

He caught up to the little sedan two blocks later and tailgated her home.

Chapter Ten

✤

Thank heavens Rebecca wasn't back yet from work, Julia thought. The windows of the lower floor were dark. The outside light over the stairs to her apartment burned faintly, frail and insubstantial against the colorless twilight sky.

Ross's motorcycle rumbled up the street, and a warm trickle of pleasure coursed through her. He hadn't just ridden away. She'd fully expected him to, after her idiotic behavior. When he shut the engine off, the silence seemed to ring more loudly, like a guilty conscience.

"Mind telling me what that was all about?" he asked, dismounting and hanging his helmet on one handlebar. His leather jacket creaked as he approached her. It was impossible not to stare at his strange new haircut—evidence of his willingness to conform to the image of Christ—but she tried anyway, turning her key ring to find the house key with great concentration.

Regardless of the new, shorter haircut, his physical presence—male, dangerously attractive—was enough to buckle a woman's knees. He probably wasn't even aware of it, but that didn't make it less powerful. If she acknowledged it, if she let herself enjoy looking at him, somehow that would make her part of it. She couldn't allow that. She had to reduce him to a spirit without a body or she'd never be able to keep herself from temptation.

"Julia?"

The faint scent of leather and cologne teased her nostrils. "You shouldn't be here," she said, her head still down.

He placed one finger under her chin and tilted her head up, forcing her to look. Lord help her, he was so big. So beautiful. His smile flashed briefly in the dim light.

"Sure. Throw on some jeans and we'll go for a ride."

Temptation pulled at her. Of course she couldn't go. Of course she had to end the evening right here, on the sidewalk.

She averted her head and his hand fell away. "I don't have any jeans. Women aren't supposed to wear men's clothes." Which was a little inconvenient when she wanted to hike or ski or simply weed Rebecca's garden, but the will of Melchizedek, backed up by the letters of Paul, always came first, particularly before selfish personal comfort.

"You must have something. I feel a little awkward standing here on the sidewalk. How about you invite me up? Then I can see where you live."

A worldly man in her apartment at night? Julia paled at the thought of what would happen if they were discovered. Even if they were sitting across the room from each other, drinking tea and discussing the Sermon on the Mount, the scandal would be dreadful, and Derrick would be justified in never speaking to her again.

"No," she mumbled finally. "I can't do that."

Ross considered her for a moment, evidently marshalling resources of patience for her ineptitude. This was why Elect girls didn't look Outside for male company. It was just too complicated. They didn't understand the standards of godly behavior.

"Can't invite me in, or can't go at all?"

It had to be done. "Can't go at all."

"Julia," he said softly, "how am I supposed to get to know you and your church if I'm always outside, standing on sidewalks? I can't come in, you won't come with me. I may as well go back to Seattle."

Father, forgive me. I don't know what I'm doing, she prayed in despair. She had to act quickly, or he'd leave. She scrambled for the compromise that was the least of many evils. "I'll run in and change, and be right back in two minutes. Then we can go for a ride. Okay?"

"If I want to talk to you, I guess it'll have to be." He turned away and stood with his hands on his hips.

She dragged her gaze away and ran up the steps and into her apartment, yanking off her stockings and dress in a haphazard path to the bedroom. This was crazy. How was she supposed to do God's will when it meant walking such a razor-fine line between obedience and condemnation?

She pulled on clothes so old they were a scandal, and a warm jacket on top so she wouldn't have to wear his leather again and smell his scent against her skin. Her fingers were rubbery as she hurried to lace up her sneakers. Maybe the Lord would protect her while she was doing His work. Maybe He'd keep her from temptation. Maybe He wouldn't allow any of the Elect to see them.

She ran back down the stairs with fifteen seconds to spare. "Okay, I'm ready," she announced.

He leaned on the motorcycle's seat, his long legs stretched out in front of him, arms crossed. "Let's go, then, before your landlady catches us."

"Don't make fun of me."

He got to his feet. "But it's so juvenile, Julia. You're in your twenties, and you're still worrying about being 'caught' when you go out at night. It's nobody's business." He handed her the spare helmet. She pulled it over her hair and did up the chin strap, slowly, clumsily, but without any help from him. If he was going to criticize her, he didn't deserve the courtesy of a reply.

"What have you got on?" he demanded, as if he'd just noticed. He swung his leg over the seat and tilted the motorcycle upright, staring over his shoulder at her clothes in dismay.

"This is all I have."

"You can't ride in a skirt that straight. How are you gonna get your legs around me?"

Only the thought of this man's immortal soul kept her from turning around and running back up those stairs. "I will manage." She placed her left hand on his shoulder and started to swing her leg over. The old black skirt snapped taut like a bandage. "Uh-oh." Suddenly she saw what he meant.

Eyes narrowed, he shouted over the roar of the engine, "Hike it up, baby. While I try not to say I told you so."

Baby. He called me baby. She fought off the sudden pleasure, and got down to business. Julia pulled her skirt halfway up her thighs and plunked down on the seat, feeling for the foot pegs. Ross looked down, under his arm.

"Whoa."

"Just drive, will you?"

"Are those bare legs?"

"Drive!" she shouted, and banged him on the shoulder. Shocked at herself, she clutched him around the waist. She felt reckless, uninhibited, saying what she wanted to and showing more leg than she ever had in her life. This must be what worldly girls felt like all the time. No one watched how *they* spoke or thought. No one cared. For those who knew the freedom of service to God, this was the forbidden, deceptive lure of bondage to the world.

Ross chuckled, as if he'd read her mind, amused creases forming in the corners of his eyes. He kicked the bike into gear.

Now she knew what to expect—the wind, the roar of the engine, the sense of vertigo as he took the turns and she leaned with him at acute angles that courted disaster. He gave the bike the throttle. They swept down the highway like the wind itself, pouring into the turnoff to the far end of the lake, and soon the black mirror of the water appeared through the trees. The road skirted the very edge of the beach littered with driftwood logs and weathered outcroppings of rock.

On the far side of the lake she looked across the water to the lights of Hamilton Falls glittering against the black backdrop of Mount Ayres. Ross slowed the motorcycle to a stop and parked where the shoulder widened and the ground sloped down to a stand of alders. A silvery strip of sand was just visible at the bottom.

The motorcycle's engine ticked as it cooled in the warm silence. Ross peeled out of his jacket and dumped it over the seat as Julia hopped off, pushing her skirt down with both hands. Ross clipped their helmets to a set of rings behind the seat.

"Come on," he said. "This looks like a good place for a break."

He led the way through the trees. Dry grass brushed Julia's calves as she followed him. Cooling earth released the scent of hay and dust and the thick summer foliage of the alders.

The water lapped softly against rocks scattered at its edge. Ross seated himself on the packed sand, and Julia dropped down beside him. She brushed a few flattened tendrils of hair away from her face. Her cheeks and forehead felt as if they'd been rubbed all over with fine grit sandpaper.

One wrist on an upraised knee, Ross glanced over. "Do you ever take it down?"

Her hand stilled on her hair and fell away. "Only to wash it."

"I want to see it."

"No." Only a woman's husband ever saw her hair down. Anything else was indecent.

He reached up and ran a hand through his own hair.

Her heart hammered in her chest and she lost the battle not to stare. He looked wild and elemental, a force of nature temporarily stilled for her benefit. Her insides turned soft and molten while her skin prickled with an awareness and anticipation that felt almost like fear.

The moon's edge rose above the mountain and bathed them in a faint light. His eyes glittered, pale silver in sockets filled with darkness, as he held her gaze. "Take it down," he whispered.

She couldn't. She wanted to. Slowly, she reached up and pulled the elastic out of her braid, threading the strands apart with her fingers, working her way up to the crown of her head. Her curls, released from captivity, sprang around her temples and bounced off her shoulders. She shoved the elastic in her pocket and searched for words to break the spell.

"There. Happy now?"

His teeth flashed white in a grin. "Very. All we need now is a leather mini. And maybe a tank top to match." He rolled onto both elbows, tipping his head back to look at the sky. His white T-shirt stretched across his pectorals, hugging his biceps.

She'd begun to shiver with tension. It was an effort to straighten her legs. Leaning on her hands, she crossed her ankles with fake nonchalance. "You will never see me in a leather mini," she said with finality.

He made a face that was supposed to convey regret, then quirked an eyebrow at her. "A week ago you would have said I'd never see you on a motorcycle, either."

"It's just that it doesn't look good, Ross."

"Does everybody mind everybody else's business here?"

"It isn't that at all. We have to watch our example for our own sake, the sake of the Elect and the sake of people who might be looking on. People like you."

"How can it look bad to me if I'm the one who wants you to ride with me?" He shook his head. It sounded circular even to Julia. But there it was. "Okay. Start at the beginning for me. What's an example?"

"It's how you appear to people on the Outside. We don't go to movies. We don't dance. We don't listen to worldly music." She recited the words like an incantation against evil. "We don't wear pants, we don't have short hair—the women don't, anyway—we don't swear. We don't wear jewelry. We don't wear makeup."

"So...what *do* you do?"

Julia floundered to a stop. "We're examples of Christ's life."

"But how?"

"I've just *told* you."

"Julia, from what I remember, Christ didn't go around not doing things. He was a positive force. He healed. He taught. He did things for people. He loved. So what do you do?"

"His Spirit lives in us. That's what makes the fellowship so beautiful."

"Beautiful? It sounds passive to me."

She turned on him. "Passive? Do you think that denying myself day in and day out is passive? Do you know how hard it is to wear mourning when you're a teenager, and all the other kids at school are in bright T-shirts and shorts? Do you know what it's like to know I could be as pretty as my sister if I just had a little bit of makeup? How much I'd love to wear a miniskirt?" She scrambled to her feet. "Don't you dare call me passive. Living the way Melchizedek asks us to is harder than anything you'll ever do!"

Her voice shook and she pressed her lips together, turning away to look down the silent, blurry beach, her arms crossed angrily on her midriff. If only she could stop shaking. The wind ruffled across the sand, tossing a few grains farther to the east. In time, she thought irrelevantly, the whole beach could be changed that way.

Something tugged on the hem of her skirt. "Hey." She looked down her nose at the man lounging at her feet. "Sit down. I apologize."

She allowed herself to be coaxed down beside him. Her hands still trembled and her throat ached. She wished she could walk away and hide in the wavering shadows under the trees. Or run up the slope to the highway. She'd never hitchhiked in her life, but right now she was willing to try.

"I have some idea of how hard it is. I gotta admit, seeing my hair all over the barber's floor felt a little weird."

"Why did you do it?" Julia asked stiffly.

He shrugged. "I didn't see any guys like me in the parking lot the other night. So I figured if I was going to come to a service I should show a little respect."

She wanted to thank him, but she was still so upset the words wouldn't come.

"You say you have the Spirit of Christ." Ross tossed a pebble out toward the center of the lake, where the moonlight made a glittering track toward them. "So logically you would do the things He did. What about helping out at the food bank? Volunteering for a suicide hotline? Or doing something for troubled kids or at the homeless shelter?"

Julia had a sudden vision of Alma Woods ladling soup at the homeless shelter—and withholding bowls from people who couldn't tell her why they weren't working. Or of Madeleine, cool and lovely, trying to talk an anorexic teenager out of slitting her wrists. Impossible. The Elect decried the fact that there were homeless and troubled people in a world overrun by the minions of Satan. People in need could come to the Elect, but the Elect could never go to them. It would look like you were grabbing for attention, doing something so unusual. "Come out from among them and be ye separate," the Bible said.

She wondered what would happen if she organized the young people for a Friday night of sorting cans at the food bank, instead of going to someone's house, playing parlor games that had been in vogue at the turn of the century and filling up on a potluck supper.

Impossible. The Shepherd would be coming for a Visit before you could say "in this world, but not of it."

Ross glanced up at her. "No, huh?"

She shook her head.

"So you live a life of self-denial, and everybody watches each other to make sure no one's denying less than the others. You know what that's a setup for, right?"

"Judgment." The shame of it washed through her, scalding her conscience, scouring away the thoughtlessness and small denials that she called her example.

"I'd say so." He paused so long that a pair of eyes winked open in the grass. A rabbit bounced and swerved when Ross spoke again. "That includes me, doesn't it? People would judge you harshly for seeing me."

"I...they..." Her innate honesty fought with discretion. How could she tell him the only reason she was here was to save his soul? Especially when it wasn't true. Not anymore. "Not as long as we spend our time talking about God."

"Is that all?" Ross's voice was too soft, too compelling. And too close. "I can think of other things we could talk about." He slipped an arm around her and her body went rigid. "Julia, you're shaking. Still afraid of me?"

He was too close and too warm and he smelled of clean cotton and that cologne. He touched her jaw with one finger and turned her face toward his.

"No," she whispered. His eyes were shadowed and dark and soft. "Of me."

Chapter Eleven

❧

Cold common sense rushed in and stopped him before he leaned any closer. Her newly liberated curls brushed his cheek as he sat back and took a deep breath of damp air, banishing her warm, clean fragrance and clearing his head.

What had he almost done?

He was working. Cultivating an informant, not a woman. This was no ordinary girl with a pair of soft lips and peachy skin that begged to be touched. This was a follower of Melchizedek the all-controlling, a cultist. And he had almost kissed her.

He sat back, resting on both hands, forcing himself to stay put. He had to save the moment before she realized what was going on.

"How can you be afraid of yourself?" he asked, giving her his full concentration to make up for his physical withdrawal.

"I—I—" She struggled for a moment. "You tempt me," she whispered.

Despite himself, a shot of adrenaline scissored through him. "I do?" he managed.

"Your motorcycle—riding with you—I don't think I should see you anymore."

Uh-oh, this was bad. He'd moved too fast. But somehow he couldn't prevent himself from asking, "Don't you like riding with me?"

She dropped her head on the arms crossed on her upraised knees. "Yes, I like it," she moaned. "That's the problem."

"It's only a problem if there's someone else in the picture. Which there is."

Her head moved up and down. "Yes."

"Derrick Wilkinson." He latched on to the subject fervently, hoping it would distract her. "I wouldn't go out with anybody named Derrick Wilkinson. Don't tell me. He wears wool pants and a boring tie and has about twenty pens in his shirt pocket, right?"

She giggled and lifted her head at last. He'd insult the absent Mr. Wilkinson all night if that was what it took to get a laugh out of her.

"Only two."

"What?"

"Pens."

"And Derrick Wilkinson is going to mind if I take you riding and talk about God?"

"*I* mind. I'm practically engaged to him. It isn't fair to be sneaking off with you at night behind his back." A single breath hitched in her throat.

She'd drawn the line, and he'd have to learn to work inside it. "Come on," he said abruptly. "Time to go."

By the time she'd reached the top of the path, he'd pulled his jacket on, started the motor, and had himself under control. He tried not to look at her woebegone face as she put on the helmet, tried not to enjoy it as her hands slipped around his waist.

His mind was firmly on the investigation as he walked her to the bottom of the steps attached to the side of her Victorian house.

"Rebecca's home," she whispered, glancing anxiously at the curtained windows on the bottom floor. The pattern of the fabric was backlit from within.

"I guess that means I don't get a cup of tea." He followed her up to her landing and watched as she fitted her key in the lock.

Humor seemed to help. She smiled for real, and dimples appeared at both corners of her mouth. Enchanting. "Don't stop," he said. "I've always wanted to do this." Gently, he pressed a thumb into the delicate depression in her cheek.

Her smile and the dimple faded as her gaze locked on his mouth. He found himself holding her chin, his fingers fanning out to touch the angle of her jaw, the soft whiteness of her throat in the faint moonlight.

"Ross—" she said, trying to twist out of his grip, and his brain short-circuited. He dipped his head and kissed his name into silence.

She made a small sound in her throat and stiffened, pushing at his upper arms. He deepened the kiss and parted her lips, tasting, exploring. Her struggle stopped and he felt her body soften, yield and finally lean into him. She met him at last, accepting him, then wooing him.

The sweet rush in his blood was like nothing he'd ever experienced. It was more than desire, it was like falling into a golden glow of warmth and generosity, soothing his wounded heart and making him forget his worries just for the moment. He pulled her harder against his chest and sank into her kiss, drowning in that sweet giving that told him without a doubt there had to be something severely lacking in her relationship with what's-his-name.

He pulled his mouth away and came up for air. "I want to see you again," he said. "To talk about more than religion."

With an intake of breath, she searched his face. "You can't."

"Why?" He dipped his head and nuzzled her cheek. "Mr. Pens in His Pocket?"

"Partly."

"And?"

"Ross, you have to go. Rebecca heard the bike. She'll give us ten minutes and then look through the curtains."

"Sounds like you've done this before."

"That's none of your business," she said primly, and stepped out of his arms.

"One more kiss."

"No." She stepped inside, and he distinctly heard her turn the lock.

The ride back to the motel cooled him down and brought him back to reality. He needed to think about what was important, not about kissing his informant. He paged Ray, and within minutes, the motel room's phone rang.

"Did you find her?" he demanded without preamble.

"No," Ray replied glumly. "She and the girl were already gone. From what the director said, she probably left right after she talked to me."

Ross was used to frustration and the stop-start nature of investigations, but this hit too close to his heart. He sat on the bed and curled over the pain, his elbows on his knees and the receiver pressed to his ear.

"Could you pick up anything?" he asked, once his voice was under control.

"Not much. The woman is in her early fifties, wearing a printed cotton dress and a gray sweater. Brown eyes, gray hair pulled up in a bun. Calls herself Miriam, no last name."

"Biblical alias," Ross murmured.

"Could be. I ran the first name through NCIC anyway, and took some pictures back down there, but no match."

"Not if she's been underground for a long time. What about the girl?"

Ray paused. "Looked to be about five, dark hair, gray eyes. Seemed in good health, according to the director."

"Five?"

"Yeah. How old did you say your kid was?"

"She was seven on October 16th. And she has blue eyes."

The long-distance connection hissed in the silence.

"You think maybe this Miriam is pulling something on you?" Ray asked at last.

"I don't know what to think." A moment ago, Ross had thought he couldn't stand the pain of having missed the woman and the child at the shelter. Now he'd welcome that pain over the yawning emptiness inside him as hope drained away.

"One last thing," Ray said. "When they left, the woman mentioned they'd be heading east. Something about a fruit festival and a pitchfork."

Ross rubbed his eyes. "There are hundreds of fruit festivals going on in the summer all over the state. She may as well have said she was going to South America for all the good it'll do me." He had no idea what the pitchfork was all about. If she was a Sealer, it could mean anything from an item on a shopping list to a reference to Satan.

"Thought I'd pass it on."

"Thanks, Ray. You did good. I guess I can only hope she calls again."

"If she does, what do you want me to do?"

"Give her my pager number, and get a lock on the phone she calls from. If she's heading this way maybe it'll be close enough for me to get to without jeopardizing this case too much."

"You think it's a hoax," Ray said flatly.

He sighed. "I've had leads over the years, but none of them have ever led me to Kailey. And this description doesn't look like a good match. For all I know, it could be someone from an old case, out of jail and playing head games."

"Speaking of cases, how's it going?"

A good question. One that had about six different answers.

"Good. But you know what?"

"What?"

"Next time I come up for transfer, remind me to put in for something simple, like drug enforcement."

The telephone on her bedside table shrilled like an alarm clock, and Julia groaned and fumbled for the receiver.

"Good morning!" Claire's cheery tones felt like little rocks of reality hammering on her skull.

"What's up?" She sat up, cross-legged, and peered at the clock. Nine-thirty. Good grief.

"Oh, nothing yet. But it's so beautiful out I thought we could get a bunch of the kids together for scrub, if the diamond down at the lake is free."

"Softball?" Resistance pooled below Julia's solar plexus. She didn't want to play a dumb softball game, she wanted to see Ross. And how come they always referred to themselves as "the kids," anyway? Most of them were in their twenties, and Derrick was thirty-one. The Shepherd told them they should be childlike, but this was taking it too far.

"Sure. What do you think? If we each made half a dozen calls we could get enough together for two teams, if the Kowalczyks haven't decided to round everybody up for a hike or something. They were talking about that at prayer meeting. I could call John and find out."

"I don't think I will today, Claire. Thanks, though."

"Julia, you love softball. Are you feeling okay? You sound a little strange."

"I'm fine." A reckless idea suddenly seized her. "Hey, I know. Why don't we all meet down at the food bank and volunteer to sort food for them? They were posting notices for a drive downtown and I bet they could use the help."

Silence.

"Claire?"

"Sort food?" Claire repeated, as though Julia had suggested robbing the food bank, not volunteering.

"You know, for the homeless. I don't know what's involved but I'm sure they'd be willing to show us. What do you think?"

"I think we should ask Melchizedek about it," Claire said slowly. "Those people are affiliated with a worldly church."

"So? It's still more useful than playing softball."

"Julia, are you sure you're okay? Elaine Bell says Madeleine told her sister-in-law that you invited that biker for dinner last night. I couldn't believe it. I told her she shouldn't go around spreading gossip."

"It isn't gossip," Julia said sharply, throwing off the covers and swinging her legs over the side of the bed. What did Ross have to do with sorting food? "And Madeleine invited him, not me. It was at their house."

"Madeleine? Then it's true? He actually came to the Elder's for dinner? On that motorcycle?"

"And he didn't even knife anyone to death. Come on, Claire, the man is interested in coming to God. Owen and Madeleine are always inviting people to dinner. What's the big deal?"

"But he's a *biker!*"

"He is not. He cut his hair. He's coming to Mission tomorrow, so you can see for yourself."

"Mission!" Claire was practically hyperventilating. "Wait till the kids hear this! If you change your mind, we'll be down by the lake. 'Bye."

Julia severed the connection. If she called Claire back, the line would be busy as the scoop went out along with the invitation to play softball. For the first time in her life, she had deliberately distanced herself from her best friend. Or was it just that she had changed over the course of the week and Claire had not?

One thing was sure, though. She'd been right about the food bank idea. Claire's first reaction had been to seek Melchizedek's approval. The right thing to do wasn't really right until he approved it. Otherwise, it was suspect. Like Ross. Suspect until she'd mentioned Melchizedek's name, and then suddenly front-page news as he took on the glow of prospective conversion.

Dissatisfied in both body and mind, she started a pot of coffee and padded into the bathroom for a shower. She was just drying off when the phone rang.

Ross!

"Hello?" Her voice was its most welcoming, a little husky, eager.

"Hi, dear, it's Mom."

Disappointment weighted her shoulders down. "Hi."

"I was just talking to Madeleine and thought I'd give you a call. I hear your little mission went very well last night."

Her *little mission*. Her mother was the only woman in the world who could demolish an accomplishment in five words or less. Julia straightened her spine.

"It isn't my little mission. It's Melchizedek's."

"Of course it is. We're just instruments of help, like Joshua and Caleb holding up Moses' hands. Dad and I were having a little study on that very subject this morning."

"Oh?"

"I just wanted to make sure you were praying about this, and keeping things in perspective."

"What things?" Julia unwrapped the towel around her hair and began to pat it dry with one hand.

"We're all anxious for a soul to be saved, but not at the expense of one of our lambs."

"Whose expense?" She felt like a lawyer, trying to get a reply from a slippery witness.

"Yours, dear."

Now she'd lost track of the beginning of the conversation. "Are you advising me to be careful I don't get involved with Ross?"

Her mother hesitated. Blunt words could cause offense, without the cloak of biblical references and the language the Elect used in Gathering. "I know that you care for Derrick, dear. The thought never occurred to me. Besides, who could ever consider getting involved with—

with someone like that? Who rides a motorcycle and all.
Is it true he wore a leather outfit to dinner?"

Julia rolled her eyes. "It's only a jacket. He took it off,
Mom, when he went into the house. He didn't come to
the table in it."

"I can't imagine Owen allowing *that*. Well, I hope their
example will lead him to what's right."

"I'm sure it will." *Get off the phone, Mom, so he can call.*

"Madeleine says Melchizedek invited him to Mission.
Is he going to come?"

"As far as I know."

"Is he coming with you?"

"Not that I know of." *Please let him come with me. Let
him sit with me.*

"That's good. We want him coming for himself, don't
we? Not for you."

"Of course." Had her mother always spoken to her this
way?

"Your father's waving at me, dear. We're going out to
breakfast with Alma Woods and Rebecca. 'Bye."

Julia hung up so quickly that it took a moment for her
mother's last words to sink in. She and Dad were going
to breakfast with Rebecca.

By lunchtime, everyone would know that Derrick
Wilkinson's intended had gone riding with that biker in
the middle of the night.

Chapter Twelve

✤

She was listed in the phone book as J. McNeill, with no address, a thin disguise for a woman living alone. Ross dialed Julia's number and she answered on the first ring.

"Hey. It's Ross."

"Hi!" No doubt about his welcome there.

"How was your night?"

"Fine."

"What did you dream about?" he teased.

"None of your business. Besides, I prayed for forgiveness."

Somehow he knew she wasn't teasing anymore. "Because I kissed you?"

"No. Because I kissed you back."

He was losing her. If she was praying for forgiveness already, he had to do something fast. He couldn't wait until Sunday night. "Let me make up for it. Let's go for a ride."

"Oh, Ross." Dismay weighted both words.

"I promise I won't kiss you again. I won't even touch you. We'll just go for a ride and leave it at that. Okay?" *Let her say yes. Let me not have damaged the investigation so soon.*

After a long hesitation in which he saw himself being posted, not to drug enforcement, but to a desk job for the rest of his career, she said, "All right."

She was waiting on the steps when he cornered into the driveway and killed the engine. She was wearing a day pack and that same skirt.

"Julia, we're going to have to do something about your clothes."

She looked down and spread her hands. "But this is all I have."

"Come on. We'll go into town and buy you a pair of jeans."

"I couldn't!"

"Yes, you can. That skirt isn't safe. If something happened and I dumped the bike, you'd scrape everything off those legs, right down to the bone." She fiddled with the helmet straps as though she'd forgotten how they worked. "I mean it, Julia. Either we buy you a pair of jeans for safety or you don't ride with me anymore."

Her eyes were big and blue and beseeching, and her teeth dented her lower lip as upbringing battled with the desire to ride. He let her take her time.

"Okay," she said at last. "There's a Denim Depot on the corner of Second and Lake."

"Good choice," he said gruffly, and straightened the bike. "Get on."

She hiked up her skirt and mounted a little more gracefully this time. A few more rides and she'd be a pro.

When they got to the store, Julia entered with criminal caution, after checking both sides of the street. She grabbed a couple of items and hid in the fitting room.

"Ross!" she hissed from behind the door.

"What?" he whispered back, leaning on the cubicle frame.

"If anyone comes in, tell me, okay?"

"I don't know any of them, Julia."

"You'll know."

He probably would, at that. The clerk with the stud in his nose and the two teenagers with ball caps on backward and low-slung pants definitely didn't fit the Elect mold. Other than that, the store was empty.

"What do you think?" Behind him, the dressing-room door opened, and Julia modeled in front of the mirror.

"Wow." Her cheeks flamed red. She had curvy hips that made her waist look even smaller, and for the first time, she wore color—a teal-green T-shirt. It brought out the fire in her hair and the creamy texture of her skin.

"The T-shirt should be black, but I figured, in for a penny, in for a pound. If I'm caught wearing jeans it won't matter if I'm wearing color, will it?"

There wasn't much of an answer he could make to that. "You look great, and what's more, you'll be safer. Now, let's get out of here." She paid for her purchase, and Stud Nose pushed her skirt into a plastic bag and handed it to her. "Want me to case the street before we go out?" Ross asked at the door. She looked down at the bag in her hands and blushed again. "Anyone else would have thought you were going to rob the till, not buy a pair of jeans. Can this much guilt be worth it?"

She lifted her chin as they walked out onto the sidewalk, and slid onto the passenger seat behind him. "Don't laugh at me. These jeans are a safety precaution. You said so yourself."

He rolled up the shopping bag and stuffed it into one of the saddlebags. Mounting the bike, he revved the engine and leaned back. "Yes, I did. You are definitely safe with me."

This time, instead of going around the lake, he took a cutoff that directed them to the top of Mount Ayres. The road wound higher and higher, offering them views out over the lake and down the long valley in which Hamilton Falls lay. The sun fell hot on his back, Julia's knees gripped him tightly, and the wind in his face smelled of green hay and wild roses.

There were days when he loved his job.

At the trailhead, he offered her his hand and they set off. Despite the sun, the wind at this altitude was cool. Julia pulled on the black sweater she had tied around her waist as they hiked through a meadow blooming with lupine and Indian paintbrush. At the spring, they sat on a grassy bank and Ross pretended to take in the view down the mountainside. Water bubbled up out of the rocks to their right and rushed down the slope with a sound like wind in the pines. He glanced at her.

"Nice place to grow up," he said. "I suppose you've hiked all over these mountains."

Julia nodded. "Over the mountains, around the lake, you name it. Eating and team sports seem to be our principal forms of entertainment."

"You don't sound very happy about it." Would she respond? Or were negative comments about her religion forbidden, too?

"I don't know what it is with me lately. I'm seeing things differently. Having doubts. Finding fault. I've always thought our fellowship was the most wonderful thing in the world. Now it's getting on my nerves."

"So what's really wrong?"

"Oh, I don't know." She sighed. "I guess I'm just disappointed. Claire—my best friend—called me this morning to organize a baseball game. I suggested we go down to the food bank and help out, and she just closed up."

"You can't do charitable works all the time, Julia."

"Once would be nice. They say faith without works is dead, but I don't know what my works are supposed to be, if it isn't helping other people out. Then again, we're supposed to keep our works secret, so how do I know what people are really doing? All I know is what I'm not doing."

"What about your sister and her husband? Isn't he the top of the heap around here?" Nice segue. He had to get her talking about the children.

"Yes. They do things, though. They have the poorer members of the Elect over for dinner. Melchizedek is there a lot. And of course, when Phinehas—he's the senior Shepherd for the state—is in town, he stays with them or with my parents."

Ross bit back a cynical comment and said instead, "I liked Owen. Nice guy."

Julia smiled fondly. "He's the nicest man in the world. He met Madeleine when she moved to Spokane to start nurses' training. Naturally she couldn't have a career once she was married, so she only had a year there."

Ross chose his words carefully. "It must be hard on them, with their little boy so sick."

Julia's shoulders slumped. "It's hard on all of us. I feel guilty any time I'm not at the hospital. Madeleine is the world's best mother and it just kills her that she's powerless to do anything."

"Have they figured out what went wrong?" Rita had said the test results were inconclusive. It wasn't likely Julia would know any more.

"They say it's gastrointestinal bleeding, but they've never been able to tell us exactly *why* he's bleeding. He's been sick for years, poor little kid. Practically since he was a baby. No one has ever known."

Unresolved sorrow and love trembled in her voice. Ross hated himself for pushing this line of questioning, but he had to. Everett was going to want answers. "Have you ever seen any kind of pattern in his illnesses?"

"What do you mean?" She swallowed. She didn't seem to think the question was odd, but maybe she was just focused on controlling her voice.

"I mean, has it always been the same thing, or did it start out mild when he was a baby and continually get worse, or what?"

The pending tears seemed to abate as she thought about it. "I never noticed any pattern, but then, we're so scared and so close to it, it's never occurred to me to look for one. He's such a fragile kid. But like most kids with illnesses, he always seems to get sick at the worst times. When I graduated from junior college was one. It took me four years to do a two-year degree because my parents wouldn't help with the tuition. They were pretty upset that I didn't get married right after high school. I didn't go to the ceremony anyhow because it just celebrates pride, but Rebecca was going to have a hymn sing for me. Needless to say, none of the family got there. We were all at the hospital. Then, a couple of weeks after Hannah was born—same thing. When Owen got the principal's job. That was horrible. Owen's first day of term was a mess because he wanted to be at the hospital so badly he couldn't keep his mind on his work."

The sixth sense that Ross had developed over the years began to tingle. Patterns. Patterns were always a place to start. Was Ryan being used somehow to placate an angry God at important times in their lives? Was there some kind of weird rite being performed in secret? He hadn't been able to find such a pattern in the other kids' deaths; in fact, the families had been so forthcoming with the investigators that he'd pretty much written them off as tragic accidents and left it at that.

But Ryan's case was different. It wasn't a onetime accident, but a series of episodes. He couldn't very well ask Julia point-blank about the placation theory, and risk upsetting her to the point where she refused to talk at all.

He changed the subject. "What made you stay in Hamilton Falls instead of moving away like your sister?"

She tilted her head. "Not everyone moves to the big city, you know."

"I know. Look at me. Still in Hamilton Falls after a week."

"My family is here. I wanted to be near the kids. And the job at the bookstore is enough for me to live on until—" She stopped, then went on quickly, "Rebecca charges me hardly anything to rent the suite. Everything was so easy that at the time I was convinced it was God's will that I stay."

"And of course there was Derrick." He hadn't missed that little hesitation. Enough for her to live on until she got married? And women gave up their careers anyway after the ring was on their finger? How archaic could you get?

If she detected any sarcasm in his tone, she didn't show it. "There has always been Derrick. Loyal guy that he is." *Unlike me*, he read in the unhappy downturn of her mouth.

He shrugged out of his jacket and laid it on the grass. The sun was hot up here. He stretched out and put his hands behind his head. "Tell me about him."

She pulled up a stem of lupine and began to pull the flowers off one by one. "I've known him all my life, so it's hard to know what to tell."

"Start with the important thing. Do you love the guy?"

She fumbled with the flower stem and it fell to the ground. "I care about him. He's been proposing to me since I was eighteen."

Ross blinked. "What do you tell him that keeps him coming back?"

"I've managed not to tell him anything so far."

"The poor guy. I'd have cut you loose after the first time."

The dimple in her cheek deepened briefly and he watched it, fascinated. "You have to understand about Derrick, though. He's been preparing all his life to be Deacon some day."

"What's that got to do with proposing to you?" The social customs of this group confounded him. Being a teenager was hard enough without having to navigate through a labyrinth like this. How did any of them survive it?

"A hundred years ago, when the first Shepherd came to Washington, only certain families showed him any kindness. They gave him a place to stay and became what we call the Firstfruits. That means the men in those families—ours, the Traynells out east of town, and a family on the other side of the lake—were made Elders. Permanently."

"You mean it's a hereditary title?"

"Yes. My great-grandfather, grandpa, dad, they were all Elders. Then when Dad got older, his health wasn't so good. We don't have any brothers to pass the title to, so when Madeleine married, Dad asked that the title be passed to Owen. Meantime, there's always a backup from a lesser family or younger sibling, called the Deacon. My husband. Derrick."

Ross lay back on the jacket, taking this in. "What happens if you fall in love with someone else?"

"Well, I haven't, have I? Derrick's been living for this all his life. It's just a matter of us setting the date now."

"Which you haven't done. Mostly because you haven't said yes, yet. Julia, something tells me you're not exactly committed to being Derrick's ticket to the big time."

"I'm not a ticket to anything. He loves me."

"I'm sure he does." She gave him a narrow-eyed glare. "I mean it. But how has he managed to chase everyone else off and keep you to himself?"

"What do you mean, everyone else?"

He gestured at the valley below them as if it were teeming with men. "All the other guys who wanted to take you out."

She made a derisive noise. "What guys? You obviously don't know what it's like to be the sister of Madeleine McNeill."

"I spent an entire evening with her and didn't fall in love with her once."

"Would you be serious?" She leaned back on her elbows and gave him an exasperated look.

"I am serious. In fact, I'm so serious I'm considering giving old Derrick Wilkinson a run for his money."

"What?"

"Who says I can't be the next Deacon?"

"Are you crazy?" She sat bolt upright.

"Why not? I cut my hair. After that, anything's possible. You're not in love with Derrick, so maybe you'll fall in love with me."

Wickedly, he grinned up at her. So he'd promised he wouldn't kiss her again. That didn't mean he couldn't tease her a little. Open body language and his patented lady-killer grin worked on ninety-nine percent of the women he knew.

Then again, ninety-nine percent of the women he knew didn't have a lifetime of training in self-denial.

She turned her nose up at him. "I have no intention of falling in love with anyone as conceited as you. I don't know anything about you. What are you doing in Hamilton Falls, anyway?"

"You can't blame a guy for trying. And I told you the other night." He sobered, playing the part. "I was passing through. Escaping."

She bit her lip. "I'm so sorry, Ross. I didn't mean to be flippant. Here I've been dwelling on my family's problems and totally forgetting how much you've suffered, too."

He shrugged. "You sounded like you needed to talk. And don't worry about me. The pain becomes part of you after a while. You learn to live with it, like a fake hand or something."

"That doesn't sound very appealing."

"Consider the alternative."

"So your employer said you could take off for as long as you needed?"

"Not exactly. I'm between positions at the moment. And was that a sneaky way of finding out more about what I do for a living?"

"No, of course not. But it's nice to have an idea of who you are."

"What I do isn't who I am." Now, there was a whopping big lie. His job—no, his vocation—as a cult specialist was a huge part of who he was. His past with Annie and the Sealers and his drive to succeed as an investigator dovetailed with his faith that this was the path God had called him for. But it was time for her to think less about him and more about them.

"Care to share my jacket?" he asked.

"The view is just fine from here, thank you." After a long moment, she turned to find him watching her. "Ross." Her tone held warning. "You promised."

"I did, didn't I?" He closed his eyes and relaxed under the sun and after a moment, despite what she'd said, he felt her stretch out next to him. The wind fanned over the two of them, bringing the sound of water splashing on the rocks below. A hawk wheeled lazily in the updraft.

Beside him, Julia sighed, a sound of desolation. He rolled to his side and rested his head on his hand, looking down into her eyes. She was watching the hawk. "What is it?"

"I was just thinking of a girl I knew in school."

"Yeah? Who?"

"Jenny Kurtz. She works for the police."

"And why were you thinking of her?"

"You told Melchizedek you saw me and—and you thought maybe God could still do good work on the earth."

"I did. But I still don't get the connection."

"She used to tell people I was in a cult. She'd make up stories from things she'd read and tell people we did them. But we aren't a cult. We just believe in God." She looked up into his face. "What do you think we are?"

This was a switch. The informant was putting his investigation back on track. He gazed into her eyes, eyes that were clear and honest and completely without ulterior motive or guile. There was only one thing he could say. "This Jenny doesn't know what she's talking about," he said gently, smoothing an errant strand of hair out of her eyes. "But I know one thing."

"What?" The breeze died, leaving them in a vast, waiting silence.

She had rolled her head toward him, her face so close he could touch it with a breath. "You don't love Derrick Wilkinson." With one fingertip, he traced her jawline.

"Yes, I do," she whispered, as if reciting a lesson. The sun caught in her eyes, gilding the tips of her lashes.

"But you like being with me." Aimless as the breeze that puffed over them, he let his fingertip drift down to her chin.

She seemed to be losing the thread of the conversation. "I'm not supposed to feel this way about an Outsider."

He felt the potential of passion like the wind racing across the meadow, coming closer and closer. Just by leaning down he could take her sun-warmed sweetness and consume it with a kiss, drawing it into himself like a talisman against the dark.

But he couldn't. He couldn't offer this woman anything, even leaving her odd religion out of it. It wouldn't be right to lead her on any further, no matter what Harry Everett thought he had to do. That would mean pushing "cultivation of the informant" past the boundaries of investigative license straight to "grounds for suspension."

And it might mean breaking her heart.

Chapter Thirteen

❧

If she let herself cry, he would see her in the side mirrors. Julia drew on years of training in silence and clenched her teeth, willing the tears back to where they'd come from. She should have known better. Bad enough she had been so forward as to lie on that jacket with him. Worse that she had lain there waiting for his kiss, throwing her self-control away under the magic of his touch. She'd been dumb enough to allow him intimacies she'd hardly allowed Derrick, for heaven's sake, and blurted out her feelings on top of that, and now look.

This was what came of playing with the wolf. This was what came of putting her own selfish desire ahead of what she knew was right. He'd bundled her back down the mountain and onto the bike like an embarrassed parent hustling a misbehaving child out of Gathering.

Julia gripped his waist as the motorcycle dipped into another turn, and wished she were at the bottom of the lake.

"Where do you want to eat?" he shouted over his shoulder, the wind grabbing the words.

"I don't care." Maybe he wouldn't hear her.

No such luck. He probably read lips. "You don't care where or you don't care whether it's with me?" he hollered. "What's the matter back there?"

She plastered on a smile and the wind immediately dried it to her teeth. "Nothing!" she shouted brightly.

"Glad to hear it. I could use some home cooking."

"Some what?"

"Home cooking! You know. Steak. Something simple."

Only a man would think steak was simple. "I don't have any steak."

"I'll settle for fried eggs. If I'm allowed in your apartment in the daytime?"

Julia struggled to understand him. One minute she thought he was going to kiss her again, the next he had rolled away in disgust. Now he wanted to go home with her for lunch. A trickle of joy seeped through the confusion and humiliation.

"Julia?"

"Yes, you're allowed." It would be all right to invite him to lunch in broad daylight. After all, he'd been to Madeleine's for dinner. Melchizedek himself was going to visit. He was no longer a Stranger, not really, and something like lunch was harmless. It wasn't like she was inviting him in at night.

He decelerated down the long grade into town. As they cornered into Gates Place she stiffened with a gasp of horror.

"What? What?" Ross demanded. "Don't do that, woman, you'll make me lay this thing down."

"I can't go home like this!"

"Like what?"

"Wearing jeans!"

"Too late. We're here."

He pulled into the driveway and cut the engine. With a sense of relief so heady it was like a lungful of pure oxygen, she saw that Rebecca's car was gone. She was safe for one more day. Could a person actually die from a heart attack brought on by guilt?

Ross followed her up the stairs and into her apartment. She threw open the curtains and light flooded into the kitchen. He stood in the middle of the adjoining living room and looked around, taking in her pictures, her books, the half-finished embroidery draped over the arm of the couch, held down by the needle stuck in the upholstery.

She opened the refrigerator door and pulled mushrooms and broccoli out of the crisper.

"I'll do that." He took them and began opening drawers, looking for a knife.

"That side." She pointed. "You can cook, too?"

"You think just because I'm a mechanic and ride a motorcycle I have no culinary skills? Mom ran an equal opportunity kitchen. Everything my sisters learned, I learned too. After that I graduated to laundry and the finer points of dusting china."

Julia tried to imagine Derrick or Owen doing laundry and dusting china and failed.

"She was stuck on me having a real career for a while there," he went on, "but she got over it. She thought I should be a lawyer or a doctor."

"A regular job has its benefits," she pointed out.

"I have a regular job. Most of the time." Mushrooms fell in precise slices on the cutting board. "Nothing breaks down more regularly than heavy equipment."

When the water boiled, Julia fed linguine into it. It was a sin to envy a worldly woman she would never see—

the future Mrs. Ross Malcolm. The man was not only gorgeous and an expert kisser, he could fix the car when it broke. He could cook. He could even dust china. She battled a sense of unreality. Why was he here in her kitchen? Why was she even entertaining the thought of his life skills when it was completely impossible that she would ever get to enjoy them?

He isn't Elect, she told herself. And even if he came to Gathering with her, even if he became Elect himself, he'd still be off-limits. She would be married to Derrick by then, with nothing to do but watch Ross get mobbed by single women every Summer Gathering, year after year, until he chose someone far more pretty and interesting than she.

"Hey." He bumped her shoulder.

She looked up, startled, and felt her knees go weak at the warmth in those gray eyes, the way his long lashes veiled them as he looked down at her. Her breath backed up in her chest.

"What do you want me to do with these?"

She blinked as he indicated the neat stack of vegetables. "Oh. Um, sauté them. Thanks."

"Coming up. Where do you go when you do that?"

"Do what?"

"Stare off into the distance like that."

She blushed the unbecoming color of beets and turned down the flame on the boiling pasta. "I was having an out-of-body experience." Wishing she were someone else.

"Stick around. I like you in this one." He smiled, and Julia felt her knees go as spongy as the mushrooms.

Where, she wondered, was she ever going to find the strength to bring this to an end?

Ross left shortly after they heard Rebecca's car pull into the driveway.

"I can't believe it," he said crossly when she'd fidgeted around the room like a fly trying to escape. "What's wrong with having a man over to lunch?"

"Nothing. It's just that you can't stay too long. It'll look bad."

"I thought we went through this already. Do they think you're going to elope with me after the entrée?"

"Of course not."

"Then why does it look like you're guilty until proven innocent?"

Julia gave up trying to explain. Single women didn't entertain a man alone. Period. Lunch had been okay. A couple of hours of conversation, no problem. But when the day stretched into late afternoon, people could think the worst, and often did. In her case it was particularly dangerous because it would look as though she were cheating on Derrick.

Ross lived in a world where his behavior was his own business. He could do and say anything he liked. The sense of freedom she'd felt earlier was just an illusion. She lived in a fishbowl because she was the sister of the Elder's wife.

"All right, Julia. Have it your way. I'm gone."

"Goodbye," she said softly on the landing. His eyes were level with hers, though he stood one step below. The memory of what had happened the last time they stood here filled the air between them.

"Thanks for the pasta. I'll call you tomorrow."

What for? Why did he bother? "I won't be home in the morning."

"I know. We could go for a ride when you get home."

"Not on Sunday, I'm afraid. And then there's Mission in the evening."

"Of course." He paused a moment as if to get his words in order. "You're sure it's okay if I come?"

Her heart gave a leap and she struggled not to gasp or weep at the unexpected gift. He still meant to come despite her idiotic behavior! "Of course. Anyone can." *Thank you, Lord. I don't deserve this.*

"Even bikers?"

"Even them, hard as it is to believe."

"Can I pick you up? Say at a quarter to seven?"

And roll up to the door astride a motorcycle? What a sensation *that* would cause. Such a thing had never happened at Mission in her lifetime or anyone else's. But then, neither had she been accosted by a biker in the parking lot before, and look what had happened since then.

"I don't think so, Ross. How about I meet you there?"

After a moment, he nodded. "See you tomorrow, then."

With a light touch, he smoothed her hair behind her ear and cupped her chin.

"Ross..."

"What?" His eyes were deep pools of slate framed by those incredible lashes.

From somewhere she summoned the strength to say, "Please don't."

"I won't. But I still think you're making a mistake."

He clunked down the steps, his boots heavy on each riser, and kept his back to her as he put on his helmet, fired the motorcycle up, and roared out of sight.

Making a mistake about what? She turned and went back inside. He's still coming to Mission. He's still coming. It's a miracle. Dear Lord, what was she going to do? She forced herself to calm down. Nothing. This is not up to you. You can't save his soul, only he and God can.

But who was going to save hers? She thought of his kisses. Derrick never kissed her that way. She'd read in the paper once that two people couldn't really fall in love until they'd exchanged some kind of chemical in their saliva when they kissed. Was that what was wrong with her?

Not that she was in love with him. She was just infatuated. This was what she got for playing with the wolf. God wouldn't let her be tempted past bearing.

The good Lord had pretty much pushed her to her limit, though.

Sunday was a day of rest. After Gathering in the morning from ten till twelve, lunch for eleven people at Madeleine's house to celebrate the news that Ryan could come home the following day, an afternoon with an energetic three-year-old who simply would not go down for her nap, and the drive back home to change due to a mistimed sip of milk, Julia was more than ready for it. But there was no hiding from the current of nervous energy that started up inside her around five o'clock, when she was finally able to shut herself into her apartment.

This must be what drug addiction is like, she thought as she knelt by the bed, trying unsuccessfully to pray before Mission. Her skin felt as though it was just barely holding her together. Blood energized by adrenaline fled through her veins. She would never hear a word of Melchizedek's sermon if Ross was anywhere in the room.

I hope he doesn't come.

Oh, Lord, please let him come.

God didn't listen to such selfish prayers. She got up and threw open the closet door. She didn't have a thing to wear. All her clothes looked dull and monotonous and, well, black. It was hopeless. The women of the Elect dressed to symbolize sacrifice, not to be attractive. And not for the first time, Julia wondered if that was really what God wanted from half His creation.

The parking lot at the Mission hall was nearly full. She could get a seat on the center aisle, she thought as she hurried inside. He'd see her right away and come and sit with her.

Or maybe not. She'd forgotten about Derrick. He would see the seat on the aisle and assume it was for him. But even if he got there after Ross, he would spend the whole service staring at them, making sure Ross didn't so much as bump her shoulder. People would notice. People would talk.

Oh, this was awful. She bowed her head and opened her Bible to Job and his patience during his trials.

The advantage of sitting on the aisle was that she only had to lift her head a little to see people as they came in. Here were Madeleine and Owen, with Hannah between them. Owen flashed her a smile as they made their way to the front row. Alma Woods and her bevy of cronies came in afterward, bulky clothes rustling, T-strap shoes clacking on the hardwood floor. They sat in the third row, gossiping about everyone they saw as if it had been a month instead of a week since they'd done it last. The room was filling up now, and still he hadn't appeared. She closed her Bible and laid it on the chair beside her. Someone in flat heels tiptoed past, trying to be quiet. Dinah Traynell, in a new high-waisted dress with a—good heavens. It wasn't even homemade. Who was she trying to impress?

A horrifying thought struck Julia. Her mother had quizzed her about Ross yesterday. Had she been spreading her guesses as truth? Were the single women feathering their arrows before Ross was even in the room?

The Bells came in like a decompressing steam train, all noise and "shhhh!" as Linda and Jim herded all their children into the back row, closest to the washrooms. There was a step in the anteroom and Julia's body tensed as if someone had wound her up like a toy. Boots. Bikers' boots. She lifted her head as Ross stepped into the doorway—and blinked. Stared.

He wore brand-new black jeans and a white collarless shirt, with a black Western-cut jacket. His jeans fit those long legs like a worn glove, making him look like a kestrel, sleek and fast, in a room full of threadbare crows. Julia felt her breath back up in her throat.

New black clothes for Mission. Attention-grabbing clothes that were far too sexy, but new and black nonetheless. He was doing it for God, the best way he knew how.

Silence swept over the room. Even the Bell children suspended their animation for a second, staring at the exotic stranger.

He looked worldly and dangerous and completely comfortable. His heels struck slowly on the floor as he strolled the empty distance between the door and the back row of chairs. *Let him see me. Let him sit with me.* Owen turned, saw who it was and half rose from his chair. No! shouted Julia in her mind. With me!

Clunk. Clunk.

Never had it taken anyone so long to walk to a seat. He was behind her now, coming up the aisle. Would he see her? Would he see the seat beside her and know it was for him?

Clunk. Clunk.

Ross eased into the chair next to her and she breathed in an intoxicating whiff of cologne and fresh cotton and relief. Something inside her melted at the bigness of him, the controlled strength, the way both contrasted with the stark black and white of his ensemble. The avid stares of everyone in the room settled on the two of them like frost in an ice storm. She straightened her back.

"Hey," he whispered, smiling into her eyes. His shoulder bumped hers gently.

"Hi," she whispered back. He handed her her Bible and she took it. "Glad you could make it."

He settled into the chair, crossing one ankle over a knee, as he thumbed through the hymnbook someone had given him at the door. He stayed that way, seemingly absorbed in the words he was reading, until Melchizedek announced the first hymn. She needn't have worried that he'd do something indiscreet, like kiss her hello, or that he'd try and talk in the Silence before the service. He was evidently sensitive to the behavior of others. He'd taken his cue from the people around him and acted as they did. Her respect for him went up another notch.

They rose for the hymn and her voice dropped automatically into the alto part.

> The new day dawns, that millennial morn,
> The world and the flesh passed away.
> Sinners and saints are alike gathered here
> On the strand at the end of the way.
> And what will the final judgment be
> On the shores of eternity?

Ross glanced at her and switched from melody to bass, their two voices blending, the notes crossing and overlapping to form a counterpoint to the melody sung by everyone else.

> Reality has new meaning now,
> And we learn the results of truth;
> Priorities change as we realize
> How much we had left to do.

> The charms of the world appear differently
> On the shores of eternity.

Julia felt as if more than their voices were blending. They were making music together, a music that was more than the artificial creation of notes on the page. He hit a low B-flat that resonated deep inside her with a physical intensity. She vaulted up an arpeggio of four notes and he had to take a breath in midphrase, as if he'd lost his place.

> The Elect who have given their lives to God
> And lived out His Truth here below
> Will know what it means to stand on the shore,
> Reaping in joy what they've sown.
> For in sweet fellowship with Him they will be
> Throughout all eternity.

Julia sat down with a gasp and bowed her head for Melchizedek's prayer. She struggled to make sense of his words behind closed eyelids, but the attention of her whole body, her ears, her very skin, was filled with Ross. When he shifted, her blood sped up. When his elbow touched hers, goose bumps broke out on her arm. She had never experienced this, never. He was like a roaring waterfall of sensation, and Melchizedek's voice faded into empty vowels and consonants, signifying nothing.

After the last hymn, Melchizedek announced that there would be a young people's meeting the following Friday. "It will be at Jim and Linda Bell's, and the topic I'd like you all to think about—" here he glanced from Dinah to Claire to the Kowalczyk twins to Julia "—is one concrete way we can silently witness for the way of the Elect. You may bring a guest if you like."

A guest? Melchizedek hadn't looked at him, but Julia knew perfectly well he'd meant Ross. Once that happened, the gates would open and the invitations would start. He would have been accepted.

As Melchizedek made his dignified way to the door to shake hands with people as they filed out, Ross leaned over to whisper. His breath fanned her ear, and she shivered.

"Is he including me?"

"I think so."

"Are you cold?"

"No. Not at all."

"I don't know anything about witnessing for the Elect, silent or otherwise."

"I think he just means for you to listen."

"What happens?" They stood up and moved down the row of chairs, joining the flow of people heading for the door. Julia tried to explain.

"Each of us—yes, even the girls, you don't have to give me that kind of look—stands up and speaks on the topic—hello, Alma, I'm fine, thanks. Yes, this is Ross Malcolm. No, he isn't that kind of biker, he rides for recreation. Ross, Mrs. Alma Woods. Then Melchizedek will do a wrap-up and message for about half an hour. Hi, Linda, this is Ross Malcolm." Ross—the rat—turned that lady-killer grin on Linda in the middle of one of her breathy sentences, and she melted in a puddle on the spot. "Stop that."

"She stopped talking, didn't she?"

"Where was I?"

"A message for half an hour."

"Right. Then we sing for a while and then everybody stampedes the kitchen for—hi, Mom, Dad. You remember Ross Malcolm."

"Hello, young man," her father said to Ross. "Nice to see you again."

"I couldn't stay away," Ross said with such conviction that Mark McNeill blinked with approval.

"Really. Well. We look forward to seeing you next week too, then."

"Hello, Mr. Malcolm," Elizabeth said, her voice tinged with the kind of warmth Julia knew could only have been engendered by Melchizedek's unspoken endorsement over the young people's meeting. "I'm Elizabeth McNeill, Julia's mother."

"You have a lovely daughter, Mrs. McNeill."

"Thank you. I understand you were a guest at Madeleine's recently. Did you enjoy it?"

The blood washed into Julia's cheeks and she turned away to greet someone she hardly knew.

"Yes. Julia was kind enough to invite me."

"And what did you think of their home, Mr. Malcolm? Such a godly spirit. Such peace. Here she is now. Hello, darling." Elizabeth leaned over and hugged her eldest daughter.

"Yeah. Absolutely." Ross took Julia's elbow. "Want to introduce me to that blonde? Didn't I see her in your pictures?"

Julia, thankful to have somewhere else to look, waved Claire over, and her best friend clicked up on brand-new one-inch tapered heels. Julia blurted the first thing that came into her head. "Nice shoes. Did you sneak off to town without telling me?" Was everybody decked out in Ross's honor? Was she the only one in an old dress and last summer's pumps?

"No, I've had these for a while. Hello," Claire said with an engaging smile, "you must be Mr. Malcolm." Julia barely had time to make the introductions when Madeleine and Elizabeth maneuvered Ross into their circle.

Claire leaned over and spoke in low tones to Julia behind Ross's broad back. "Isn't this something? Everybody wants to meet him. He's the hottest news since Lara and Marshall had to get married."

Madeleine frowned at them.

"Would you keep your voice down?" Julia begged. Her sister left Ross to her mother and tapped Claire's arm with the spine of her hymnbook.

"Claire, what kind of Spirit is that?" she chided with the smile that Julia knew disguised disapproval. Julia hoped Ross couldn't hear her friend being bawled out like a five-year-old. "Mr. Malcolm isn't here to be 'news,' he's here for the salvation of his soul. Shame on you for embarrassing him."

Ross laughed at something Elizabeth had said and turned to Julia, maneuvering her out of the little group. "Nice bunch of people," he said. "But right now you've got to tell me where the little boys' room is." She pointed. "Thanks." He strolled toward the door.

Claire spoke in a breathy whisper, completely ignoring Madeleine's warning. "Ooh, Julia, he is some kind of gorgeous. You'd better watch your step."

"I don't have to. Everyone else is watching it for me."

"You should just hear them talking. Derrick is chewing nails. I could hear his teeth grinding from two seats away. Now, don't give me that look. What is he supposed to think, with you sitting with another man? What are you trying to do to him?"

"I'm working a mission. Nothing more." Uh-huh. That was some mission up on the mountain. And what about that little scene by the lake? She squelched the mocking voice inside her head. As far as she was concerned, she'd bypassed "mission" entirely and was walking in some uncharted territory with only her feelings for a guide.

And so far they were more likely to get her in trouble than help her out.

"Don't let his looks tempt you," Claire said earnestly. "Believe me, I know what can happen when you do. Look at my sister. She wants to come back to the Elect, but she'd have to leave Andrew. She'll never leave the kids, and he'll never let her take them. Looking Outside only means heartbreak."

"I know, sweetie," Julia said, squeezing her friend's shoulder. Claire's distress over her sister's unhappy choices distracted her momentarily from Ross. Yet that insistent voice that had been living in Julia's head all summer just wouldn't go away. They all defined themselves by the love of God, but their code forced Elaine to choose between the man she loved and the God she worshiped. God's love was said to be wider than the heavens and higher than the sky. Why did the Elect force it inside the narrow confines of their way? Seen with the eyes of the Elect, Elaine's choice should be obvious: she should put her salvation before earthly love and renounce her worldly husband. Seen through the eyes of love, Elaine shouldn't even have to contemplate such a choice.

Julia knew there was no reconciling the two points of view. Since Ross had ridden into her life, though, she'd found herself able to think from both sides of a question. To the Elect, that ability was fatal. It meant the Devil was working in your mind. There was only one side. Ross had—

Ross. She looked over Claire's shoulder toward the washroom entrance. Where was he? Had Derrick trapped him in there and challenged him to a duel? Maybe she'd missed him and he'd slipped out the door already. The hall was practically empty and Melchizedek was looking at her expectantly. She walked to the door and shook his hand.

"I'm so pleased your friend was willing to come this evening," Melchizedek said. "And amazed that his appearance has changed so markedly. The Spirit must be taking control of his life. Do you think he enjoyed sitting under the sound of the gospel?"

"I'm sure he did." Julia had no idea. She certainly hadn't heard any of it. "Has he come by?"

"No, I'm anxious to speak to him myself."

"That's odd. He went to the men's room ten minutes ago and I haven't seen him come out."

"Would you like me to check? Everyone's gone now."

"Oh, no, don't trouble. I probably just missed him and he's out in the parking lot waiting for me." Embarrassed, Julia scurried out the door. She'd finally been able to emulate Madeleine and bring someone to Mission—only to lose him the way she lost scarves and keys.

She barely had time to sweep the parking lot with an anxious gaze before a hand clamped her elbow. "Julia."

She jumped. "Goodness, Derrick, you scared me!"

"I've been standing out here for fifteen minutes, waiting for you." He tugged on her arm, and unwillingly she went with him to his car. "Where's your friend?"

"In the men's. He'll be out in a moment and I'll introduce you."

"That'd be nice. I seem to be the only one in town who hasn't met my girlfriend's new man."

"Derrick!"

The lines around his mouth drooped. "Well, what am I supposed to think? I don't see you for days, and suddenly you turn up in Mission, making a big production out of sitting together."

"It wasn't a production. We came separately. I'm the only person he knows."

"He knows Owen and Madeleine, from what I hear."

"He wouldn't be comfortable up at the front."

His hurt gaze accused her. "I think you should let Melchizedek take over. If there's a mission to be worked here, he should be the one to do it."

"What you think and what Melchizedek thinks are two different things."

"It looks bad, Julia. How can you shame me in front of everybody?"

She frowned. Shame him? "This isn't about you. This is about a person's soul."

"Do you think about his soul when he smiles at you like that?"

"Oh, for heaven's sake." She turned away and scanned the parking lot again.

Where on earth was he? A few stray clumps of people stood here and there. The motorcycle was nowhere in sight. Had he walked, or merely parked it discreetly down the block? Now that she thought about it, she hadn't heard him arrive in the first place. As she stood looking from one end of the lot to the other, completely mystified, Melchizedek came out the door and locked it behind him.

He looked around for her and waved. "I checked. No one there," he called, before striding down the path to his apartment.

"He's not in the bathroom?" Derrick asked. "Where did he go, then?" Satisfaction at losing the competition was all too visible in his face.

"I—I don't know," Julia said.

No one there. No one here. Ross Malcolm had ditched her. And Derrick had to be the one to witness it.

"Would you like to go somewhere and talk?" he said, bending over her, all solicitousness now that she had been completely mortified.

She shrugged him off, distracted, and walked to her car. She had already forgotten about him by the time she turned the key.

Chapter Fourteen

❧

Ross washed his hands, mulling over the cast of characters in this weird investigation. As he pulled a paper towel from the dispenser, he shrugged his shoulders a little, unaccustomed to the restriction of the new jacket. The sacrifices he made for an investigation. He hoped the OCTF would reimburse him for the new mufti when he submitted his expense report.

He slam-dunked the balled-up towel into the trash can, and leaned against the sink thoughtfully. Try as he might, he couldn't connect Melchizedek's sermon, exclusive and arrogant as it was, with aberrant behavior, so it wasn't likely Ryan's parents were being urged to it from the pulpit. The people were another matter. Conservative to the point of social isolation. But isolationism wasn't a crime. None of their behavior led him to think they were anything but a harmless splinter group.

Or at least, the kind of harm he'd seen wasn't the kind he could prosecute. "Them" versus "us" thinking. The privileged, sanctified few against the rest of the world. The refusal to accept fellowship with the rest of the body of believers. Separating the women from the mainstream as effectively as any Middle Eastern group.

The kind of thinking that would be deeply ingrained in his daughter by now, wherever she was. The old pain in his heart had scabbed over into a kind of fatalistic hope. Some day, if he investigated enough people and ferreted out enough cults, God would lead him to her. Some day he'd walk into a house with a prayer and a search warrant, and there she would be.

Except he had no idea what she looked like now. No idea if she knew who he was. Or if she did, how her view of him had been shaped by hatred of the Outside.

The thought of Insiders versus Outsiders led him back to Julia. How could she have survived in a household where the parents' favoritism was so overt? No wonder she'd been so hard to approach. If she had any self-esteem at all, it was her own doing, and probably hard-won at that, with all this emphasis on humility and self-sacrifice.

And there was old Madeleine, jumping on Claire like a cat on a toy. She'd been happy enough to let her mother sing her praises. What was it with that woman? She had everyone worshiping at her feet, but look out if you turned the spotlight on anyone but her. So much for humility. The only person who showed real humility in this crowd was Julia.

Thankful to have something to smile about again, he ran a glance around the washroom. Thick yellow paint covered plain concrete-block walls, so thick in some places that it looked like cake frosting. The kind of work done by zealous but unskilled volunteers. On the right wall, opposite the door, was a ventilation grille, and as he reached for the door handle, he heard voices. There must be another anteroom on the other side of the wall.

"Madeleine, I'm sorry to follow you in here, but I can't stand it." The desperate murmur got his attention. Ross stepped under the grille and listened. "I can't pray. This is standing between me and God. I need your forgiveness."

"There's nothing to forgive, Michael. Ryan's illness was God's will."

Michael? The doctor?

"Nothing to forgive? Then why do you despise me? I can see it in your eyes when you look at me...or refuse to look at me. Nothing is the same anymore, Madeleine. I've destroyed our relationship, haven't I?"

"You're my brother in the Spirit." Madeleine's voice became more gentle and controlled the more emotional Dr. Archer became. "That hasn't changed."

Her control seemed to goad him. "At least you'd look at a brother! It's like I don't exist anymore for you. I tell you, I can't stand it. Forgive me, hate me, do what you like but at least show me some emotion! It's all I—" He stopped, and a cold silence fell.

Ross's eyebrow quirked up in anticipation. Madeleine and the good doctor? Did her adoring parents know what she was up to? Or her husband?

"What emotion do you feel you deserve?" Madeleine asked, a hint of a tremor in her voice. "I'm a happily married woman."

"And Owen's worthy of your love. I'm not. I know."

"Self-pity is a sin, Michael," she told him. "That's what is standing between you and God. You're looking for sympathy in the wrong place."

"I'm not looking for sympathy, I'm looking for forgiveness."

"Only Melchizedek and God can give you that," she snapped. "You'd do better to concentrate on healing other women's sick children."

Ross blinked. Madeleine, the role model, showing her claws again? Had that little wobble in her voice been rage, not sorrow?

"Madeleine, wait—"

Ross heard a sound like the snap of a flag, as though a woman's skirt had been pulled aside in disgust, and the door closed. He straightened. Definitely rage. Something big and nasty was going on here. If ever there was a perfect chance for a few questions, this was it.

The corridor was empty when he stepped out of the washroom. He pulled the anteroom door open and saw a middle-aged man with his back to the door, one shoulder against the wall, slumped in defeat.

"Hey." Ross put a hand on his shoulder in masculine comfort. "You okay?" Dr. Archer looked up, surprised. Ross shrugged and tried to look sheepish. "I couldn't help but overhear. My name is Ross Malcolm. It's none of my business, but I bet if I prescribed a cup of hot coffee, it would do you good. Want to join me?"

The doctor studied him for a moment, evidently weighing the desire for solitude against a chance to be an example to the famous prospect. He held out a hand and Ross shook it. "Michael Archer. Why not?" Archer allowed Ross to steer him out a side door onto the street. Ross didn't feel too hot about leaving Julia in the lurch, but he'd call her and explain later. The opportunity to learn more about Ryan's case was too good to ignore.

He found a café on the corner, the kind where the neon signs really had to work at getting through the nicotine film on the windows. Perfect. Ross would bet a month's salary the Elect wouldn't be interrupting them anytime soon.

"Thank you," Archer said as their coffee arrived, along with a cinnamon roll the size of a sofa pillow. "You're a good man."

"Want to split this with me?" The sofa pillow was so fresh it bowed in the middle as he tried to cut it.

Archer smiled. "Thank you, but no. I'm not helpless. I feel badly about taking you away from J—er, from your friends for nothing."

"It's okay. Can I do anything for you?"

The smile faded, and Archer's forehead furrowed with pain as he poured milk into his coffee, turning it the color of a muddy spring river. "There's nothing anyone can do."

"Are you sure of that? Sounds like you and Julia's sister have some fences to mend."

"I don't understand where you came from." Archer fixed him with a look.

Ross deliberately ignored the underlying question and answered the obvious. "Like I said, your voices carried into the men's. Through the vent. Sorry I eavesdropped."

"It could have been worse. It could have been Mark. Or Owen." Dr. Archer sighed. "It's an old and not very interesting story."

"I'd still like to help."

"You can't forgive me and she won't," Archer said. He dropped his head into his hands.

"You could forgive yourself," Ross suggested gently.

"How can I do that? I can't tell her what's wrong with her son. She's right. It's my incompetence keeping him from being completely well. Years of it. Years." His voice hitched to a halt.

"How long have you been in love with her?" Ross asked, his tone quiet and matter-of-fact.

Archer looked up briefly, surprised, then an avid look crossed his face at the possibility of relief—of talking about what haunted him without the initial shocking confession first.

"I came to Hamilton Falls fresh out of medical school. Pediatrics. They didn't have a specialist here, only a GP, so my practice grew pretty quickly. Madeleine was about ten then. She was such a delightful child. When she got too old to need a pediatrician I still saw her sometimes, when Elizabeth would bring Julia in for poison ivy, a sprained ankle. You should have seen her. At eighteen she was the loveliest thing you ever saw." He shot Ross a sudden guilty look, as if he'd remembered to whom he was talking.

Ross unrolled the pastry and tore it into sticky pieces. "A man in his thirties. A young woman. It happens." Ross could give him understanding. If he wanted penance, he'd have to go talk to Melchizedek.

"I'd get up in the middle of the night and pray for forgiveness. My thoughts were base, carnal. Unworthy of her. I loved her, even then. Sometimes she'd come and talk to me about nursing, get my opinion on what I thought of it. I'd tell her it's a suitable career for a woman. I treasured every single moment, hoping..." He paused. "It was I who encouraged her to start, though some of the more traditional folks here objected. When she met Owen..." He paused again. The memory was painful. "Stupid. I should have known she wouldn't settle for someone so old. So limited in his prospects. I couldn't offer her what Owen has."

"So you offered her what you could. You looked after her kids."

"So well one of them has never recovered."

Ross looked up, startled. "What?"

"Oh, I don't mean his illnesses have any one cause." Archer reached over and helped himself to one of the pieces of the roll. "I mean indirectly. Through my own inability to diagnose the problem. To figure out what's wrong."

"Didn't the specialist tell you that?" Ross waited. Rita Ulstad had explained Ryan's charts to him, but maybe Archer could give him an insider's view. A guess. A speculation. Anything.

"All he would say is that Ryan suffers from a chronic infection that causes internal bleeding. But I knew that already. What I don't know is what causes it. And believe me, I've been up enough nights trying to find out."

"Surely there's been some indication in the tests."

Archer lifted a shoulder, then took another piece of roll. "I've done so many blood tests I've practically exsanguinated the poor child. We've done surgery. EEG scans when he had seizures and then postseizure lethargy. Even a feeding catheter, with poor Madeleine doing round-the-clock care, to see if he would thrive. She won't ever have a nurse, and she's right. Ryan is only comfortable when she's with him. I can see it, you know. She's the most loving and involved parent I've ever known. A real example to all the young families in town." He dropped the roll in his saucer and contemplated his coffee. "I just can't understand it. Not at all."

"Have you done any kind of blood screen?" Ross asked cautiously. "Do you have facilities for toxicology here?"

Archer quirked an eyebrow at him. "You sound almost as educated as Madeleine. I hope not for the same reason."

Ross smiled, inwardly cursing himself for the slip. "No. I made it through two semesters of premed and dropped out." He'd completed two semesters to prove to his mother that the career she envisioned for him fit him no better than a white lab coat, and changed majors. To administration of justice.

"A shame. To answer your question, no, we don't. This is a small town. They do that kind of thing in Seattle or Portland, but not here. I doubt a toxicologist would have any more to add than the GI specialist who operated on him. Besides, he's scheduled to go home tomorrow. I just can't tell Madeleine that we have to keep him in for a few days more to run another blasted test."

Ross could just detect a hint of affronted professional pride, carefully held in check since pride was a sin. Dr. Archer drained his cup and set it in the saucer with a clink.

"Thank you for coffee," he said. "And for allowing me to bend your ear."

"No problem. I'd like to get together again. I feel more comfortable talking to you than to Owen or Melchizedek." There, that should hook his interest and guarantee carte blanche for another visit.

Dr. Archer gave him a searching look. "But I did all the talking."

Ross shrugged. "Your turn tonight, my turn another night. I'll be around for a while."

Archer smiled. It looked sincere. "Call me at the office any time."

Outside the café, Ross watched as Archer pulled away from the curb in his sober late model sedan. He walked back to where he'd parked his motorcycle and sat on it sideways, legs crossed at the ankle, thinking.

There was no evidence of bodily harm to the children of the Elect. Even the other two deaths he'd looked into had been explainable and competently followed up on by the investigator. But in one family, the danger seemed very real. If Owen and Madeleine were such wonderful parents, and Archer such a dedicated physician, why couldn't anyone find out what was making the kid so sick?

A memory stored in the case files in his brain surfaced. Back before Christmas he and Ray had been on surveillance, cracking sunflower seeds and swapping stories. There was little else to do while you were staked out. But Ray had told him something that had made his blood run cold. He wished he'd paid more attention, but the target had come out of the house about then, and everything but their case was crowded out of his mind.

In light of that memory fragment, the little byplay between Claire and Madeleine took on a darker cast. *He's the hottest news since the wedding,* Claire had whispered behind him, and Madeleine had squashed her. Why? Out of consideration for his feelings? Consideration for people's feelings hadn't stopped her from dealing a harsh blow to Archer. Or was it for some other, more selfish reason?

What was going on in this family?

Why was Ray's case ringing bells in his memory?

He slewed around on the seat and fired up the engine. The drive over to the station didn't take long. He parked the motorcycle in the back, where no one would see it, and let himself in the rear entrance. He picked up the phone and dialed Ray's number. It wasn't urgent enough to page him, but he still needed to know. Voice mail clicked on.

"Ray, it's me. When you get in in the morning, page me. No, I'm not hounding you about this Miriam woman. Not yet. Remember that case with the mother and the kid you told me about? I need some details. This thing in Hamilton Falls...I'm starting to wish it were nothing but a nice, simple cult."

Chapter Fifteen

✤

"Two weeks of sniffing around and this is what you come up with?" Harry Everett said incredulously the next morning. "I pay you time and a half and I still have no grounds?"

Ross tipped the wooden chair back and propped his boot heels on Harry's steel-and-laminate desk. "In a nutshell." He took another sip of his third cup of toxic coffee.

"What am I supposed to tell the lieutenant?"

"Just what I said. There is a superconservative bunch of people here that you could call a cult under some definitions. He ought to be glad they're living in his town keeping the crime rate down. But there is no criminal activity."

Everett glared at him with eyes narrowed in suspicion. "Your informant's got you conned, Malcolm."

Ross wasn't offended. Harry really wanted to crash a cult and make a bunch of arrests—maybe even make the State News section of the Seattle *Post Intelligencer.* Too bad. It wasn't going to happen. "There's no child abuse in general. No weird sacrificial rites. No black altars in their houses. Just a bunch of people living in a time warp."

"'In general'? What does that mean? You've got to have *something*."

Ross lifted his boots off Harry's desk and got down to business. "That's the part that has me worried."

"I'm warning you. Quit playing with me."

"The Blanchard kid...I'm wondering how anybody can be sick so much and not have somebody figure out what's wrong. It doesn't make sense."

"What do you mean? You've seen the kid's file. It's about a foot thick with everything that's gone wrong with him since he was born. Of course it doesn't make sense. Neither does cancer, but I don't arrest John Doe's family when John Doe comes down with it."

"You might if it had been induced somehow."

"Induced?" Everett looked as though disbelief were causing him physical pain.

"What if someone wanted him to stay sick?"

Harry leaned back in his chair and closed his eyes. "That's the weirdest theory I ever heard, and trust me, I've heard them all."

Ross shrugged. "It isn't even a theory. It's just a feeling."

"Yeah, well, keep your feelings to yourself, and start coming up with facts. Bellville's paying your expenses and he wants answers. And what's with this expense report that showed up on my desk this morning?"

"I had to get some clothes. To fit in. Make it look like I'm conforming."

"What do you think this is, Narcotics? They might have the budget for hot rods and gold chains, but we don't. Or clothes, either."

"You'll sign it though, right?"

"Yeah, I'll sign it," Everett agreed unhappily. "Just keep the rest of this weirdness quiet, will you?"

Ross loped down the front steps of the station. What he ought to do was get himself out of Julia's life and let the good folks over at Child Protective Services take over. They probably would anyway, once he could get something solid behind his hunch. But the thought of the sweet warmth in Julia's eyes when she smiled at him, the honesty in every word she spoke...the mess he was going to have to make of her life...

"Hi, Ross!"

With a jerk, he oriented himself. Front of building. Main Street. Julia, standing on the sidewalk, tilting her head to look into his eyes.

"Are you okay?" Dimples dented her cheeks as mischief colored her smile. "What did they do, sentence you to life without parole?" With her chin, she indicated the police station behind him. "Did you get a speeding ticket or something?"

Cover story, quick! What else would a biker be doing in the police station? He couldn't very well say he was investigating her family and daydreaming about her smile.

He took her elbow, and strolled in the direction of the bookshop. "I can't believe anyone takes a thirty-mile-an-hour speed limit seriously in this town. They got me coming down the hill the other day."

She nodded sympathetically. "It happens to everybody. They hide behind that laurel hedge on the edge of the high school property and knock off tourists by the dozen."

"And I fell for it." He felt slightly guilty that she'd accept a shoddy last-minute lie like that one so easily. "What are you doing, footloose and fancy-free? Don't you have to work?"

"I was at the post office getting stamps. It's lunchtime."

It had been ten-thirty when he'd gone to see Everett, and in between paperwork and trying to reach Ray and trying to convince Harry there wasn't any criminal activity among the Elect, the morning had disappeared.

"Want to eat somewhere?"

She blushed. He noted with careful attention the way the blood rose in her neck and cheeks, then receded, leaving her skin creamy and soft. She had great skin, despite what the endless black wardrobe did to it. She'd probably never had a blemish in her life. But then, if a woman didn't smoke or drink and spent her time hiking around the hills like something out of *The Sound of Music,* it wasn't surprising.

"I wasn't fishing for an invitation," she said in a low voice.

"It wouldn't matter if you were. I'd still like to have lunch with you. I went to a place yesterday that was pretty good. Some diner. Not very fancy but good."

"Ross, that's all the way at the other end of town. I have to be back at work in forty-five minutes."

"It'll take two minutes if we ride."

"Plus twenty for the speeding ticket."

"Be nice."

"I can't ride with you in public. It would break the rules."

He grinned down into her eyes. It wasn't even his lady-killer grin and look—there was nothing quite as rewarding as having a woman stare at your mouth like it was all she wanted in the world. "You're breaking the rules just being seen with me."

"Not any more." She sounded a little dazed. "You have the official stamp of approval."

He stopped at a Chinese café and held the door for her. "Why's that?"

"Melchizedek called me last night when I got home and asked if I thought you'd be coming with me to prayer meeting Wednesday. I said I didn't know." The waitress handed her a menu and she buried her nose in it.

Oops. Last night. He'd better clear that up right away. "Hey, Julia, about last night..." Instead of taking the menu and sitting across the table, he slid into the booth beside her.

She wriggled aside to make room for him, but kept her attention on the soup of the day. "It's all right, Ross. You don't have to explain."

"I ditch you in front of all your friends and I don't have to explain? That's taking submission a little too far."

She blushed again. He'd never had this effect on a woman before.

"It's got nothing to do with submission. I don't have any claims on you. We came to the service separately. You can do what you like."

Ross frowned. This wasn't like Julia. He wasn't going to get anywhere if she spent any more time talking to Melchizedek. Obviously they'd discussed more than the guest list at Wednesday's prayer meeting.

"You invited me somewhere, and I accepted. I owe you an explanation for cutting out in the middle," he said gently. "I had to talk to someone about something important, and there wasn't time to find you."

"Talk to whom?" she asked, plainly puzzled. She knew how many of the Elect he'd met, after all. He would tell her the truth...as far as he dared.

"To Dr. Archer."

Her eyebrows went up, and she politely refrained from staring at him, turning her attention back to the menu instead. "Really?"

"We got to talking in the men's. It got kind of involved, and I didn't want to stop. A professional, educated man's perspective. You know."

He'd let her think he meant the life of the Elect. That he was considering joining up. On such allusions and omissions were cover stories built.

"Oh."

Somehow, he didn't have that feeling of satisfaction that weaving a good story usually gave him. In fact, he felt downright crummy about it.

With an internal sigh, he looked at the list of dishes marching down the laminated page of the menu and tried to concentrate. The waitress appeared to take their order, and when she'd gone, Ross deflected the subject. "So there's a prayer meeting Wednesday? What does that involve?"

"What you'd expect. Prayer."

"I haven't prayed since the last time I laid a bike down, and I was twenty-two then."

"Is that the only time you pray? When disaster is about to strike?"

Conversations with his Father were as much a part of him as breathing. Ross often struggled with the knowledge that, much as he wanted to direct his own life, it wasn't a good idea without getting input from on high first. Something as simple as a conversation could sometimes have life-altering consequences without God's guidance. And sometimes even more with it.

But that wasn't part of his cover story. And if his experience with cults was any indication, he would need a little divine guidance now.

"I lost the knack about the time my wife was killed," he said. "How do you pray?"

Julia hesitated, and glanced around. "It's not really proper to talk about it here."

"What's wrong with talking about something you love?"

"It's private. We're not like the scribes and Pharisees, praying in public."

"I don't want you to actually do it. Just tell me about it."

"Well, all right." She lowered her voice. "First, we pray for Melchizedek and Phinehas and the other Shepherds. For their missions and well-being. Then for the other members of the Elect, which believe me, can run to quite a list. Then last you pray for yourself, for what you need to stay true to Melchizedek's words."

Lord, they've put you in a box and expect you to work miracles from inside it. Help me now.

"What about other people?" he asked. "You know, others who believe in God who aren't Elect. Do you pray for them?"

"Worldly people? We pray that God will direct a Shepherd to them."

"So someone outside the Elect can't be saved unless they come through a Shepherd?"

"It says, 'Who shall be saved except them that hear the gospel.' And the Shepherds carry the gospel."

"But many pastors and priests do. Do you really think that all the people in the world have to come to God through a Shepherd?" The whole body of believers were not saved because they hadn't come to God through the Elect's leaders? Ross was torn between disbelief and pity.

"It's not up to us to say," she said, but she sounded less sure. "That's human thinking. It restricts God's power."

"I'd say that funneling God's power through one set of men with one set of beliefs is not only arrogant, it's dangerous. Almost blasphemous."

Her eyes narrowed. "Just how much do you know about God, anyway?"

"Well, now, look who's here," a voice said above them.

Ross closed his mouth on his answer and looked up to see two guys in shirts and ties standing at their table. One was about twenty, tall and skinny, with a spiral notebook bulging in his pants pocket. The other was looking at Julia as if she'd just run over his dog.

"Hi, Derrick," she said, in a tone that just missed being welcoming. "Hey, John, how's it going?"

Derrick. The infamous Derrick Wilkinson, her future husband, who really did wear wool pants on a warm summer day and had two pens in his pocket. *This* was what she had to look forward to for the rest of her life?

"Mind if we join you?" the skinny kid asked. "They said we couldn't get a table till one o'clock."

"Sure," Julia said without consulting Ross. "We just got our soup."

At least he'd had the foresight to sit beside her. Watching Derrick Wilkinson snuggle up to Julia across the table would be more than he could stand this morning.

"Ross, Derrick Wilkinson and John Kowalczyk," Julia said, pointing her soup spoon at each of them in turn. "Derrick works across the street at the lawyer's office, and John does landscape design with his brother."

Ross reached across the table to shake hands. "Ross Malcolm," he said. "Funny how we identify ourselves by what we do, isn't it?"

"What do you do for a living?" Derrick asked.

Ross grinned and shrugged. "Nothing, at the moment. I'm on vacation."

"He's a heavy equipment mechanic," Julia supplied. Derrick looked down his nose at him, or would have if Ross hadn't been the bigger of the two. Evidently mechanics didn't rate very highly on the Hamilton Falls social scale.

"Are you a lawyer?" he asked Derrick.

"No. Paralegal. I couldn't afford to go to law school."

There didn't seem to be any polite rejoinder to make to that. The guy had a chip on his shoulder they could saw up at the mill.

"Julia and I were just talking about prayer meeting."

He hadn't touched Julia since taking her arm on the street. Now, under the protection of the tablecloth, he touched her elbow with his own. Maybe it was because she looked soft and feminine and touchable in a booth overflowing with defensive testosterone. Maybe it was just because he wanted her to remember there were other fish in the gene pool. She didn't need to settle for this one.

Straightening slightly, she went very still, but she didn't pull away.

"So what I want to know is, does it do any good?" he asked, dropping his spoon in his empty bowl.

"The prayers?" Julia asked.

"Depends what you mean by good," Derrick said, as annoyingly evasive as any attorney Ross had ever heard.

"I guess a person could feel they contributed to world peace or something," Ross allowed thoughtfully. "In a nonparticipatory way."

John frowned. "But everyone participates. That's part of what makes it so powerful."

"But don't you think that getting out there and doing something would add to the effect of your prayers?"

Both men turned horrified eyes from him to Julia. He lifted an eyebrow. He could almost hear what they were thinking—poor Julia, consorting with the publicans and sinners.

"World peace isn't in our hands. It's in God's," Derrick said.

"It's in everybody's hands," Ross shot back. "A Christian doesn't hide behind God's back. Do you want to abdicate your responsibility?" Both Derrick and John bristled, as if he were accusing them personally. "I'm using the figurative you, of course."

"I think God answers our prayers," Julia put in, her tones soft and logical. "And I'm using the literal our."

Blessed are the peacemakers, for they shall prevent a food fight. "I'm glad to hear that," he said. "How?"

John seemed to be a sensible man. As the food arrived, he settled in for an active debate. Old Derrick was still red in the face and was probably going to have galloping indigestion the rest of the afternoon. Ross felt a secret satisfaction at the thought. If he did anything else on this case, he was going to broaden Julia's horizons on the subject of the opposite sex.

At a particularly hot point in the debate, Ross felt a flicker of movement under the table. Julia slipped her foot out of her low-heeled pump, and he forgot the rejoinder he'd been about to make. His breath caught as her stocking-clad foot slid over the instep of his boot and pressed gently in warning, heating him right through the leather and his sock.

It worked, but probably not the way she'd intended. The pressure of her foot made him lose track of the conversation, and Derrick and John were off on a tangent about the governor's latest antics. He didn't care. He was having a conversation of his own.

Above the table, he ate Chinese food and contributed innocuous mumbles to the topic. Risking a glance to the side, he saw he wasn't the only one affected. Above the high neck of her blouse, color washed into Julia's cheeks.

Did she know what she was doing to him, right there in public? She asked him a question, something about whether he was enjoying his lunch, lifting those long gold lashes with utter innocence, her soft lips parted.

"Uh," he said. Mr. Intelligence.

The hands of the clock over the cash register dragged past 1:05 and Derrick started. "Uh-oh, got to go. They hate it when I'm late. I'll pick you up for prayer meeting, Julia." He pointedly excluded Ross. Fine. Ross could care less. He was absorbed in watching Julia lick sauce off her thumb.

"Bye-bye," she said, waving with the other hand and ignoring her intended's aggressive tone. "It's been fun."

At least Ross had the patience to wait until the other men were safely out of the restaurant before turning back to her. His lashes veiled a gaze so intense that she nearly swayed toward him for a kiss before she remembered where she was.

"Do you have any idea," he rasped, "what you're doing to me?"

"No." She'd only wanted to let him know in the most direct way she could that it was futile to take Derrick up on a challenge. He would spend the rest of the afternoon in argument if it meant winning his point. But the contact with Ross's foot was so absorbing that she couldn't help herself.

His wonderful mouth was inches from hers. He slid an arm around her and dragged her closer.

"Don't, sweetheart," he murmured in her ear. "Not unless you're ready for me to take a big jump over the line."

If there was anyone else in the restaurant, she couldn't hear them. She was only aware of Ross and the way he was looking at her.

She pulled back, fighting for sanity through the fog of her disloyalty. "I didn't mean—I have to go back to work. I'm late already."

"Call in sick. Say you ate something that disagreed with you." When she hesitated, he leaned close. She breathed in his scent, shivering as his breath beat softly against her ear as he spoke. "Spend this afternoon with me."

She was drowning, dying in the fire that enveloped her. Her skin hurt with the need to feel his arms around her.

"No," she gasped, drawing on her last reserve of strength. "I have to go."

He straightened and paid the bill. She followed him out of the restaurant in a daze of longing, imagining what might happen if she tossed aside everything for one afternoon and went with him.

The summer air and the swish of traffic, the smell of exhaust mixed with evergreens and hanging flowers and coffee, brought her out of it. Reality. She was standing on Main Street two blocks down from the bookshop. Derrick was probably looking out the window of the lawyer's office right now, counting on his wristwatch the minutes she and Ross had been alone. Her parents could drive by, or any of the Elect, and see her on the sidewalk with Ross. What did they look like? Were they leaning toward each other, barely restraining themselves from falling into an embrace?

"Julia?" he asked. "Are you going to make that call and come with me? We could go somewhere down the road, have a nice dinner, and then have a moonlight ride back."

"I can't," she said, and shut her mouth on the hateful words. The story of her life. Can't do this, can't think that, can't say so-and-so.

"Why not?"

"A thousand reasons." She glanced towards the lawyer's office. "The most immediate being that I have to work."

"You can take a day off once in a while, can't you?"

"I can't just disappear. It would look bad. And I couldn't tell anyone where I was going. That would be even worse. I'd get a Visit from Melchizedek. He'd probably have me Silenced for a year."

"Silenced? What is this, the Mafia?"

She waved a hand in negation. "Not like that. Being Silenced means you can't speak to anyone in Gathering or at any function, even a family dinner. Some people call it shunning. My parents would never get over it. Neither would Derrick. In fact, his position as Deacon would probably be jeopardized."

"Who says you have to tell anyone anything? How can you live like this, Julia? I'd go nuts if I thought my whole church was watching every move I made."

She shrugged, and crossed her arms, hugging herself to find a little comfort. "That's just the way it is. If you don't do anything wrong, then it shouldn't be a problem when people watch you." A silence fell while he looked at her as if she'd been speaking in code and he was trying to decipher it.

"You know, we'd get a lot further if you hugged me like that."

Bless him for finding something to laugh about at a moment like this. She felt her spirits lighten and even managed a smile. "I have no intention of going any further with you."

"I know what you mean." The smile still lurked in his eyes, but his tone was serious. Soft. "I don't know what happens to me when I'm with you. Rationality goes out the window and I find myself wanting to kiss you against my better judgment."

"That's how I feel, too." She had been living with this guilt and forbidden feelings so long she could identify with his completely. Understanding him was one thing. Doing what he asked was another.

"Do you want to kiss me?" he asked, his voice brushing anticipation along her skin. Voice and eyes were all that held her motionless on the sidewalk, but she felt their power all the same.

"You're over the line," she whispered.

"Wanting to doesn't put me over the line."

"It's the appearance that does the harm, not the reality."

He drew back and the warmth leached out of him, replaced by the cold formality of two acquaintances meeting on the street. She realized she was on the verge of losing something very precious, something whose value she had only begun to learn.

"Well, I guess there isn't much I can do about that. You have my number if you change your mind." He didn't even smile as he turned and crossed the street.

Words balled into an ache in her throat as she watched him stride away. She couldn't let them out and call him back. She was going to be the future Deacon's wife.

At least she got as far as the bookshop before the tears rose up and choked her.

Chapter Sixteen

❧

Julia had no idea that pain and loss could make a person physically ill. Getting through the week took a monumental effort, and she didn't know whether Ross went to the Wednesday-night prayer meeting because she didn't go. Finally, on Friday morning she laid her conscience flat with one blow and called in sick.

"I think I've got some kind of flu bug," she lied, wincing at how nasty the words tasted.

"Don't come and infect me with it, then," Rebecca replied briskly. "I've been waiting for this. You've been looking peaked all week. Besides, with a voice like that you'll scare the customers away."

She was hoarse from crying, spiritless with depression. She stayed in bed all morning, ignoring the phone, reliving every moment she'd spent with Ross, but that only made her cry, too.

"Get out of bed and act like a woman," she finally

scolded herself. She pulled on the most ancient skirt she owned and staggered out to the kitchen.

Only one message blinked on the answering machine.

"Hello, Julia, this is Linda Bell. I'm so thrilled that biker is coming to Gatherings on his own. Do you think he would like to come for a light supper before the young people's meeting tonight? There'll be a spread later but my kids won't last that long. Oh, and I mean you too, of course. Give me a ring back and let me know. Bye-bye."

Ross invited for supper at Linda Bell's? She must be bursting a gasket at being out of the loop for the hottest gossip in town. Every word, glance or inadvertent touch they shared at supper would be public knowledge by lunchtime the next day. Julia's relationship or lack thereof would be written up on the wall for everyone to pore over the way a Hasidic Jew pored over the Law, making interpretations of every jot and tittle.

The doorbell rang and she jumped. Maybe it was Ross. Maybe she hadn't messed things up completely, and she could still redeem herself.

She tottered to the door and looked through the window. Owen Blanchard stood there, his back turned to her, his tie a little loose and his hands in his pockets.

Owen? Hastily she tucked her shirt in, and tried to smooth her hair away from her face. She was supposed to be sick. A hot, swollen face was a symptom of just about any disease, wasn't it?

Her brother-in-law turned with a smile as she opened the door. "Hi, Julia. Feeling better? Rebecca said you had the flu." She gestured for him to come in, and he followed her into the living room, taking the easy chair while she perched on the couch.

"Can I get you a lemonade or something?"

"No, thanks. I only stopped by for a minute, to see how you were. We missed you at prayer meeting."

It took all her willpower not to ask if Ross had been there. "I thought it might be a flu bug, but it must have been one of those twenty-four-hour things. I'm okay now. How is Ryan?"

The smile faded from Owen's face and the pale shadow of pain settled in its place. "His progress isn't as rapid as we'd hoped," he said slowly. "He threw up this morning. Lina's hardly left his side. And now here you are with a flu...I wonder if he could have caught it somehow? Dear heaven, Julia, he's in no shape to be battling flu. Not when he just got out of the hospital."

"Have you called Michael?"

"Yes. Madeleine is almost at the point where she wants to ask him to put in the feeding tube again, just to get some nutrients into his body. But I just can't face it."

Julia's face crumpled with distress. "Is there anything I can do or bring? Can I stay with him so you two can at least get out to Mission?"

He shook his head. "Lina would never go."

Julia had to agree. "No, of course not. I just thought—"

"I know, and I appreciate the thought. You're so unselfish with your time, Julia. That's only one of the things I love about you." He smiled affectionately.

Julia smiled back, swatting down the uncomfortable realization that the only reason she was so unselfish with her time was because she had nothing else to do with it.

Owen straightened and changed the subject. "Speaking of your time, I hear Linda has invited you and Ross Malcolm for supper."

"How do you know that?" she asked. "I just got the message myself."

"Oh? Didn't you talk to her? I thought you'd been home sick."

What a tangled web we weave... "I turned the ringer off while I was sleeping, and the machine picked up."

"Oh, of course. Linda talked to Madeleine earlier, and when I heard about it I thought I'd wander down here and have a Visit."

A Visit. Uh-oh. To the Elect, a Visit didn't just mean one person going to another person's house. Oh no. A Visit meant someone perceived you had a need—for help, for correction, for encouragement. And a Visit from Owen, her Elder, meant someone thought she had a serious need. Could a person be Silenced for having wicked thoughts about an Outsider instead of the man she was practically promised to?

"Well," she said inanely. "That's kind of you."

Owen went straight to the point. His voice dropped to that intimate, sonorous timbre that convinced people to give their lives to God. "I've been doing a lot of thinking about Ross Malcolm. How serious do you think he is about joining us, Julia? Do you think he's sincere?"

"I—I believe so," she stammered. She felt as though she was breaking Ross's confidence, even though she knew it was Owen's business to ask questions like this. "He seems to be serious about coming to Gathering, and he pays attention when Melchizedek speaks."

"Yes, he does," Owen agreed. "You're not proving to be a distraction in that sense."

Julia shrugged off the little jab. Self-esteem was just self-interest in most cases, wasn't that what the Shepherd said? This was Owen, who loved her. He wouldn't deliberately phrase something in a way that would hurt.

"And his appearance has certainly changed. God must have given him a revelation. Does he plan to go to the young people's meeting?" His calm blue gaze held hers.

"I don't know." Julia bit back the urge to apologize.

"How do you feel about him?" Owen asked, his voice dropping even lower. This was the tone the Shepherd used just before issuing the invitation to the Stranger to give his life to Jesus. It was filled with the hush of anticipation and the sense that the angels were hanging on every word.

"I—I, well, he's a friend." The angels slumped in disappointment, shaking their glossy heads.

"I didn't mean it that way. I meant, do you have...feelings for him? Does it matter to you whether he comes or not?"

Her hands were freezing. How come she was perspiring, then? She wished she could pull Rebecca's crocheted afghan off the back of the couch and hide from Owen's loving scrutiny. "I enjoy his friendship," she admitted finally. "He's interesting to talk to. He's kind. I like him."

"Are you sure that's all it is?"

Her memory flashed on the way he had kissed her beside the lake. The angels covered their eyes, fluttered against the ceiling in agitation, and faded away through the plaster.

"Why are you asking me this, Owen? Is there something wrong with me seeing Ross?"

"No, not at all. I'm just very concerned that you might fall into the Devil's trap and be deceived. He's the kind of man who attracts women. It's easy for our flesh to get carried away."

He made it sound so cheap and soulless. Perhaps that's what he thought relationships with people outside the Elect consisted of. Just empty flesh getting carried away.

"I haven't been carried away," she said firmly.

"Has he tried to...take advantage of you?"

If anyone but her brother-in-law had asked her that, she'd have shown him the door. She was tempted as it was. "No."

"But perhaps he's attempted to—how shall I say this? Seduce your mind and heart away from God?"

"Why would he?"

"To take you Outside."

"He's a friend, Owen. He's seeking God himself. He doesn't have any reason to do that." Did aggravating her into thinking for herself constitute seducing her mind?

"Claire tells me that you've been acting strangely lately. Separating yourself from your friends. Is that true?"

"No, of course not. I just didn't want to play baseball last weekend."

"She says you suggested something outlandish instead."

She huffed a laugh of disbelief. "Helping out at the food bank? That's not outlandish. It seemed reasonable, considering that Jesus tells us to give to the poor and feed the hungry."

"He meant in a spiritual sense, Julia."

"I don't think that was all he meant."

"Well, our thinking has no place in this. We need to seek after God's thinking, as Melchizedek tells us."

A rush of impatience so strong it was almost anger swept through Julia, and it was only with the greatest effort that she prevented herself from snapping at her brother-in-law.

"Be careful," Owen cautioned her. "I would hate to see you drawn away and deceived if Ross's motivations turn out to be less than pure."

What about your motivations? Julia wondered. What on earth are they? "I will," she promised, the lie cold on her lips. Affront and impatience battled angrily inside her, though she kept her face calm.

"I know you will," Owen said complacently, and got up. Julia started to her feet, but he wasn't finished yet. He wandered over to the bookshelf, where her pictures were ranged in a clutter of silver and porcelain frames. He touched one of Derrick and herself, taken last summer during a hike along the river.

"Derrick came for a Visit with me a few days ago," he said. "He was quite upset."

"Oh?" She closed her eyes for a moment. Would this never end?

"He's afraid, Julia. Afraid that your relationship with Mr. Malcolm is going to jeopardize his Deaconship. The announcement hasn't been made yet, after all." Julia stayed on the couch, holding his gaze, waiting. After a moment, Owen filled the silence. "I have to sympathize with the poor guy. He hasn't seen you in a couple of weeks, he says. He's getting worried."

"I don't know why. Everyone knows he's the most suitable for the title."

"And everyone knows that isn't all there is to it. He can't be Deacon without you as his wife." Owen made an impatient movement, and the picture fell on its face. "Don't play games with him, Julia. It's been settled for years. Why not say yes and put the poor boy's mind at rest?"

Julia turned her face away before he saw it set with rebellion. Why should she settle for a boy when she wanted a man, with a man's responsibilities and thoughts? Why was no one asking about what she felt? Why did she sense that the only reason Derrick loved her was because he loved the Deaconship too? And why did this strike no one but her as backward?

Ross was right. She was Derrick's ticket to the big time, and she was done with catering to his and everyone else's feelings before her own.

"Julia?" Owen said, reminding her that he had asked a question.

"All right," she said.

"All right, you'll marry him?"

"All right, I'll set his mind at rest."

Owen smiled. "That's our girl. It will make him so happy. Well, I'd best be going. Madeleine will be wondering what's happened to me."

"Give her my love," Julia said, and practically bounded across the floor to open the door for him. "And a special hug for Ryan."

"I will. See you Sunday. Enjoy the young people's meeting."

She smiled for an answer so she wouldn't have to lie. Then she locked the door behind him and picked up the phone.

Ross returned the page so quickly she thought he must have been sitting next to a phone himself.

"Is the offer of a ride and dinner still open?" she asked abruptly as if she hadn't spent most of a week in total agony at being away from him.

He paused, and with a sudden stab of apprehension she wondered if he'd changed his mind. He could be packing up to leave, for all she knew. Or at the very least, he'd go to the young people's meeting without her, and take someone home who knew her own mind.

Getting acquainted with one's mind was a more painful process than she'd anticipated.

"It is," he said at last. "Nice to hear from you and all that. Aren't you going to the meeting?"

"I just had a Visit from my brother-in-law, and from what he said I may as well put on those jeans and ride through town in a—" she tried to think of the most shocking thing a woman could wear "—a red tank top."

"You wouldn't get any argument from me." A smile colored his tone. "What did he say?"

"He wanted to know if you were seducing me away from the Elect."

"What did you tell him?"

"I said no, of course. What I don't understand is why he thinks that thinking on my own means I'm getting ready to leave."

"Sometimes learning to think for ourselves unsettles people. Especially if they're used to having their thinking done for them. Rules and regulations create a nice, safe environment where you know what the expectations are, but I've found it doesn't allow much room for growth with God."

Julia thought of the young people's meeting tonight. She'd been to dozens of them since she'd reached the Age of Understanding, which the Elect estimated to be twelve. The age where a child could be expected to make her own choices in matters of the Spirit, as Jesus had done when He'd stayed in the temple and allowed his parents to leave without him. But really, there wasn't a choice. Had never been a choice. She could go to the meeting and hear what she'd been hearing all her life. Don't do this. Don't wear that. Say this and not that. Think this and not that.

The prospect of a ride and dinner with Ross, in comparison, seemed like the kind of freedom she'd only read about in books.

"You seem to know a lot about God," she said.

"I only know what He means to me," he replied simply. "And what He's done for me."

"But how can that be?" she asked, more of herself than of him. "You aren't Elect."

"God is bigger than the Elect, sweetie. He can't be forced into the boundaries of one group's belief."

Melchizedek had always said that couldn't be true. Worldly people in worldly religions were deceived, and that was that. But here was Ross, who seemed to have a better handle on spiritual matters than she did, proving Melchizedek wrong.

Melchizedek couldn't be wrong. He was the mouthpiece of God.

But what if he wasn't?

Lord, help thou mine unbelief. The cry of the sinner echoed in Julia's head. If Melchizedek was wrong, then the Elect were wrong, and everything she'd stood for all her life was just a big lie. She'd lost her childhood and half her womanhood wearing black and believing she was one of the chosen people.

But what if she wasn't?

Nausea that had nothing to do with imaginary flu bugs began to roll in her stomach.

"Julia? Are you still there?"

She took a deep breath. "I'm here. But I'm very confused."

"I have a solution for that. Let's get out of Dodge."

Running away never solved anything. But she could look at it a different way...as running toward something. Taking action, as Ross had said in the restaurant.

She just didn't know what it was yet.

"All right," she replied. "Now?"

"Yes, now. It's a beautiful day. By the time you get those jeans on, I'll be there."

Chapter Seventeen

✤

"Any preferences on where we're going?" Ross shouted over his shoulder.

The wind had plastered a lock of hair against Julia's lips. She pulled it away. "No," she shouted back.

"How about taking in a festival?"

"I've never been to one. Melchizedek says they're frivolous."

Ross laughed, and accelerated up the on-ramp to the highway. "Sounds like a good enough reason to go."

"There are some within riding distance of here," she shouted. "If we're going east, we could try Ainsley, Pitchford or Middleton. Pitchford starts today, I think, but it's ninety miles away."

For a second he forgot to shift, and the motorcycle whined in complaint. He kicked it into gear.

"Pitchfork?"

"Pitchford. As in the Pitchford Plum Festival. I read

the entertainment section of the paper in the bookshop, but don't tell anyone."

He pushed the bike to the upper limits of its speed range. "Pitchford it is."

A shiver that had nothing to do with wind speed crept up his back. God's hand was in this, no question about it. Should he let Julia in on the real reason they were going? Bad enough he'd encouraged her to give the young people's meeting a miss so that he could get her alone and learn more about her sister and their family life. Worse that he'd caused her to break the rules about her example. But tell her that he was looking for a woman and child he'd never seen?

She'd given up a lot for him, and would probably end up giving more once they returned to Hamilton Falls. The least he could do in return was let her in and share the quest.

It wouldn't hurt to have another pair of eyes to help him, either.

When they rolled into Pitchford, they found roadblocks set up all around the downtown area, and tents containing booths and stages where local musicians played.

He was thankful it wasn't as crowded as some of the big-city events where he'd done surveillance. Still, finding a strange woman and child wasn't going to be easy. He had to enlist Julia's help.

She was bending over a table where a vendor had spread a sparkling trove of bead necklaces. But from her expression, you'd think they were the contents of a Spanish galleon.

She looked up when he stopped beside her. "It's such a sin to look at these," she said with a last reluctant glance. "I shouldn't tempt myself. It only makes it harder. But then

I see something like those sea-glass necklaces and I literally have to march myself away."

To put action to words, she squared her shoulders and walked in the opposite direction, where there was a stand selling sausages wrapped in pastry. He bought four and offered one to her, then looked up at the pricing board. "Two lemonades, too, please."

Something about the sign caught his attention. A design was painted on either side of the booth's name—a snake with its tail in its mouth, and within the circle of its body, a depiction of the planet Earth.

An apocalypse symbol. He'd seen variations of it in a number of his cases.

Something—a feeling of impending change, maybe, or a sense that something big was about to happen— made him marvel at the intricacy of God's plans for his life.

"What organization runs this booth?" he asked the proprietor, a teenage girl with a ring in her left eyebrow.

"My church," she said. "That'll be three bucks."

"What church is that?"

"We're a forward-looking group that focuses on heaven, not earth," she replied, as if she'd read the marketing literature and knew it by heart. "We concentrate on the joy of the future rather than the sins of the present."

Ross ignored the cognitive dissonance that told him a kid like this should be out playing soccer and focusing on being a kid, not reciting somebody else's cant. "Do you have a name?"

She nodded. "We recognize each other by the sign of the Seventh Seal. Would you like to come to one of our services? It'll be right after the fair closes tonight, in the town square."

Thank you, Lord. Thank you, Ray. And thank you, Miriam, wherever you are, for talking about pitchforks where someone could hear you.

"I'll look forward to that," he said. "Do you know someone named Miriam?"

The girl nodded. "That's my aunt's name. A bunch of women in my church use it. I picked Deborah, myself. You know, the prophet? But my mom still calls me Lisa, even though she knows I hate it."

Had he really expected Deborah/Lisa would just point and say, "Oh, sure, she's right over there"?

He took the lemonades and handed one to Julia. "Come on." She looked up in surprise at his tone. "We have to talk."

He led her some distance away, where people lay on the grass on blankets and ate picnics out of baskets. Normal people. Ross couldn't remember the last time he'd eaten a picnic lunch. Even as kids, his family had tended more to concrete basketball courts and takeout, not leisurely homemade lunches.

"What's wrong, Ross?" Julia asked. "Is the sausage bad? Mine was pretty good."

"Want another one?" He handed her the second sausage and took a fortifying bite of his own, stalling for time. He'd made the decision to tell her about Kailey, but how much further should he go? He had to talk about how Annie's disappearance had changed his life without revealing how it had propelled him into cult investigations—and the whole reason he was in Hamilton Falls.

"There are a few things I haven't told you," he began.

She bit into her sausage and gazed at him, waiting. What had happened to Kailey had been such a huge part of his inner life that he'd actually never given any thought to how he might broach the subject aloud. And he was becoming more and more convinced that somehow, some way, the little girl with Miriam must have been Kailey. Otherwise, why had the Lord gone to all the trouble to direct him here?

"Remember how I said that my wife and daughter had been killed by a drunk driver?"

She nodded, and her eyes filled with compassion.

"Well, that wasn't quite true." He looked up, but her face hadn't changed. She merely waited for him to tell her in his own time. "I've never been married. About seven years ago, the woman I was living with joined a religious group called the Church of the Seventh Seal."

Julia sat up and glanced back toward the food stalls. "Didn't that girl say something about them?"

"I know. It may not be the same group. If it is, they've changed some." Maybe they were going public, targeting a different demographic and easing up on the frumpy look for women. "Anyhow, the group I knew is one of those groups with guns, hiding out in the hills and waiting for the end of the world. Anne took our daughter with her. Kailey. It took me a year to find them again so I could serve her with custody papers, but when I did they disappeared, and I've been looking for them ever since."

She stared at him as if she'd never seen him before. Which, in a way, she hadn't. "You have a daughter? Alive?" She sounded a little winded. "You're single? Not a widower?"

"Yes. And no. But an odd thing happened. Some woman named Miriam called an old friend of mine trying to find me, and she told him that Annie is dead and she—Miriam—has Kailey. Until I talked to my buddy, I didn't know for sure that Kailey was alive. I really was on a road trip looking for some kind of solace." He gave her the ghost of a smile. "Which I think I might have found."

Sure, she was a little shocked, but if he hoped for an answering smile, he was disappointed.

"I suppose it amounts to the same thing, Ross, but you didn't have to lie about being married. Nobody's going to condemn you for your relationships before you knew God."

"That's what drove me back to God," he said gently. "I had no one else to turn to."

She didn't seem to hear him, focusing on some internal struggle. Then she looked up. "But about this woman, Miriam...you don't think she kidnapped Kailey, do you?" Julia's voice filled with the beginnings of fear for his sake.

"I don't know. It doesn't look like it. I think she was trying to get her back to me. But there are two problems. A, she left the message and disappeared again, and B, the description we have of the girl doesn't match what I know of Kailey."

"What do you mean?"

He explained about the age difference and the girl with gray eyes.

Julia sat up. "How old do you think Ryan is?"

"I know how old he is. He's four." He didn't tell her the reason he knew was because of the information in the little boy's file.

"But he doesn't look it, does he? They wouldn't let him start preschool because he was so small and sick. If these people haven't been feeding Kailey properly, she's not going to thrive. She could be seven. She just might look five because she hasn't had vegetables and grains and things that are good for her."

He fought down the surge of hope. "That still doesn't explain the eye color."

"Ross, a baby's eye color can be completely different from a child's. Look at my friend Claire. Her baby pictures have big blue china-plate eyes. Now they're green. They started changing when she was in elementary school."

He gazed at her thoughtfully, almost afraid to let himself hope. But where he couldn't put hope safely in human hands, he could put it in God's. And the Lord seemed to know what He was doing today.

"You could be right," he acknowledged. "The reason we're here isn't because I wanted to set you on the path to perdition by taking you to a fruit festival. It's so we can look for this Miriam and the little girl. My buddy says she told someone about a festival and a pitchfork. This is about as close as it gets to both."

Julia was already on her feet, picking up their cups and napkins. "What are we waiting for?"

"The description I have of Miriam is that she's in her fifties, wearing a flowered cotton dress and a gray sweater, with her hair pulled up in a bun."

"Except for the flowers, that describes half the women in the Elect," Julia remarked. "But the good thing is, there aren't going to be any Elect here. That's got to narrow the field some."

"I have a feeling the older generation of Sealers have standards of appearance that Melchizedek would approve." He caught up to her by the trash bin. "We're going to put some thought behind this. The area isn't that big. If each of us searches the fair in a grid, one from each side, we can meet in the middle and compare notes. Say, by the sausage stand in thirty minutes."

"Done."

"And no sneaking peeks at necklaces."

She rolled her eyes at him. "Don't worry. I know how to focus."

No doubt she did. Ross watched her until she disappeared into the crowd, and began quartering the booths and stalls, looking in shops, sliding into and out of groups of people, searching constantly for a woman with gray hair worn up. He had no idea what Kailey looked like now except for the sketch Ray had been able to get. Any little girl he saw chasing her friends on the grass or darting into a booth could be his daughter. He'd once thought he would just know when he saw her again, with some internal knowledge special to fathers, but in the long, hard years in between he'd come to learn that it didn't work that way. At this rate, they'd both have to go in for genetic testing before he'd know for sure.

If he found her.

"Got a quarter for my grandma, mister?"

A grubby urchin held out a hand and jerked her shaggy head at a woman in a wheelchair. The chair was parked against a sunny wall behind the barricades, and a hat lay on the ground with a few coins in it. He dug out some change and gave it to the little girl, who ran and dumped it into the hat. Ross looked them both over. The girl had light eyes, and the woman's hair was jammed up under a sun hat so he couldn't tell whether it was in a bun or not, nor could he see her face clearly. But she wore stretchy brown pants. And there was the chair. Ray hadn't said anything about an identifier so obvious as a wheelchair.

With a sigh, he turned away, and met Julia a few minutes later at the sausage stand.

"Any luck?"

She gave him a rueful look. "Everywhere I looked there were dark-haired kids and grandmas with buns. Just not together, or not the right age, or not dressed the way you said. You?"

"The same." He sighed. "It was worth a try. The next thing to do is wait until this Seventh Seal group has its revival or whatever in the town square. If they're all to-gether it'll make the job simpler. Not easier. Just simpler."

The wait until six o'clock, when the fair would pack it-self up, seemed interminable. They amused themselves by window-shopping at the booths, but Julia couldn't buy any of it, and he'd long since memorized every booth and its contents. They called a hamburger and a soda at the drive-in dinner, and finally they heard an amplified voice coming from the park.

Show time.

The makeshift podium was on a stage set up at one end of the park. Fortunately there couldn't have been more than sixty or seventy people, and from what he could tell, they were mostly Sealers.

Talk about preaching to the choir.

But when the speaker introduced himself as Moses, leader of the Church of the Seventh Seal, the one whom God had ordained to lead his people to eternal life, Ross gripped Julia's hand in a sudden convulsive movement.

"It's them," he said quietly. "The ones Annie and Kai-ley were with. Keep your eyes open."

Working the edges of the crowd, sticking to the older generation, he asked questions in a respectful murmur. Do you know a woman named Miriam? Did you know Annie DeLuca? Do you know what happened to Annie's daughter?

The answer was always no, but they could be lying. "Don't talk to strangers" was a warning given to more than little kids.

Preaching to strangers was a different matter...although there seemed to be precious few of those. The crowd knew Moses well, shouting hosannas in agreement with whatever he was trumpeting from the podium. Some-thing about Armageddon and being prepared for the final fiery trial. Ross wondered if people ever got tired of hearing about it. He'd only been listening for twenty minutes, and already he was sick to death of the subject.

The crowd parted, and he saw the woman in the wheelchair. Her sun hat was gone. She clutched a woven bag of some sort in her lap, and her eyes were fixed on Moses with fervent adoration.

Ross moved closer, and knelt by the chair. Somebody moved, and the light fell across the woman's face.

With a shock, he recognized her.

This woman had answered the door the last time he'd ever seen his daughter. Every detail of that meeting was burned into his mind's eye, including the suspicious gaze the woman turned on him now. Maybe she'd gained weight and now used a wheelchair, but that expression hadn't changed one bit.

He knelt by the chair, gripping the base of the arm rest. "Do you remember me?"

She frowned. "Nope. Sorry."

"I remember you. You knew Annie DeLuca."

"So?"

"So I'm looking for Annie's daughter, Kailey. She's supposed to be with a woman named Miriam, who was trying to find me. I'm Kailey's father, Ross Malcolm."

"And I'm the prophet Deborah. Prove it."

He wasn't sure if she was introducing herself or being sarcastic. "I don't have the papers with me, but I have her baby picture." He pulled it out of his wallet and showed it to her.

The woman sniffed. "That don't prove anything. Could be any kid."

"Do you know where Miriam is?"

"Nope."

"Do you know someone who would know?"

"Nope."

Ross resisted the surge of frustration that commanded him either to shake the woman or bang his head on the arm of her chair.

Behind him, Moses wound up with a thundering exhortation, and the crowd, including the woman in the wheelchair, applauded enthusiastically. Then she got to her feet, folded the chair up, and handed it to someone, who moved off into the crowd with it under his arm.

Ross regretted the handful of change he'd given her. Nothing like being taken in by the Sealers a second time.

"Can you tell me anything at all that would help me find my daughter?" he said desperately, tagging at her elbow, Julia in tow.

"Maybe she's gone to Seattle," the woman said over her shoulder. "Maybe she's here. Maybe she's at the shelter where all the homeless people go. Who knows?"

Homeless people?

What shelter? The only one he knew about was in Seattle. But—

And then he knew. He'd been talking to Miriam all along.

By the time he'd recovered his senses, she'd melted into the crowd and he and Julia were left standing alone on the grass, where nothing moved but the Sealers' trash blowing in the breeze past their feet.

Chapter Eighteen

❦

"Where are we going?" Julia took the helmet he handed her. Though she no longer fumbled with it, in the time it took her to buckle the chin strap, Ross already had the motorcycle started and his helmet on.

"The sheriff's office."

He must be going to report the woman. Julia hung on to his waist as he took a corner about ten miles an hour too fast. Miriam could be arrested for half a dozen different crimes, in Julia's opinion, child endangerment being the greatest one.

They pulled up outside a brick building similar to the one that the police department shared with the mayor's office in Hamilton Falls. But instead of marching in there to report Miriam, Ross took her hand and led her to a bench next to a planter box full of flowers.

He pulled her down next to him. "Julia, I don't see how to get around this. There are things you have to know before we go in."

She'd seen him outside the police department in Hamilton Falls earlier in the week. He'd said it was for a speeding ticket, but was it?

"You're not on parole or something, are you? Where you have to check in?" The words came out hesitantly, and he lifted his head with a huff of laughter.

"Parole? No."

Well, that was a start. "What, then?"

"There is something else I told you that wasn't quite true."

Oh, no. He was married, after all. Or not married, but in a relationship. Or in a relationship and getting married.

"Don't look like that," he said. "I'm not a criminal, I promise. I'm a cop."

"Are you married?"

"No. Single father. Julia, did you hear what I said?"

He wasn't married. It didn't matter, anyway. She was the one who was in a relationship and getting married, wasn't she? She lowered her head in her hands. "I think I'm losing my mind."

"I know I let you believe I was a mechanic, but that was just a story I tell sometimes when I'm off duty. I needed to get away from police work, find solace, like I said. A vacation that's part travel and part spiritual break. Just me and the highway and God. If people know I'm a cop, sometimes they act strangely around me. It's easier to use the—the cover story."

Compared to what she'd been expecting, the news that he was a policeman seemed wildly unimportant. Nice to know, but not really relevant.

"So why tell me now and not in the park?" she asked. "When were you going to get around to telling me who you really are?"

"I was working up to it," he said with a smile. "But in order to claim Kailey I need to have the law enforcement establishment behind me. And I need to use the computer in there." He jerked a thumb at the building behind them. "Are you okay with this?"

She shook her head, feeling as though there were bees buzzing in her skull instead of happily functioning brain cells. "It doesn't matter if I'm okay with it. You are what you are. Is there anything else you'd like to tell me? Otherwise we have a child to find, right?"

He bent his gaze to look into her eyes. "I'm a cop, a single dad who really wants to find his daughter and a guy who thinks you're the most remarkable woman he's ever met."

In spite of herself, she smiled. That didn't sound like a man who was committed elsewhere, did it?

They went into the sheriff's office at six forty-five, and by seven-thirty Ross had everything he needed, including the information that there was indeed a county shelter at the other end of town. Ross wasn't able to get the woman who answered the phone to confirm that Kailey was actually there, but he was determined to go down in person anyway.

Julia had to admit that having the law enforcement establishment behind you certainly got the job done. Ross had paged his "old friend," who turned out to be his partner in Seattle, and prevailed on him to go down to his apartment and transmit the original petition for custody and Kailey's birth certificate out to the sheriff's office. While he was waiting for the fax, she stood behind his chair as he downloaded an image of Kailey's baby fingerprints from the missing children's archive in what he explained was the National Crime Information Center. That kind of attention to detail told her Ross wasn't about to allow anything to come between himself and his daughter, not at this late date. Julia couldn't blame him. But she was less worried about the legalities of reuniting father and daughter than about the emotional effect it might have on the little girl.

When they parked in the miniscule parking lot belonging to the county shelter at the far end of town, she discovered she wasn't the only one worried about it.

"She doesn't know me," Ross said as he tilted the motorcycle on its kickstand. "The last time I saw her, she was sixteen months old. She took one look at me and screamed."

"I think we should go back and find Miriam," Julia said uneasily. "Think how you would feel if you were Kailey and these strange people appeared with no warning to take you away."

"That woman made it plain she wasn't going to help. More than that—if she left Kailey here unsupervised and uncared for I'm going to track her down myself and arrest her for endangerment."

Julia waited while Ross pushed open the door of the shelter for her. "Maybe I should try to talk to her first," she persisted. "Prepare her for you. A woman might be more reassuring to a little girl who's lost her mom."

Ross nodded, and stalked across the bare hallway to face the woman sitting behind a battered metal reception desk. "I'm Kailey Malcolm's father," he said, laying his black-leather identification folder and the fax on the desk in front of her. "Investigator Ross Malcolm, Organized Crime Task Force. I'm here to take my daughter home."

The woman's brows wrinkled. "Where is her mother, Investigator?"

"Her mother is dead." Ross's mouth flattened to a grim line, as though the words hurt. "The woman who brought her here isn't her mother. She's been trying to bring Kailey to me, and I just now tracked her down." That was putting it very mildly and charitably, but Julia saw he was trying to phrase it in a way that wouldn't make the specter of Child Protective Services suddenly appear.

If it hadn't already. The thought chilled her. Kailey could be on her way to a foster home right now, snatched out of his grasp at the last moment.

The woman gazed at him over the rims of her glasses. "Kailey DeLuca was assigned a social worker when she arrived. Let me see if Renee Iverly is still here. Most of the day staff have gone home."

For a moment Julia thought Ross was going to push past the woman and do a forced search of the shelter. He gripped the edge of the desk and controlled himself while the woman spoke to someone on the phone. A door opened down the hall and a tall, rangy woman dressed in a black tunic and tights walked into the reception area.

"Investigator Malcolm?" she asked, extending a hand to him and then to Julia. "I'm Renee Iverly. Come with me, please."

With every delay, Julia's tension rose another notch. She could only imagine what Ross's feelings were. He made them very plain once they were ushered into a cluttered office rather than into a room where there were kids.

"I've been looking for my daughter her whole life, ma'am. Annie took Kailey when she was a baby and ran off with a religious cult. I just got the information that she was in Pitchford this afternoon."

He put the papers on her desk, and she read through them rapidly. She seemed to find what she was looking for, and laid them down, clasping her hands on the crumpled pile.

"I understand your feelings, Investigator. You've been very proactive in providing the birth certificate and your original petition for custody. And you say the child's mother is dead? The woman who left her here wasn't her mother?"

"No. She's been trying to find me, I assume to deliver Kailey to me."

"What is she, a misdirected package? The poor child is being treated as abandoned. We were about to contact CPS on her behalf."

Ross's hands clenched. "I'm here now. I'm prepared to give her the home she deserves." Julia caught her breath at the years of frustrated longing in his voice.

"Let me tell you how the system works."

"Ma'am, could I just see my little girl?"

"In a moment. I want to set your expectations. You can't just walk out with the child. There are steps to this. To protect her." She gave him a kind but unyielding look, and Ross reluctantly sat back in his chair.

"What steps?"

"The case of abandonment seems pretty clear, so this should be straightforward. As her social worker, I can authorize supervised visits—"

Ross bolted up in protest, and she held up a placating hand.

"As I said, there are steps that must be followed, Investigator. We'll need to do a criminal check on you, which obviously won't take long. There will need to be a home study, a look at your employment, and so on, and then you and I will go before a judge and get her officially released from the county's custody. Did her mother have parents who might contest your right to the child?"

"No," Ross said through clenched teeth. "They're dead."

Ms. Iverly nodded. "Then it shouldn't take long to close the case. I'll get the background check initiated first thing in the morning, and get on Judge Olafsen's docket. Where can we reach you?"

Ross gave her his card, and indicated the pager number. "Now," he said in a voice so gentle it made Julia shiver, "about that supervised visit?"

Julia knew all too well what it was like to be skewered by that steely gaze, and hoped the woman could see beyond the badge to the father's heart.

Ms. Iverly was evidently used to dealing with desperate parents. "She's still in the playroom. We get the smaller ones ready for bed first. Follow me."

Outside the door, in the dimly lit hallway, the do-it-my-way-or-else cop dissolved and an uncertain father took his place. When Ms. Iverly paused at a door covered in finger paintings, he took a shaky breath.

"What if she hates me?" he whispered. "I don't know what Annie's told her about me. Or about the world outside the cult, for that matter. I couldn't stand it if she—if—"

"Just wait here," Ms. Iverly said. "By the door, where she can see you. I'll tell her who you are."

Inside, half a dozen children played, cutting up construction paper and coloring pictures on the floor.

A dark-haired little girl with Ross's eyes sat alone on a cushion at the table, carefully cutting pictures out of a magazine with orange-handled blunt scissors, her lower lip caught between her teeth.

The social worker walked quietly across the room and knelt by the table, and the child glanced up, startled.

"Hi, Kailey." Kailey clutched the pair of scissors, as if she were afraid they would be taken away. "Are you cutting out pictures?"

Kailey nodded. "See?"

Standing beside Ross just inside the door, Julia had an awful vision of the pictures slashed, the child acting out her hatred and disappointment on paper in the absence of her father.

"Goodness. Did you cut out all these? May I see one?"

"Here." The child fanned through a little pile of cutout people on the table. Carefully, she laid a picture of a man and a woman pushing a child on a swing in Ms. Iverly's palm. "This is the best one."

The social worker held it up for the two of them to see. No slashes. No cuts. It was a little uneven, and the scissors had slipped once across somebody's knee, but other than that it was a very careful piece of work.

"That's my daddy," Kailey said, as if explaining something the older woman couldn't possibly know.

"I see that."

"He loves his little girl, even though he's mad at her mommy."

"How do you know that, sweetie?"

"He told the mommy to stand over there while he pushed the swing."

The woman glanced at Ross. "Do you miss your mommy?"

She nodded. "Not Miriam, though. She's always mad at me, even when I get people to bring her money."

Julia's heart broke at a small child learning such survival skills.

"Do you think about your daddy a lot?"

Kailey turned back to the magazine and began to cut another picture out with precise little snips of the scissors. "He's going to come and get me someday. We stopped moving with the church so now he can."

"He can find you now?"

"Mm-hm."

"Did Mommy tell you that?"

Disdain wrinkled the child's small nose. "Uh-uh. I just know."

"Did you like it with the church?"

She shook her head vigorously. Gently, Ms. Iverly brushed a strand of the shaggy hair out of the child's mouth.

"I have to weed the garden, and pray a zillion times a day. And ask people for money, even crabby people. I wish daddy would hurry up." Kailey's voice trembled a little on the last words. The doubt underlying her stubborn hope caught at Julia's heart.

"Kailey, would you like to meet your daddy? He loves you so much. He's been looking for you for a long time."

The child stopped cutting. "When?"

"How about now? See that man over there?"

Her uncertain gray gaze locked on Ross, then returned to the social worker, begging her not to be playing a trick, to be making a promise that would never materialize. "That man?" The scissors were motionless in her hand, poised for a piece of paper that had fluttered to the floor.

Ross clutched Julia's arm, and she felt the tremors coursing through it. Julia touched his hand gently and gave him a little push, blinking back tears.

Ross walked slowly to the table, and Ms. Iverly stepped back to lean against the wall.

"Kailey?" His whisper cracked, and a lump rose into Julia's throat at the raw emotion in it. The little girl still did not move, but watched him carefully as he approached, as though she were a wild creature who might break and run at the least alarm. "Sweetie?"

He knelt beside her chair, tears swimming in his eyes. "Hi, baby. I've been looking for you for a long time." Her solemn eyes took him in, detail by detail. "You stopped moving, didn't you? So I could find you. What a smart girl."

The scissors dropped on the floor. Neither father nor child paid any attention.

"Daddy?"

Julia could see the effort Ross made to give her time, to stop himself from hugging her right away, so she could adjust her mental picture from the idealized perfection of the people in her pictures to this wet-eyed man in the scuffed leather jacket.

"Yes, baby. It's me."

"Daddy!"

Kailey flung herself off the chair and into her father's waiting arms.

Later that evening, Julia considered calling some-one—Rebecca, her mother, Derrick—to let them know where she was and when she'd be back. Then she thought about how she'd explain where she was: ninety miles away, unchaperoned, at nine o'clock at night, with a non-Elect man.

That would go over well. Even the fact that he was a cop wouldn't stop the scandal.

No one would consider Ross's feelings or the fact that he had to appear before a judge early tomorrow, or how heroically he was controlling his impatience and frustrated love. His little girl had allowed him into her heart so suddenly and completely that even Julia, who had been taught that modern-day miracles were a publicity stunt perpetrated by worldly churches, was tempted to believe.

The phone in this motel room didn't work, anyway. In fact, it wasn't much of a room—just a nightstand between two beds. But the sheets were clean, and there was a bathroom, and they were a short walk away from Kailey, who had just been persuaded to go to bed. She was terrified that Ross wouldn't be there when she woke up, so he had made himself comfortable on a plastic chair next to her cot until she'd fallen asleep.

Even then, he'd had a hard time tearing himself away. Julia thought he'd be just as happy to spend the night right there, watching over her like a grim, wary eagle, but Renee had convinced him that the pale, hollow-eyed look would not be the best way to present himself to the judge.

Julia patted the blanket, which was sturdy and warm, on the far bed. "I'll take this side, if you want to be closer to the door."

Ross shook himself out of his abstraction. "Sure it's okay with you to share a room? They probably have another one if you don't feel right about it."

"At a fruit festival? I don't think so. We were lucky to get this one, and that was only because it's on the other side of town."

"It looks bad." He smiled, as if they shared an inside joke. Which, she supposed, it was.

"But I know the truth. I know how badly you want to be there at the crack of dawn when Kailey wakes up. Besides, we're in this together."

The moment the words were out of her mouth, she regretted them. Regardless of the kisses they'd shared and the emotions they'd been through, she had no claim on him. They weren't a couple. And what she'd just said sounded as if she were asking for some sort of commitment about the future.

But he only nodded. "I don't know how I would have made it through this without you."

He held out his arms and she went into them like a homing pigeon, as if it were the most natural thing in the world to seek comfort and shelter there.

After a moment, Ross set her away from him. "You want to go first in the bathroom?"

Well, that answered her unspoken question, if nothing else. She was worrying about mistaken assumptions, and he was worrying about who got the bathroom first.

It helped to have a sense of humor when there was a man around.

"I wish I'd known this was going to be an overnighter." She looked in her purse, just in case at some point she might have stashed something more useful than a comb in there. "My kingdom for a toothbrush."

"I keep an emergency overnight kit in the bike in case I ever get stranded," Ross said. He handed her a small case. "Toothbrush, toothpaste, shampoo—samples from the drugstore—twenty bucks. And a granola bar."

She seized the little case like a starving person. "Shampoo? You're kidding." She gave him a quick hug of sheer happiness. "That's worth more than twenty bucks to me right now. I feel like someone dragged me backward through a hedge."

"Help yourself."

She emerged twenty minutes later feeling like a new woman, and Ross took the kit and disappeared into the bathroom with it.

"I guess the first thing on the agenda tomorrow is a shopping trip," he said when he returned. "Kailey's clothes are so old I wouldn't use them for shop rags."

With a pang, Julia thought how much fun it would be to shop for a girl who wasn't required to wear black. Madeleine made all Hannah's clothes, with the requisite ruffles and elongated hems, but they were still black. She would love to take Kailey on a spree and buy pint-size jeans and sleeveless sundresses and neon-pink T-shirts. Neither she nor the child had ever had any such thing.

Even a dream as simple as that was impossible.

She pulled the blanket up to her chin. It felt very strange to be in a room with a man, and stranger still to go to bed fully clothed.

Ross collapsed onto the edge of his bed with a sigh that seemed to come up from his feet. "I still can't believe it," he said quietly. "Half of me expects to wake up any minute now. She just took to me. Just like that."

"Maybe Anne didn't portray you in as bad a light as you thought," Julia said, trying to be fair. Only Kailey's behavior would tell them for sure.

"It's that Miriam woman I'd like to get my hands on. Leaving my daughter on her own just on the off chance I'd figure it out in time. The only reason we did is because God led us here. Otherwise the chances of me missing her and CPS taking her into the foster-care system would have been too high for me to beat."

"Do you really think God had anything to do with it?" The question was wrenched out of her, past years of conditioning not to talk about spiritual things with Outsiders.

But Ross wasn't an Outsider. Not to her.

His gaze was gentle and uncritical, with certainty behind it. "Absolutely. I don't believe in coincidence. Not with this many pieces scattered on the board, moving around for days until they came together right here. You and me, Kailey, the Sealers. No matter how careless she was, even Miriam couldn't fight the design. It's humbling, is what it is."

Without warning, he got up and sat beside her, and took her hand in a hard grip. His fingers were warm and solid and very sure. He bowed his head.

"Lord, I thank You from the bottom of my heart for bringing Julia and Kailey and me together today. I praise You for Your design, and love You with everything I am. You make me want to serve You for the rest of my life, just to show You my gratitude. But I know You know my thoughts even before I do. Thank You, dear Father. Thank You."

When Julia dared to look at him again, his eyes were squeezed as tightly shut as his fist around her hand, and a tear trickled slowly down the side of his nose.

She felt so unworthy of God's love—or Ross's, for that matter—that even tears wouldn't come. The prayers she'd prayed were so dry and selfish...all form, no function. Not like this. Not from the heart, offering praise, offering the very self to the One who loved it most.

She felt crushed, lifeless. Dust.

Gently, she unwrapped Ross's fingers and slipped into the bathroom to find him a tissue.

Even then, in the protective dark that gave away no secrets, the tears wouldn't come.

Chapter Nineteen

❧

The illuminated face of his watch told him it was six-fif-teen. Quietly, so as not to wake Julia, he knelt by the bed for a few minutes of communion with God.

He slipped out of the room and jogged the half block to the shelter, where he took up his station, on the plas-tic chair next to Kailey's cot. He'd promised he'd be there when she woke up. Nothing would have prevented him from keeping that promise.

Somewhere out back, half a block away, a rooster crowed to welcome the sun, and Kailey opened her eyes with a gasp, a sudden movement prompted by fear.

"It's okay, sweetie. I'm right here." His voice was low and soothing, a contrast to his thoughts. If he could just get his hands on the Sealers, just once, for doing this to her...

"Daddy?"

"Yup. I'm here."

She scrambled out of bed, a borrowed nightie about three sizes too big wrapped around her like a sheet, and into his lap. He held her close, breathing in the scent of freshly laundered cotton and clean child.

"I thought I had a dream."

"No, sweetie. This is real. We're going to ask the people here if you can come and live with me. Would you like that?"

"Do you live in a camper?" From her eager tone, a camper was the epitome of comfortable living.

"No. I live in an apartment in a big town."

"What's a 'partment?"

"It's a building where everybody gets their own set of rooms. It has a park across the street, and a pool downstairs where you can swim."

"Can I swim?"

"I'll teach you. Your mom used to swim like a fish, so you probably can, too."

"Mommy died and went to join the army in Heaven. Miriam said I had to be good or I'd die, too."

"Miriam was being mean, and she wasn't telling you the truth."

"I'll be good, Daddy. Don't leave me behind."

"Sweetie—" his voice broke "—even if you were as bad as you could be, I wouldn't leave you behind. We're going to live together forever."

Judge Olafsen wasn't terribly happy about hearing Ross's petition in his living room on the weekend, but when Renee Iverly explained the mitigating circumstances he relented.

When the papers were signed and they were on their way back to the shelter, Renee turned to Ross. "Usually I order a home study and all that before I release a child. We're still going to do that, but I'm going to award you provisional custody, pending its results. Your devotion to Kailey has been obvious to me and to all the staff. I think if we kept the two of you apart any longer, that would do more harm to her than if we released her right away."

"How soon is right away?" Julia asked, when a glance at Ross told her he was struggling to speak past the lump in his throat.

"As soon as we get back and I do the paperwork."

She was as good as her word. Julia had never seen a woman give so much of her own time and care to other people's children. She could be going to a festival or boating on the lake on this sunny morning, but instead she was slogging through a pile of paperwork so that one small family could be reunited.

Julia had heard Melchizedek say that worldly people did good deeds for their own gain, while the Elect did them for the glory of God. But every day she spent with Ross, it seemed, some teaching of Melchizedek was proven wrong. If the Elect did good deeds, such as inviting the less fortunate to dinner, they did it among themselves. They certainly didn't reach outside the boundaries of the group. The bastion of rules and caution that had protected her from the world outside was crumbling, precept by precept and line by line, and she was getting a good look at the view outside it.

Maybe living in the world wasn't such a bad thing, if it were populated by people like Renee and Ross. It had its Miriams, too, of course, but on the whole, the Renees and Rosses gave it hope.

Ross and Kailey emerged at last from Renee's office. Ross slung his jacket over his shoulder, gripped Kailey's hand in his, and grinned at Julia as if the weight of the world had been lifted from his back.

Which it had, when you got right down to it.

"You are the happiest man I've ever seen." Not even Owen had been this radiant on his wedding day, and she'd been judging men's looks by that standard for years.

Ross grabbed her around the waist and kissed her soundly, then knelt and kissed Kailey with relish. "I'm the happiest man on the planet. I have my two best girls with me, it's a beautiful day, and I think even the Lord is smiling."

"Does He smile?" Kailey wanted to know. "He's getting ready for a war."

Ross picked her up and walked out the door of the shelter, Julia close behind.

"Well, shrimp, Miriam didn't tell you the truth about a lot of things. I bet she didn't tell you the truth about God, either. He's not some kind of mean old general, ordering an army around. He's full of love and joy, and you know what?"

"What, Daddy?"

"So are we. And that means God is right here inside us, doesn't it?"

Kailey was silent, trying to puzzle that one out.

Ross kissed her, then glanced at Julia. "So...rumor has it that it's illegal for three people to ride on a motorcycle in this state. We need to get back to Hamilton Falls. Any suggestions?"

That was easy. "I'll take Kailey on the bus."

The two of them sat in the back of the bus, with Kailey on her knees on the seat, waving at Ross every few minutes as he followed them on the motorcycle. Even after the twentieth time, he still waved with just as much enthusiasm as the first. Kailey was delighted at the attention.

"My daddy has the biggest, baddest motorcycle in the world," she told the woman sitting in front of them.

Julia had to laugh. "He could drive a junker and you'd still think it was the biggest, baddest one," she teased.

The little girl looked from Ross to Julia. "Are you going to marry my daddy?"

"I don't know," Julia answered, groping for the truth at the suddenness of the question. She just didn't have it in her to whitewash a story for this child. "He's my friend, but I don't know if he wants to marry me. Even if he did, you're more important to him right now."

"Where are we going, then?"

"To my house. Daddy's on vacation in the town where I live. Maybe he'll let you sleep over."

"Do you live in a 'partment?"

Julia considered this seriously. "Yes. On the top of an old house. My friend Rebecca lives in the bottom. You can see into the tops of the trees from my front window."

"Do you have a little girl?"

"No. I have a little niece, though. She's three."

"Does she live with you?"

"No, she lives with her mommy and daddy and brother. Except her brother's sick so he's in the hospital."

Julia felt as though she'd stepped out of time since they'd left for Pitchford. As soon as she got home she was going to call Madeleine to find out how Ryan was. As the bus rolled into Hamilton Falls, trailed by the rumbling motorcycle, she tried to come up with an explanation for missing the young people's meeting and staying away overnight. She'd been trying since last night, though, and was no further ahead than when she'd started.

There was one thing she did know.

"Ross, where are you staying?" she asked when they got off the bus and walked over to where he'd parked the bike. Kailey immediately clambered up on it, and he held it steady for her.

"I've got a motel room. Paid by the week."

She looked at him doubtfully. "Are you going back to Seattle with her?" She hadn't thought about it until this minute. What if he said yes, strapped the little girl to the seat and they rolled off into the sunset, never to be seen again? What would she do then?

He shook his head. "I'm still on vacation. I thought about spending a few more days here."

"In the motel?"

"Sure, unless you have a better idea."

She had two bedrooms. One was full of Rebecca's late husband's stuff that she couldn't bear to throw away—including his mother's antique brass bed. There was nothing to amuse a child with in a motel room, whereas at her place there was a box full of Ryan's and Hannah's toys and books. There were snacks and juice and games and...well, why couldn't they stay with her?

It was impossible. Melchizedek would be on the doorstep like an avenging angel as soon as he heard. And what on earth would Rebecca say? Brass bed notwithstanding, she'd probably evict her.

Julia's mouth set stubbornly. How could she be evicted for offering shelter to a little girl who had been neglected and abused her whole life? Whose idea of a wonderful place to live, Ross had quietly told her, was a camper?

"I sure do," she said. "You guys can stay with me. Come on, Kailey. Let's go make some lunch while your dad gets his stuff and checks out of his motel."

"Julia, are you sure about this? Rebecca probably won't approve."

"I'll deal with Rebecca." She lifted Kailey down from the seat of the bike and grasped her warm little fingers in her own. "See you over there."

* * *

The motel room door barely had a chance to swing shut before Ross grabbed the phone and dialed Ray Harper's pager number, with the 9-1-1 emergency code that told his partner to drop everything and call.

It took Ray a minute and twenty seconds.

"What have you got, bud?" Ray's voice was breathless, as if he'd run up a flight of stairs. "Is Kailey all right? Did something happen with the custody thing?"

"No, it's fine. I've got her. They pulled some strings for me. Thanks for getting the paperwork out here so fast. That really greased the process."

"Don't mention it. As I keep reminding you, we're partners. How's the case going? If it were me, I'd bag the whole thing and get back here with my kid."

"I'm tempted. But I feel responsible for this other kid, too. There's been something I've been meaning to ask you, but Kailey drove it out of my mind. Tell me about that woman and her kid again. That one from your last tour of duty."

"Why do you want to know?"

"Because something's bugging me about this case. I want to see how it compares with yours, but I don't remember enough about it."

"I remember being on patrol for four years straight because of it. That's what messing in these family cases will get you."

Ross frowned. "Give me the details."

"You asked for it. It was when I was working down in Pasqualie. Single mom, kid sick constantly, in and out of hospitals all his life. He was about three when the hospital alerted us. They were suspicious something weird was going on."

"What happened to the kid?"

"They thought she was poisoning him. So did I. I did everything but rig the house with cameras to catch her at it."

"Did you?"

"Nope. She was pregnant with somebody else's kid and I had my case all built, ready to pop her and go to court. Know what happened?"

"You never said."

"It's not the kind of stuff you broadcast. She had her second kid and the hospital discovered the exact same symptoms."

"She was abusing both kids?" Ross's voice held his incredulity. "A newborn?"

"No. It was a *disease*. The second kid by a different father proved it was genetic, that she was a carrier of some kind. And there I was with the D.A. ready to go, a bunch of nurses lined up to be witnesses in court. I was ready to arrest her when I found out. But by then it was too late. The hospital called my lieutenant and made a big stink about it—as if they hadn't called me in the first place. I got hauled into Staffing and laughed back down to patrol for my crazy witch-hunting ideas."

Cold sweat prickled on Ross's forehead. He could be in the same position if he wasn't careful. "How did you find out?"

"Linda Chang over at the forensics lab. I was planning to use her for a witness. To do that I had to get her a blood sample from everybody, kids and mother. She's the one who found proof of this disease." Ray paused. "I'm telling you, you don't want to touch these mother-and-kid cases. It's too easy to see something that isn't there."

Ross shook his head slowly. "I've got to find out, one way or another. Wrap this up quickly and get on with my life." A life that looked completely different from the one he'd had a week ago.

"I'm telling you, don't do it."

"Right, Ray, I'm going to just drop it and let the kid suffer? Maybe die?"

"I'm not saying drop it. Just don't go as far as prosecution. It's suicide."

"Yeah, for the kid."

"Three weeks away and I forget how stubborn you are. Look, at least talk to Linda before you go and do something stupid. I just saw her in the cafeteria. She was on her way back to her office."

"Ray, I can't talk right now. I've got to get Kailey settled. Julia's waiting for me."

"I warn you. The body count is piling up. We got some kind of nutcase running around here with lamp cords and duct tape. If you don't catch her now you might have to wait a week."

"Ryan doesn't have a week."

"I rest my case. Hang on while I transfer you. I'll give her the condensed version and you take it from there."

Cold dread churned in his stomach while he waited. Then the call went through with a click. "Dr. Chang?"

"Yes. I understand you want to talk about a case." She sounded about twenty years old, but with her record in court, she was probably closer to forty.

"I appreciate whatever help you can give me."

"I've got about ten minutes before some stomach contents get here. Tell me the details."

The woman did not waste time. He flipped a page in his notebook and launched into a description of Ryan's short life, the patterns it contained and what little he'd managed to learn from Rita, Julia and Dr. Archer. When he finished, he added, "My informant is a pediatric nurse at the hospital. The administration isn't listening, so she came to us. She's suspicious that the kid's being abused, but has no proof. Ryan's been released and has been home less than a week, and the last I heard, they were talking about opening him up again and sticking in a feeding tube. I've got to tell you, Dr. Chang, I don't know much about medicine, but I know I'm worried about this situation."

Over the static of long distance, a pencil scratched on a note pad. "I hate to ask you this, but do you know how difficult to prosecute these cases are?"

"I already had a lecture from my partner. But I also need to know if there might be the possibility of abuse."

"There might. It sounds to me, based on all those symptoms, that your informant has good instincts. But that's not enough. Tell me more about the mother."

"I don't have much, but I do know she's been the center of attention her whole life. Parents adore her, friends think she can do no wrong. They're in this church that thinks she's a saint."

"A certain type of personality needs that."

Ross went on, "She plays mind games with the doctor. She's in total control as far as the kid's care is concerned. Never leaves his side."

"What about the father? Is he distant? Does he control other aspects of her life?"

"I wouldn't say that, but the church lays down the law along traditional lines. Men have all the say."

"Uh-huh. And the pattern of abuse is a clear signal. You noticed that every time there's an event in the family to take the attention off her, the child gets sick."

"Yes. The family blames the kid's fragility. I wondered if it was something else—some kind of religious rite."

"That would be easier to believe. Investigator Malcolm, have you ever heard of Munchausen's syndrome by proxy?"

The ugly words chilled him as she gave his fear a name. "I've heard of it. Never been involved in a case, though."

"This mother fits the profile in many ways. Have you done any research on it?"

"No, but Ray told me what happened on that case you and he worked on."

Dr. Chang's voice hardened. "He was operating on an assumption based on the evidence he had at the time. It wasn't until the second baby was born that we realized the evidence could go both ways."

"It can in this case, too."

"I wouldn't say so. From what you've told me, the pattern is consistent with events in the family. Ray's case was completely different."

"I'm not going to start a witch-hunt and prosecute someone with a reputation for being an exemplary mother."

"But the majority of women who fit this profile are seen that way. The maternal bond is sacred in our society, so people aren't willing to believe MSBP exists. There's a lot of research on it out there now. A few years ago there were only a couple of hundred reported cases. Now they're making TV shows about it and the pendulum is swinging the other way, attacking innocent mothers with legitimately sick kids. You're right. It's all too easy to do a witch-hunt." Dr. Chang paused. "But the victim—the child—has to come first."

Ross nodded, then realized she couldn't see him. "Of course. I'm scared I might be wrong. But if I'm right and something happens to the kid..." He swallowed. "You're short on time, here. Can you just tell me if it's possible to generate the kid's symptoms? And what might be used?"

Dr. Chang sighed. "It would need to be something easily available to the caregiver. People use anything from rubbing alcohol to ant poison to their child's own feces to create gastric distress. From your description of his symptoms it could be some form of grain alcohol. But without a blood sample, of course, I'm just guessing. You say the symptoms have been going on for nearly three years? Vomiting, lethargy, gastric bleeding?"

"From the documentation in the file, I'd say so."

"Well, I must say it would take some medical training to know exactly how much to administer over time. Otherwise it would kill him. If you think you have enough evidence, you need to do something before they put the feeding tube in. It creates direct access to his GI tract. In his condition he isn't going to be able to fight any foreign substances."

His stomach twisted as he got a mental flash of Madeleine injecting something—isopropyl?—into a tube, the fast lane to Ryan's vulnerable gastric system. "She did have some nurse's training apparently."

"But these symptoms could indicate any number of diseases. A simple ulcer, for one. Epilepsy, even."

"His doctor would have found those long before now."

"Not if he's testing for something specific. Anything outside that screen would be missed. I'm still curious about the mother. You say she's a good caregiver?"

"The best. Like I said, the community reveres her. Her husband worships the ground she walks on, and so does every other man she knows. The family doctor has been in love with her since she was eighteen."

He heard what sounded like a snort. "Not a good sign, then. She could bring the kid in bleeding from a stab wound and he'd believe anything she said. You seriously think this is how she maintains her standing in the community? This church?"

"One of the ways. Her sister's been talking to me: I'm also using her as an informant." This felt like a confessional. "When my informant, Julia, brought me to the church, everyone's attention swung to us. That's when Ryan took a downturn. And I started to get a weird feeling about it."

"Don't feel responsible for that," Linda Chang said. "If your suspicions are correct, it would fit her particular pattern. The mother sees that the church is paying attention to her sister instead of her, so her reaction could be to hurt the child...if she suffers from MSBP. And that's a big *if* at this point without hard data."

The chill spread through Ross's body. That was the problem. There were too many *if*s. The suspicions that had taken root that afternoon on the hillside when Julia had pointed out the patterns in her family life could be explained in a number of different ways. And he couldn't prosecute until he'd narrowed them down to one.

"What am I going to do?" he asked heaven, scraping his fingertips through his cropped hair in agitation.

Dr. Chang replied as if he'd asked her. "You're going to get me a blood sample, to begin with. And then you've got to catch her in the act of administering the substance, on video if possible. Nothing else is going to stand up in court."

Ross tried to imagine setting up video surveillance in the Blanchard home. That'd be about as easy as riding his bike into their living room. "This church is so conservative they don't even watch TV. And how would I get consent from the husband? He thinks she's the Madonna."

"What about the sister? Could she help? Or the nurse? Even the doctor. There's got to be a way to get to one of them. Quietly. Don't do what Ray did and get the entire hospital lined up, only to find out you're wrong."

"I'll find a way."

"I hope so. In my opinion, regardless of the cause of his illness, this child doesn't have much time."

Ross had prayed many prayers in his lifetime—thankful prayers, angry prayers, humble prayers. On his knees by the bed, he learned for the first time what it was like to pray a desperate prayer for two children who affected him deeply in different but equally powerful ways.

He would do everything in his power to get Kailey through the adjustment process and back to a normal life. But as far as he could tell, only God's help was going to get Ryan through this one.

Chapter Twenty

✦

It seemed to Julia that the thing Kailey liked most about her apartment was how soft everything was.

The second time she saw the little girl cuddled up in the corner of the couch under the knitted afghan, she put down the knife she was slicing apples with, and sat beside her. "Are you cold, sweetie?"

Kailey stroked the afghan. "It's soft. Pretty." She bounced a little on the couch cushion. "So is this. And your bed." Her tone held wonder. "Everything."

Julia smiled, and stroked the afghan too. "Not quite everything. The corners of that little table there are pretty sharp. And you don't want to clunk your head on the bathroom sink, either."

"You have a bathroom? All your own?"

"I sure do. Tonight you can have a bath if you like."

Kailey scowled. "Don't like baths. They're cold."

"Mine isn't. I have lots of hot water. I don't have any

bath toys but I have lots of soaps that smell pretty. You could have a raspberry soap or a lime one."

Julia brought her a plate of apple slices spread with peanut butter and a glass of milk. "This is just a snack until your dad gets here." Kailey ate like a kitten, with delicate bites, licking her lips after each one to make sure she didn't miss anything.

The hollow sound of footsteps on the stairs brought Julia to her feet. "There's your dad now."

She swung open the door and Rebecca blinked at her in surprise. "Julia. I didn't think you were home." She waved a piece of paper, then stuck it in her pocket. "I was going to leave you a note, but now I don't have to. May I come in?"

Julia stepped back, a little flustered. She'd been so consumed with Ross and Kailey and making life-changing choices that she'd forgotten about the possibility of being evicted.

"Sure."

Kailey covered herself with the afghan and peered over the arm of the couch. The fringe hung in her eyes like the ruff of a woolly sheepdog as she watched Rebecca warily.

"My goodness," Rebecca said, taking in the child, the half-full glass of milk, and the fact that Julia was wearing jeans. "This is different."

Julia had never before been subjected to the up-and-down evaluation of her dress. Alma Woods was quite good at it, but usually Julia and her small circle of friends were so self-conscious that they gave the older women nothing to criticize. She realized for the first time exactly what a "speaking glance" was. She stiffened her spine. Getting caught in jeans was just the beginning.

"Rebecca, this is Kailey Malcolm," Julia said steadily. "Kailey, say hello to Miss Quinn."

"Hello, Kailey," Rebecca said gently. Kailey didn't reply. Instead, she tugged the afghan over her head and made herself small in the corner of the couch.

"Are you baby-sitting, dear?" Rebecca asked. She moved a cushion out of the way and sat in the easy chair.

"No, this is Ross's daughter."

Rebecca looked confused. "Ross? The young man on the motorcycle? I didn't know he was a father. Or married."

"He isn't married. Kailey's mother died recently and Ross and Kailey have just been reunited. It's a long story."

"Long enough to explain why you weren't at the young people's meeting?"

Trust Rebecca to jump right in.

"Yes. Ross found out Kailey was in Pitchford so we went to get her."

Rebecca gazed at Julia for a moment, her eyes very blue and clear over the silver rims of her glasses. "You know that you're one of my very favorite people, don't you, dear?"

"Am I?" Julia wondered how long that would last. If she were a betting woman, she'd estimate about seven or eight minutes.

"And I know you've often come to me to talk things over when by rights you should have gone to your mother. In fact, I look on you as the daughter I never had. Which is why it distresses me that you didn't let me know you were out of town overnight."

"Rebecca, I'm twenty-six. If I want to go somewhere, I don't need to ask permission."

"I didn't say anything about asking permission. But I would have appreciated having some kind of story to give your mother, your brother-in-law and Melchizedek when they called me one after the other. Once they found out you weren't in the young people's meeting and Derrick didn't know where you were, there was a hue and cry the likes of which I've never seen before. Silly geese."

Julia gaped at her.

"It was very awkward. It's been a while since I had to play stupid, but I did it. After all the hueing and crying was done, I simply said I had no idea, and no doubt you would have a perfectly good explanation when you came home."

"Thanks." Julia couldn't think of another thing to say.

"You're most welcome. I would prepare myself, dear. I have no doubt you counted the cost before you went to Pitchford, and that it was worth it."

Julia glanced at the couch, where Kailey had partially emerged and was looking at Rebecca with great curiosity. "Yes, it was worth it. We found her in the county shelter, and it took some time to get through the legalities. She was just released into his custody this morning, and we took the bus back. Ross should be here any minute."

"Here?"

Julia nodded. Now came the part where she was going to be evicted. "He's been staying at a motel, but I think Kailey will be more comfortable here. She needs new clothes and decent food and a little bit of stability while Ross is in town. So they'll be staying with me for a little while." She took a breath and rushed on. "I realize that looks bad, and I understand it will reflect badly on you. So yes, I'll be looking for another place to live. I just hope you don't mind if it takes me a few days."

"I do mind. I mind very much."

Julia's shoulders tightened with tension. "I'm sorry, Rebecca. I'll try to find another place as fast as I can."

"I don't mean about that, you ridiculous child. I mind very much that you think I would give you the boot for providing a temporary home for two people so obviously in need of one. What kind of heartless—" she cast around for a word bad enough "—wretch do you take me for?"

Julia struggled to make sense of the collision between expectation and reality. "You're not going to evict me?"

"Evict you for caring for a child who was found in a homeless shelter? Great heavenly days, dear. I'm astonished at you."

Julia dropped on her knees beside Rebecca's chair and hugged the older woman. Rebecca hugged her back, and Julia felt the strength of her bones.

"There's Ross, too," she managed around the lump in her throat.

"If it really bothers you that much, you can come and sleep in my guest room. But for pity's sake, you have more to worry about here than lending a room to your friends. Your mother, for one thing. Dear Elizabeth is on the warpath with a vengeance." Gently, she steered Julia to the couch, where Kailey had come out from under the afghan completely, and was busy braiding each tuft of the fringe. "She isn't letting on, of course. If anyone but Melchizedek brings up the subject she freezes them out. But the Spanish Inquisition has nothing on her when it comes to interrogation. I finally had to lie and tell her I had a kettle boiling over to get her off the phone. May the good Lord forgive me."

"What I don't understand is why all the fuss. I've been on overnight trips tons of times and no one has batted an eye."

"That's what I came here to tell you, dear. Ryan's condition is worsening, and most of the family has been at the hospital since last night." She held up her hands as

Julia leaped to her feet. Kailey snatched the afghan over herself again and blinked fearfully through the fringe.

"There's really nothing you can do. He was moved to intensive care, and Michael told them not to overreact and act as though he was on his deathbed, poor wee baby, but everyone went into panic mode anyway. I would suggest you clean up and change, and consider yourself warned."

"I can't leave. What about Kailey?"

"I'll watch her until Mr. Malcolm comes. In fact, I think we might get along famously if she allows me to help her with some of those lovely braids."

Julia was becoming painfully familiar with the pediatrics ward. Even when she was concentrating on bringing Madeleine and Owen two cups of tea without spilling them, she avoided the corner of the carpet sticking up in the waiting room as automatically as she avoided the creaky board in her bathroom that had been known to wake Rebecca out of a sound sleep.

She got to Ryan's room without spilling a drop. Madeleine looked awful after a two-day vigil. Her skin was pale and drawn, and her eyes looked tearful to the point of flooding. Owen looked up from the Bible on his lap, which he'd been reading to them in lieu of going to Sunday Gathering, and got up to greet her. A cold feeling of unease tugged at Julia as she handed him his tea. If Madeleine looked drawn, Owen looked positively deathly. Julia suddenly realized that he was not the young, golden god she had always worshiped, but a middle-aged man whose greatest efforts and constant faith were useless against the unknown threat that stalked his son.

"How is he?" she whispered.

"No change." Owen's voice carried his pain the way damp air carried sound. He made an effort to smile at her. She had always been so much in awe of his position in the church she had never felt comfortable kissing him, but she did so now. "I'm glad you're here, Julia."

She was selfishly thankful that her sister and brother-in-law were both so consumed with their son that they had no time for trivialities such as where she'd been lately and with whom.

She turned to the bed. Ryan lay on the pillow, his head engulfed by its softness. He looked so small. So fragile, as if a word spoken too loudly would end his life. A tube ran into his nose.

Julia looked over her shoulder. "They've put a feeding tube in?"

Madeleine nodded, and leaned over to brush a lock of damp hair off Ryan's forehead with the gentlest touch of her fingers. She didn't seem to see the cardboard cup Julia held out to her, so she put it gently on the tray at the end of the bed.

"He couldn't keep his food down. At least this way we know he's getting nourishment while they try to find out what's wrong."

"Is it—is it the same as before?" Julia asked, frightened to put the thought into words. "It's the flu, isn't it?"

"We don't know," Owen replied, subsiding into his chair again. "We're hoping that's all it is. It came on so suddenly."

"I've never thought it was flu," Madeleine said with authority. She held her head so stiffly the cords in her neck stood out like bone. "I told Michael that from the first. If he'd listened to me sooner, we might have been able to act days ago."

"He's acting now," Owen said, looking at Julia. "They have a specialist coming up from Spokane in the morning."

"I still think we should have insisted on the GI man in Seattle," Madeleine said stubbornly. "I was very impressed with his credentials. What can they know in Spokane, for goodness' sake?" She adjusted Ryan's blankets, then peered at the digital display on the apparatus next to the bed as if checking the doctors' work.

"If it does turn out to be flu, we'll probably be glad he only came from Spokane," Owen said with a trace of his old humor, watching her.

"It isn't flu, Owen. Why do you keep believing what Michael says?"

"Because Michael's a doctor, darling."

"Oh, and I'm not. I'm just his mother, and for your information, you forget I have nurse's training."

"You were only there a year, Lina," Julia said without thinking, and Madeleine rounded on her.

"That's a year more than either of you! I don't need any comments like that from single people, thank you very much! Since when did you become an authority on children when you've never had any?"

Julia stared at her sister. Her stomach rolled over with a nauseating thud.

Owen gently led Madeleine to the other side of the room. "Come on, sweetheart, I know how hard this is on you. I know you've given the kids everything you had to give. Let's go for a walk, all right? I could really use one."

"I'm not leaving Ryan."

"Julia can stay with him for two minutes. Please."

Madeleine allowed her husband to take her out into the waiting room, and Julia sat in the uncomfortable chair. The anxiety was getting to them all. Poor Madeleine was just developing stress fractures in her spirit.

But it hurt. Deeply. No one in their family used such unkind words, or that tone of voice, either. Julia groped for some sort of spiritual strength, but there was nothing inside but a reverberating shock that anyone who professed to love her could speak to her that way. It was almost as if Madeleine hated her for voicing even the smallest of doubts about her ability to care for her children. For a few dreadful seconds she'd seen a stranger glaring out of Madeleine's eyes.

"Auntie Julia?"

Ryan's voice was hardly more than a whisper. Julia leaned over the bed, her uneasy thoughts vanishing. "Hi, big guy. I heard you weren't feeling so good."

The little boy's eyes were huge in a face that had long ago lost its baby fat. His short eyelashes were clumped together, and his hair was stuck to his forehead with perspiration. Julia dipped a tissue in the water carafe and sponged his face.

"Auntie Julia, I saw the angel from hell."

The back of Julia's neck prickled.

Ryan and Hannah had always been creative, imaginative children. Was Ryan really so ill that he could no longer distinguish between reality and fantasy? Or was there, as worldly people believed, really an angel of death hovering at this moment in the pastel-colored hospital room, waiting to take away the child she loved?

Julia huddled in the chair by the bed, cold inside and out. When Owen and Madeleine came back a moment later, the look on her face betrayed her.

"Julia, what is it? Is he worse?" Madeleine pushed the sock monkey aside and took Ryan's wrist.

But the little boy had drifted back into sleep. Not for worlds would Julia tell them what their son had seen.

Chapter Twenty-One

✣

With a white maintenance overall covering his clothes in case someone walked in, Ross paced the hospital laundry room. He hated not having his hand in everything to do with a case. Bad enough he'd had to entrust Kailey to Rebecca and dash down here with no warning, once he'd heard about Ryan's downturn. But oddly, Kailey seemed to like Rebecca, and the woman had been introducing the little girl to the wonders of making peanut butter cookies when he'd left.

Meanwhile, where was Rita? They had too narrow a window to risk any deviations from the plan. He'd seen Ryan himself earlier. Time was running out.

Soft footsteps sounded in the corridor outside, and Rita slipped into the room, closing the door behind her. "Sorry. Swing shift got called into a staff meeting and they always run long."

"What's the status?" Ross asked, hands loosely on his hips.

"I saw Julia just now, on her way out. Owen will probably leave in the next half hour or so. He's been here all evening. My colleague says that Madeleine usually runs down to the machine on the next floor around nine for a snack. That gives us about five minutes to get the sample."

"Did any of them see you?"

"Of course not," Rita said. "They know I work here, but I keep out of their way. If anyone discovers I'm working with you, I've had it. I hope you don't plan to stay long."

"No. Once you get his blood sample, I'll meet you in the parking lot. It'll go in the priority courier to Seattle and with any luck, we'll have some results from Dr. Chang in a day or two."

"Let's hope. But tell me something. If they find isopropyl alcohol, it will only prove that someone is poisoning Ryan. How will you prove it's Madeleine and not one of us nurses?"

Ross nodded in acknowledgement of the risk. "Dr. Chang told me the best way was to catch her at it on video. But I don't see how we can do that. I'm not going to stand on a ladder and drill a hole for a camera above his bed. Getting the approvals alone could take days. And from the look I got at Ryan a while ago, we don't have days."

"He'll be lucky to make it through the week, if you want my opinion. My colleague says his condition is so fragile that if Madeleine gets to him even once more, it could send him under."

Not for the first time that day, Ross clenched his teeth and prayed. It was an incoherent jumble of pleading and emotion, but the Father, the all-knowing and all-loving, would translate.

"What are you going to do?" Rita asked when the silence extended past her comfort zone.

"I think we need to bring Archer in to help us."

Rita snorted. "Get real. He's in love with her. And he's true-blue Elect."

"But if that sample comes back positive, he'll have to listen. He can't argue with the facts."

"Ross, my big leather-clad innocent, the Elect have been denying the facts for a hundred years. Look at Melchizedek and that arrogant prune, Phinehas. They think they're prophets, leading the people to heavenly glory, when Melchizedek is just an unemployed mill worker named Mitch Duckworth. Phinehas has been running this scam for so long I don't think anybody knows who he used to be."

He lifted an eyebrow. "What about the generations of McNeills and the wandering prophets and having the Elder's position handed down and all that?"

"He's a wandering prophet, all right. All of them are. They wander right in and start where the last one left off, getting weirder with every generation. Don't fool yourself. Denial of reality is an art form here."

Ross thought about the torture in Michael Archer's eyes at his inability to diagnose Ryan correctly. If Madeleine really had been toying with him for most of Ryan's life, imposing her own reality on his and playing a game that pitted her cunning against his knowledge and the authority of the entire hospital system, the effects were beginning to show. And that could just work to Ryan's advantage.

"I don't know," he said slowly. "Archer craves an answer. He feels he's failing as a man and as a doctor because he can't come up with one. If we give him that answer, the shock might just push him onto our side."

"I think it's a mistake, but this is your show," Rita said flatly. "Now, I've got to get back to work and you've got to disappear."

More than anything, Ross wanted to slip upstairs and watch while Rita took the blood sample, to make sure Ryan was still breathing. Maybe poke around and see if he could find any evidence of what Madeleine was up to. But he couldn't. He'd looked in and Ryan had opened his eyes for a moment. He couldn't risk it again.

He pushed open the door to the glassed-in staircase on the outside of the building and began the descent to the ground floor. At the landing, he ran smack into a woman.

"Oops! Sorry, miss, I—"

Julia looked up at him and smiled, as if his mere presence were a gift. Her hair glowed in the last of the daylight like Spanish gold. Longing rippled through him—longing for a warmth and promise that would be chilled forever in just about two minutes, after he'd said what he'd been holding back for weeks. Well, there was nothing left to lose, now. To do his best for her nephew, he had to tell her the last of his secrets.

"I need to talk to you."

For a moment, her heart raced. Julia took a deep breath and tried to calm her responses to his closeness and the intensity in his eyes. That penetrating look always affected her, and she was too close to coming undone as it was.

"Is Kailey all right? Honest, Ross, I didn't mean to leave her so suddenly, but when Rebecca told me about Ryan, I had to come. She's okay with Rebecca, isn't she?"

"She's fine. Rebecca's showing her how to make peanut butter cookies. And probably how to eat them, too. I mean I need to talk to you about your family."

She had already reached the turn of the stairs, but that stopped her. "My family? Why, did my father call and ask about your intentions, or something?" That was all she needed right now. So far she'd managed to avoid her parents, but it wouldn't last forever.

"Here, sit down." He stripped off his white overall and laid it on a step. She did as he asked, his odd tone and hooded eyes preventing her from doing what she wanted to do, which was to touch his forehead and smooth away the frown that seemed permanently lodged there.

He paused a moment, as if trying to choose words. "I need to come clean with you about what I'm doing here," he began.

She gazed at him curiously. "Here at the hospital? You mean you didn't come to find me? I might have known." Her attempt at humor fell flat.

"Not here at the hospital. I told you I was on vacation, taking a spiritual break, and that was true. At the beginning. But two days into my ride I was called to Hamilton Falls on a case. It involved a group we suspected was abusing its children."

Surprise stiffened her spine, and she stared at him.

"The guys at the station had me pulled off leave because crimes by small groups are a specialty of mine. I managed to gain entry to the group and began investigating the most current case. This hasn't been easy for me. I want to get that out on the table first of all. I've felt pulled in two different directions since I started, but the well-being of the victims has to come first."

"But what do abused kids in some organization have to do with my family?"

"I'm getting to that. A pattern became clear in the life of the most recent victim that worried me, so I did a little investigating. It seemed that whenever there was a major event in the family, like a wedding or a graduation or the start of a new job, the child got sick."

"That sounds like us," Julia said gloomily.

He paused, long enough for Julia to look up. She felt a prickle of unease. His eyes were gunmetal-gray, the way she'd first seen them.

"Right. Well, in my mind there might be a reason in this particular case. There's a disorder called Munchausen's syndrome by proxy where a mother hurts her child to get attention whenever the family's attention is pulled elsewhere. Ever heard of it?"

"Never." Goose bumps broke out on Julia's arms, and she wished he would talk about something else instead of some grisly case.

"I believe there's a strong possibility the mother in this case has this disorder. And she's damaged her little boy almost to the point of killing him. I intend to find out for sure, and if I'm right, stop it."

He seemed to be asking her to think about this, as if he wanted help with it. Julia ran over a list of all the people she knew. Who on earth would have done such a thing in Hamilton Falls? Nothing like that had ever been in the paper. She'd never heard a whiff of gossip. The only thing that came close was—

She stared at Ross in horror. "You're not saying—you can't possibly think—"

"I do, honey," Ross said in a gentle tone. He took both her hands in his. "I've been investigating the Elect. It could be that Madeleine has the disorder. There is a very good possibility she is slowly killing your nephew."

"No." Even to herself, her voice sounded high and wobbly. "My sister loves Ryan. She's a godly woman. The Elder's wife. You must be crazy."

"Even if I am, I can't risk it. I need to prove it one way or the other. In a moment, when you get past the shock of all this, I'll show you how. I'm going to need your help to—"

Julia pushed violently away from him and leaped to her feet. "Need my help?" she repeated. "My help to what?"

"To investig—"

"Do you mean to tell me you've been stringing me along all this time? In order to *investigate*—" she enunciated it bitterly "—my sister?"

"To help—"

"Why should I help you when all you've done is lie to me? You've been using me, haven't you?" Her voice cracked on the last word.

"Honey, your sister could be sick. If she is, we need to get help for her. And we need to help Ryan." His voice rose to a shout as she jumped up and bolted down the stairs. "I want you to watch for something. If they've put a feeding tube in, it means she could have a fast and easy way to put the poison in his system."

With a squeal of denial, Julia covered her ears. He caught up to her and gripped both wrists.

"I'm going to make you hear this whether you like it or not. I have reason to believe she might be feeding him isopropyl alcohol. Starting tonight, his condition is going to go downhill fast. When that happens, you'll know I'm right. Got that? And—"

Jerking her hands out of his grasp, she whirled and dashed down the stairs again, her footsteps loud in the silence. Ross leaned over the rail. "—and I'll be here, Julia. All night. You look after my little girl and I'll look after Ryan. Hear me?"

The slam of the outside door was his only answer.

* * *

Julia started awake with a gasp, the weight on her chest crushing the breath out of her. The cool dimness of dawn had brightened her room, but the sun wasn't up yet. She glanced around, reassuring herself with the sight of her dresser, the wicker chair by the window, her books and clothes.

Just a dream.

Ross, Ross, why are you persecuting me? What he'd said at the hospital had shocked her into looking at reality clearly. Now that she'd lost him, she knew how deeply her feelings ran. Seeing him had been like a punch, like a gift, like being whooshed up in the air and then dumped back down by the knowledge that the only reason he was interested in her was because she was useful to him.

What did the police call them? Finks, that was it. She'd heard Jenny Kurtz use the term once, and not in a nice way. She lay back in bed, struggling with the magnitude of her crime. In the meadow she'd told him all about their family history. On the beach she'd spilled her deepest secrets about how she really felt about the Elect. She'd betrayed her community and given him everything, and he'd used it all, ruthlessly.

It would take her a long time to forgive him. And even longer to forgive herself.

And in the meantime, there was Kailey.

He hadn't come back to the apartment by midnight, so she'd looked in on his sleeping daughter and wondered how this had happened—how she'd come to be looking after his child while he was—or said he was, anyway—looking after Ryan.

Because, of course, he was lying. Was this some weird, horrific way to deliver a breakup speech—to give him a reason to leave?

Regardless of what he was up to, she still had a Monday to get through, and a little girl to care for. Kailey woke with a start when Julia sat on the edge of the brass bed.

"Good morning, sweetie," she said gently, and brushed the girl's hair out of her eyes.

"Daddy?" Kailey looked past Julia, as if expecting to see her father on the threshold.

"Daddy's working. He'll be back after lunch, I think, or maybe by suppertime. Do you want to come to the bookstore with me?"

"No. I want Daddy."

Now what could she do? "I saw him at the hospital last night when I went to see Ryan. He says to say he loves you, and he'll see you a bit later."

"Want him now."

Julia had not been baby-sitting small children for four years for nothing. It took an hour, but she got Kailey fed and dressed in the pitiful sweatpants and T-shirt they'd found her in, and buckled her into the back seat of her car for the short ride downtown.

Item one on the to-do list was to spend a little time at work. Item two was to buy some clothes for Kailey. No matter what she felt about Ross, it wasn't the child's fault. Kailey's need for the basics of life was greater than Julia's hurt feelings.

She got Kailey settled in the kids' section with a book that made animal noises when you pressed the pictures. Then she spent a few minutes restocking shelves. Book by book, putting them in their places like a mason walling himself in, she made order out of chaos.

But she couldn't wall his voice out of her head. *I have reason to believe she might be feeding him isopropyl alcohol...Munchausen's syndrome by proxy...*

It was all so fantastic, so ridiculous. The words were meaningless. Probably didn't even exist. Julia got to her feet, glanced at Kailey to make sure she was still absorbed in the play book, and went to the medical and self-help section. Pulling down the first psychology book she could find, she flipped to the back and found it. Page 247. Okay. A whole chapter. So it did exist. She read the chapter reluctantly. Just because the syndrome existed didn't mean Madeleine had it. In fact, half the list of symptoms was wrong.

But half could be right. More than half.

Impossible.

She bent to look for a book on poisons. Why was she doing this? What sick, unexplainable urge was making her look for ways to prove her sister was a criminal? *Because then you can prove Ross was right,* the voice in her head whispered. *And if he's right, then maybe loving him isn't wrong.*

She was pitiful. She didn't love him. She couldn't love a man who lied to her.

Keeping Your Children Safe: A Guide to Household Poisons.

Why did Rebecca stock this stuff? This was not what she called wholesome reading. Julia pulled it off the shelf and flipped to *I.* Well. Rubbing alcohol. Easy to get and reasonable to have in the house. She ran a trembling finger down the list of symptoms. "Nausea, vomiting, hematemesis *(what was that?),* hemorrhagic gastritis, excessive sweating leading to coma."

Vomiting. Hemorrhagic gastritis. Did that mean bleeding in the stomach? No, that wasn't right. Madeleine had said he had an infection in his GI tract. That wasn't the same, was it? Ryan had been sweating, too, but that was normal if a kid had a fever. Wasn't it?

The front door bell tinkled and she heard Rebecca's voice. "Hello, dear. How are you? Yes, she's in the back."

Julia braced herself. She didn't want to talk to anyone. Maybe she could grab Kailey quietly and make it outside—

"Julia?" Derrick stopped in the doorway and brushed his hair off his forehead with a nervous hand. She blinked in surprise. She hadn't seen him since last week in prayer meeting. She'd almost forgotten they lived in the same town.

"Hello." She got to her feet and smiled. "I don't suppose you're looking for a book."

"No, I was looking for you." He crossed the room and stood awkwardly in front of her. His mouth moved, as if he were trying to choose words. Finally, he reached down and took her hand. "Julia, I've got to know something."

Here it was. Her heart began thumping in her chest and she took a deep breath to try to calm it. "What?"

"I haven't seen you in days. You didn't come to the young people's meeting, or to Gathering yesterday. You ignored me at prayer meeting. I'm sorry I was short with you last week. I want to make it up. Please tell me what I've done wrong."

She squeezed his hand, then dropped it, wrapping both arms around herself instead. Cold. What was wrong with her? "You've done nothing wrong. I just need some time by myself to think."

"Have you been with him?" She turned away and didn't answer. "I've got to know," he repeated desperately. "Because they've—Melchizedek—has sent me to bring you over to the Blanchards'. They want you to answer to the Testimony of Two Men."

Chapter Twenty-Two

Julia's breath went out of her in a rush, and she fumbled for a reading chair. "The Testimony of Two Men? You mean they're going to Silence me?"

She couldn't go through with this. No one had been Silenced in Hamilton Falls since Rita Ulstad, seven years ago. She couldn't put the Elder's family through this shame. But she had no choice. Not if they'd sent Derrick over to get her.

"I don't know yet. All I know is that they're waiting for us at the Blanchards'." Derrick's face twisted in pain. "Julia, if you have been with him like they're saying, tell me now. Don't let me find out in front of the Shepherd."

She might as well. She had nothing left to lose. Her future with Derrick was canceled as surely as if one of them had died. She got up and put her arms around him, the same way she would comfort one of the kids.

"If they're saying I was out of town with him overnight, then that's true," she confessed quietly into his shoulder. The quiver that ran through his body forced tears into her eyes. "But nothing else. Not that it matters. I'm sorry, Derrick. So sorry. I've ruined your future, too."

A gasp as he struggled to control his emotions was his only reply. He hugged her fiercely and cleared his throat. "Come on. They're waiting."

She followed him past the cash register. Rebecca looked up with a world of sadness in her eyes. "You go on," she said quietly. "I'll close up shop and take our little guest home. Don't you worry about us."

Bless Rebecca. She was the only person Julia could trust, like a rock in a stormy ocean.

Owen met them at his front door, and motioned them into the living room. Four of the dining-room chairs had been set up in the middle, facing one. Julia hesitated.

"Sit here, please, Julia." Melchizedek held the back of the single chair. She sat. Owen, Melchizedek, her father and Derrick all took their places, unable to meet her eyes. Her heart squeezed with sorrow for Owen. He looked as though one more blow to his family would kill him. She couldn't look at her dad. The pain in his face hurt too much.

Melchizedek opened the Bible on his lap and cleared his throat. "The words of Jesus, from the eighth chapter of John's gospel: 'And yet if I judge, my judgment is true: for I am not alone, but I and the Father that sent me. It is also written in your law, that the testimony of two men is true.'" He looked up.

Julia sat, frozen and isolated in her chair. Her hands clasped one another in a death grip, and her knees and ankle bones vibrated against each other with the force of her trembling.

"Julia, do you know why you are called here today?"

"No," she whispered, and her throat closed up.

"We understand that you have been spending more time in the company of a worldly man, unchaperoned, than could be accounted for by simple mission visits. Is this true?"

Julia opened her mouth, but sound refused to come out.

Melchizedek went on, "That, in fact, you did not go to a recent meeting of godly young people, but instead spent the night at an unknown location with Ross Malcolm, whom all of us know as a potential convert to the Elect." He spoke slowly, reluctantly. "You were seen in the town of Pitchford at a worldly event. His motorcycle has been seen in Rebecca's driveway at all hours. And lastly, you've been seen touching him in public places. This is going to have severely damaging consequences to his conversion if he is led to believe that your behavior is normal among us. Is it true, Julia?" His eyes begged her to say no.

"Yes," she got out.

Owen bowed his head and sighed. Melchizedek flipped to a different place in his Bible.

"Paul's first letter to the Corinthians, chapter five: 'But now I have written unto you not to keep company, if any man that is called a brother be a fornicator, or covetous, or an idolater, or a railer, or a drunkard, or an extortioner; with such an one no not to eat.

"'For what have I to do to judge them also that are without? Do not ye judge them that are within?

"'But them that are without God judgeth. Therefore put away from among yourselves that wicked person.' Julia, the words of God are clear on this point. You have admitted to ungodly behavior with this man, unbecoming to a woman of the Elect. You have worn color, signifying your unwillingness to sacrifice your human nature. You have worn men's clothing, in direct disobedience to Scripture. Did you also commit physical acts with him?"

The remains of those beautiful hours with Ross fell under the trampling, vengeful feet of the army of God. "Yes," she said, her voice still soundless, the word a whisper.

Derrick closed his eyes in pain and turned his face aside. "What physical acts?"

"We kissed."

"Did you commit fornication with him?"

"No."

"Can you prove that?"

"No."

"Did you desire it?"

"Yes."

His voice assumed the thunder of the law and the prophets. "I've called together the three men who are closest to you, who love you most. You may choose two of them. They will decide on the consequences of your actions. Do you understand?"

How could people who loved her do this to her? Was this really Melchizedek, the man who had taught her "Chopsticks" on the piano when she was six? And what would they do to Rebecca when they found out Ross and Kailey were staying there? Cold shivered over her skin. "Yes."

"There are three ways that judgment will fall. In the first, you will be put away entirely. You will be asked to move out of the Quinn house, and you will not be allowed to Gather with the Elect of God anymore. If this is your judgment, Rebecca will be asked to reconsider you as an employee. I'm sure you can see how painful it would be for both of you."

Julia struggled for breath. "Yes."

"In the second, you will be Silenced. This means you will not be able to participate in a service for a period of seven years. The Elect of God will not be encouraged to speak to you, even though you will still be numbered among us."

She may as well be dead—or a ghost, Julia thought. Seven endless years of drifting among the people she loved, disembodied and voiceless. No wonder Rita Ulstad had cracked and abandoned the Elect forever.

"The third judgment," Melchizedek went on, "comes in the event of a nonunanimous vote. The two votes must be unanimous. If they are not, no punishment can be given. You may now choose the Two Men who will decide your case. Who will you have, Julia?"

Melchizedek leaned toward her in his chair, his elbows on his knees. It was obvious he'd had a little experience at this, and expected to be one of the two. Her father had never stood up to a Shepherd in his life. He couldn't even stand up to her mother.

"I choose Owen and Derrick," she said.

Owen swallowed. Derrick turned white.

You wanted to marry me once, Julia thought. I hope that colors your decision now. No one here is going to stand up for me. I can't even speak for myself. No one wants to hear my reasons. No one cares about anything except the facade they show to the Outside.

"Owen and Derrick," Melchizedek confirmed, sitting back. "Owen, what is your decision?"

"I—I hardly know what to say. This is all so shocking I—" He paused to collect himself. "I vote for Silence," he said bluntly. "Although since this concerns Derrick the most, I believe his vote should have the most weight."

Julia fought down the urge to scream, This doesn't concern Derrick at all. This is about me. My life. And I have no say whatever here.

"Derrick?" Melchizedek prodded.

Derrick looked from Melchizedek to Julia, a hurt, hunted expression in his eyes. He held her gaze. "A couple of weeks ago this group proposed I should be Deacon," he said slowly. "Long before that, I had asked Julia to be my wife. If she is put away, neither of those things will happen. If she is Silenced, they will be delayed for seven years, since we can't live together as husband and wife under those circumstances." He paused, his gaze never leaving Julia's. "I vote for neither judgment, if Julia agrees here and now to marry me."

Julia closed her eyes as her very blood chilled, leaving her as cold as death.

Melchizedek leaped to his feet. "That's too great a sacrifice!" he exclaimed.

Derrick stood as well. "I don't believe it is. As I see it, two things will happen. The first is that no scandal will touch the Elect. The second is, no scandal will touch us personally. No one will dare to say a word about it once she's my wife. No one in Hamilton Falls outside ourselves even needs to know. And I'm sure Rebecca will be able to see the wisdom of it."

Julia tried to swallow as she felt the jaws of the future closing around her. No hope—no escape—no love—

Melchizedek regarded Derrick solemnly. "You realize what you're saying? She's no longer pure. She committed physical acts with another man and desired to fornicate with him."

Julia flinched. So did Derrick. "I realize that. But I'm willing to marry her in spite of it. If she'll have me."

"Julia? What is your decision?" Melchizedek asked.

Alarm bells sounded in her head. Time's up, she thought from somewhere far away.

Owen jerked upright. "That's the phone." He came half out of his chair. "Julia, what is your answer?"

What was left to say? No matter what she chose, she would lose something precious—either the love of her family and friends, or the possibility of real love, not the wounded substitute Derrick offered.

Her nightmare had come to life. The terrible weight bore down on her.

Into the expectant silence, a tinny voice emanated from the answering machine. "Owen, this is Michael Archer. You're not home. This is terrible. Owen, you've got to get down to the hospital as quickly as you can. Ryan's condition is deteriorating. He's in a coma. Oh, God—"

The machine clicked and rewound as Michael hung up in midprayer.

Owen was already clattering down the stairs. Julia jumped to her feet and knocked her own chair over. "Owen, wait for me!"

"Julia, come back here!" Melchizedek ordered. "We're waiting for your answer!"

"I have to be with my family!" she shouted up the stairwell, defying the Shepherd to his face for the first time in her life, and slammed the door behind her.

She doubted that Owen had even registered he had someone in the passenger seat as they tore down the highway toward the hospital. It didn't matter. She needed time to think.

His condition is going to go downhill fast, Ross had said. *When that happens, you'll know I'm right*. It couldn't be true. It couldn't. This was just a horrible coincidence, the result of poor Ryan's fragility. She tried not to think about what the book had said. Coma. She didn't want Ross to be right. Because if he was, then her carefully constructed world of right and wrong was going to come tumbling down. And she wasn't sure she could stand losing anything more.

Michael met them at the door of the ward. "Julia, I'm afraid I'm going to have to ask you to wait outside for now. Owen and Madeleine are the only ones I can allow in. I'll be back in a moment, all right?"

She nodded and sank onto the familiar vinyl couch while the swinging doors closed behind the two men. Resting her elbows on her knees, she awkwardly massaged the back of her neck with both hands.

"Here, let me do that." Two strong hands descended on her shoulders and began to knead her tense muscles. She gasped and jumped, whirling to look up at him. The impact hit her the way it always did. He was so beautiful, standing there in his jeans and white T-shirt, giving her that lazy smile. His eyes were guarded, though. Guarded and unreadable.

"Hey," he said gently, holding up both hands like a surgeon after scrubbing, "your muscles will never relax if you do that."

"Go away." Crossing her arms, she hunched over as if protecting herself, her back to him.

"No." He gripped her shoulders again, and his fingers felt so good, massaging the pain out of her neck, that her will to resist began to melt away at the same rate as the tension. The circular motion between her shoulder blades stopped, then began again. "Ready to talk?"

She had to let go of one world and leave it behind. Once again she was at the point where her next words would decide the rest of her life. What could she look forward to with the Elect? Love and approval? Sure, if she wanted to pay the price of a loveless marriage. What could she look forward to on the Outside? Ross's approval, maybe. Certainly not his love. Her own family would be lost to her. Could she live the rest of her life alone with that knowledge?

Maybe she should stop looking at it in terms of the love on each side of the scale. She'd taught herself to look for love from the community because she didn't find it in her family. But as soon as she was Silenced, what kind of love could she look for from anyone?

What she needed to do was to put this in God's hands. Really trust, instead of using Him as an insurance policy when all else failed. Because with Him she wasn't completely powerless. With Him, she could still give love. To Ryan. And for a short time, to Kailey.

"Yes," she said.

He stopped massaging and came around the side of the couch to lower himself beside her. "You sure?"

"You said he would go into a coma. Now he has."

"And you're willing to help me?"

"I don't know what I can do. She's my sister." Julia's lip began to tremble, and she willed the tears away. He made a movement as if to slide a little closer, then stopped himself. Her heart cracked. She craved his arms around her the way an addict must crave his drug. But thinking there was safety in his arms was just a fiction. Their whole relationship was based upon a fiction.

"As soon as Archer comes back, we'll talk about it," he said.

She lifted her head. "Michael knows?"

Ross nodded grimly. "He does now. I got a fast analysis on Ryan's blood. They did what they call a coma panel and it's definitely isopropyl alcohol."

"I read about the symptoms." Her voice was lifeless.

"Did you?" He gave her an appraising look. "So did I. Do they fit with what you remember from his history?"

She nodded, staring at her hands knotted in her lap. "I didn't want to believe it. I refused to. But everything was there, in a list in a book. What does Michael say?"

"He believed in Madeleine. But not enough to risk Ryan's life."

The doors swung open and Michael Archer walked over to them. "Julia," he said. He looked at Ross. "Have you been talking to her about—"

"Yes. She knows."

"How can we bear it?" Michael asked her, as if Ross wasn't there. His face was pale and rough with stubble. Perspiration matted the normally faultlessly groomed hair falling on his forehead. "She used me. All these years, she's been playing cat and mouse with me, destroying my credibility, my faith in myself, my reputation...I can hardly believe it. And yet...how can we do this?"

"I don't know," Julia said dully. "But Ryan's life comes first."

"What are you asking us to do?" Michael asked Ross, settling on the arm of the adjoining couch with a sigh of resignation.

Ross didn't waste any time. His tone was businesslike. "First of all, it isn't enough that we can confirm the alcohol in his blood. We have to tie it to Madeleine. Otherwise, it's too easy for someone else to be blamed."

"Someone else? Like a nurse? Or...even Michael?" Julia asked.

Ross gave her an approving glance. "Yes. Put bluntly, we have to catch her in the act."

"But—but that might kill him!" Michael protested. "He's hemodynamically unstable as it is. His heart is in danger of failing."

"The timing has to be perfect. We need a way to watch her with him, yet stop her before she does any more damage. That's why I need your help, Doctor."

"You need access to the surveillance system," he said.

"You have one here?" The last word rose on a note of incredulity.

Michael's lips twitched in a tired smile. "Even out here in the sticks. But only in the ICU, which is where Ryan is right now. The things are designed to look like smoke detectors. There's one over every bed."

"Are you telling me we might already have her on tape? When can I review them?"

"No, no. These are only in ICU. Ryan was only moved in here when his condition deteriorated. Up until last night he was in his usual bed in pediatrics."

Ross fought against the disappointment. "Who monitors the cameras?"

"The nurses."

"Not good enough. I can't hang around the nurses' station for hours on end. Neither can you. Madeleine will know something's up, and she's so chummy with them there's no telling what they'll spill. Can you have the feed moved to a monitor somewhere else?"

Michael thought for a moment. "That isn't really my area of expertise, but I'll go talk to the director of security and see what he can do."

"What can I do?" Julia whispered. All this talk of security and cameras was too real—more real even than reading about Ryan's symptoms in a book. She needed to go home and hide. But she couldn't. Ryan couldn't fight for himself. He needed every bit of help he could get.

"Come with me," Ross said, and took her hand.

Chapter Twenty-Three

❧

Ross and Julia sat knee to knee in an office no bigger than a closet, at the end of the hallway bisecting the intensive care unit. Banks of television monitors loomed over them on both sides. Once every thirty minutes the security officer moved from screen to screen, doing his rounds. Movement flickered all around them as the night-shift nurses entered and left through the various doors and stairwells observed by the security cameras, but Ross's attention was divided between the woman beside him and the single screen containing an overhead view of Ryan's bed. Security hadn't let him down. They'd split and rerouted the video feed so that Ross could watch Ryan from above like a guardian angel.

Madeleine just had to make one move and Ross would be down that hallway so fast the doors wouldn't even have time to shut behind him.

He leaned toward the monitor. Julia shifted uncomfortably, and he caught a whiff of her scent, that intoxicating compound of shampoo and clean cotton that made him want to pull her into his arms and keep her there forever.

"Is she asleep?" he asked in a low voice.

The shadowy black-and-white figure on the screen had slumped bonelessly in the chair next to the bed. Her head tipped back, and her mouth fell open, making her look childlike and vulnerable.

"She must be," Julia replied, watching her sister.

"You don't quite believe she's doing it, do you?"

"How can I?" Julia asked. "I don't even know why I'm here."

He sat back. Loyal to the very last. And maybe beyond. He might as well face it. Once this operation was over, it was stupid to hope he and Julia could ever be together. He'd destroyed her trust, and now he was working hard at destroying her family. Despite her affection for Kailey, he had to admit that life with him would hold very little appeal for her.

"What do you believe about me?" he blurted, and then cursed himself. Why couldn't he keep his mouth shut and leave dead romances to lie?

She seemed to flinch, then schooled her body into its previous calm. Watching the monitor in front of her, she said, "What do your finks usually think about you?"

The breath whooshed out of him in astonishment. "What?"

"That's what you call us, right? Finks? People who get you information so you can arrest other people?"

"Julia, you are not a fink."

"And you're not a heavy equipment mechanic."

Ouch. "Touché."

"It must have been fun, getting what you wanted out of me. Information and some rolling around in the grass.

Two for the price of one." He had never heard such a bitter tone from those sweet lips, thinned now with suppressed disappointment and hurt.

"Please don't do this." He'd give anything to stop her inflicting this kind of pain on herself. Especially when every word hurt him twice as much.

She gave him a cold look over her shoulder, and turned her gaze back to the monitor. "I'm not afraid of the truth."

"It isn't the truth. Not entirely."

"Oh? Which was the lie?" She huffed a sardonic laugh. "It couldn't have been the information. Must've been the rolling around."

"That wasn't a lie, either."

She rolled her eyes. "Give me credit for some intelligence. Or are you always so enthusiastic about your undercover jobs?" She gave a particularly nasty emphasis to *undercover.*

"I wanted that to happen. I wanted *you.* I've been fighting how I felt about you since the beginning."

He didn't know what he expected as an answer, but anything would be better than this silent rejection. Julia watched her sister's sleeping image on the screen. Her eyes were dry. She didn't even blink.

May as well get it all out into the silent intimacy of this little room while he still could. The chances of seeing her and explaining anything after he arrested Madeleine were nil.

"I believed you were in a cult," he began, his voice quiet and matter-of-fact. "So the fact that I was attracted to you—well, I hated it. I hate cults, period. I've been tracking them down and doing whatever the law allows to break them for years. But that was just an excuse so I could search for Kailey."

He glanced at the video screen. No change there. The changes were all in the atmosphere between them, thick with emotion and words that must be said.

"Two kids have died in the Elect since February. Then there was Ryan. In my line of work, that's enough to get a file opened. We believed you were doing some kind of sacrifice."

Julia said slowly, "Going through the ice isn't what I'd call a sacrifice. Neither is crib death."

"I know. A little investigation discounted that theory almost right away. But the thing I couldn't discount was Ryan and his history of illness. Evidence just kept piling up until finally I knew I had a case. A different one than the one I'd started with, but a case."

"But why me?" she asked, her voice so low it was almost a whisper.

He took her hand, and when she would have pulled it away, gripped it tighter. "When I first saw you, I thought you were Ryan's mother."

"Me?"

"You were crying. Grieving. Because you loved him. I knew then that between your love and my work, we might have a chance to save him."

"And you needed someone close to my family."

He paused, then forced the truth past his teeth. "Right."

"Someone you could get close to."

"Right." He could see where she was going with this. "And like I said, the closer I got, the more I wished circumstances were different. That we weren't together because of my job, but because we cared about each other. You're not going to forgive me for this, are you?"

"I don't know yet." She held his penitent gaze with her own honest one. "Let's take one thing at a time."

He gave her a crooked smile and turned back to study

the monitor, the tightness easing from his shoulders. One thing at a time. There was still hope. He felt strangely at peace in one way, and on edge with tension in another.

Madeleine stirred. Yawned. Then slid to her knees, templing her hands under her chin. He fought down a spurt of anger that she could do what she was doing and still believe that God was listening to any of her prayers. Then he stopped himself. It wasn't his place to judge her relationship with God. It was his place to get her into a position where the justice system could judge her actions. That was all.

"Are we going to sit here all night?" Julia said. "It's past midnight."

"I am. You can go home whenever you want to, you know."

"I don't want to. There'd just be—" She stopped.

He looked quickly at the screen, but Madeleine hadn't moved. "What?" She took a deep, shuddering breath, and let it out slowly. He squeezed her hand.

"There'd just be a phone message from Melchizedek telling me they want my answer. And I'm not ready to give them one."

"About what?"

She told him, in a voice so low he could hardly hear. What he did hear appalled him. "You mean that because we went to recover Kailey, you either get excommunicated or you have to marry Derrick Wilkinson? Are these people crazy?"

Her eyes were bleak. "It doesn't matter if they are or not. Either way I lose. I give up my family and friends, or I give up my independence and a chance at happiness with someone else." She gave him a wistful glance through strands of hair that were beginning to come down. "For Kailey it was worth it. But for me? I don't know."

Pain and guilt twisted deep within his gut, and he dropped her hand reluctantly. He'd done this to her. He'd allowed his disregard for the rules and his needs to override everything, and this was the result. And it wasn't even finished. The price had escalated even higher than he had imagined.

"There must be something we can do."

"One thing at a time," she repeated. "That's the only way we can get through this. You have a job to do. Maybe we should concentrate on that. Ryan is more important right now, then Kailey, then ourselves."

Always the giver, always putting someone else before herself. Admiration for her courage rose through the pain. He wasn't going to let them throw her to the wolves. Once this was behind them, he would—

"Ross! What's she doing?"

He leaned in toward the monitor. The shadowy figure that was Madeleine rose and went to the machine that administered the cardiac drip that was practically all that was keeping Ryan stable.

She looked around, then reached up and pressed the buttons. Ross was no expert on these things, but he did know that messing with those numbers was bad.

He leaped to his feet. "Call Archer! Get Security up there too," he ordered, and dashed down the corridor.

An alarm bell went off with a suddenness that made him jump, and a nurse pushed by him shouting, "Emergency in 137B!"

An emergency team ran down the hall and burst into the room, with Ross right behind them. Madeleine screamed at them to help.

"I was sitting here praying for him when the alarm went off," she wept, and one of the nurses put an arm around her and led her to the other side of the room, making soothing noises while the team worked.

Ross gripped Madeleine's arm, and she raised huge, beautiful eyes to him. "Mr. Malcolm," she said. "Are you here to help, too?"

"What did you do to that dial, Madeleine?" he asked.

"What?" The nurse glared at him. "Get out of here. Don't you see we have an emergency with this woman's child? How did you get in here?"

He pointed at the cardiac drip. "She changed the IV drip. I was monitoring the video feed. Check it."

The nurse hovered between anger and incredulity. "Who are you?"

He yanked his ID out of his pocket and flashed it at her. "Investigator Malcolm, Organized Crime Task Force. Check the system. Now."

Without another word, the nurse went and checked it, then grabbed Michael Archer, who had just joined the crash team.

"The rate is tripled! I swear I checked him just a little while ago, and it was fine."

"Leave that alone!" Madeleine exclaimed. "My son will die if you touch it!"

Ross tightened his grip on Madeleine's arm. "He'll die if you don't keep away from him. We've got you on camera, Mrs. Blanchard. I have grounds to believe you attempted to murder your son. You have the right to remain silent...."

Julia slipped into the visitors' room as quietly as she could, and to her intense relief, no one looked up. Everyone was there...her parents, Owen, Derrick. Oh, no. Even Melchizedek, despite the fact that it was painfully early in the morning. She hadn't slept at all. She doubted anyone had.

What if, once they knew Ryan was out of danger, they decided to take up Testimony against her here and now? After all, she had compounded her sin. She had betrayed Madeleine on top of everything else. Even Ryan's safety wouldn't be enough to alleviate that.

Stop thinking of yourself. There are bigger things at stake here than Silencing you.

She shrank into a corner of the couch, thankful beyond words when Michael stood and captured everyone's attention. He braced himself with one hand on the back of the nearest couch, and cleared his throat. "Mark, Elizabeth, Owen. Melchizedek. The first thing I want to say is that we've discovered the cause of Ryan's illness."

Elizabeth cried out. "Oh, thank the Lord! Thank the Lord!" Clutching her husband, she looked at Michael. "What was it, Michael? The gastroenteritis that Madeleine suspected?"

Mark patted her back, his own gaze riveted on Dr. Archer. "Will he pull through?" he asked urgently.

"Yes, he'll pull through. We got it in time."

"Got it in time?" Mark repeated. "You make it sound like cancer. It's not, is it? He's only four!"

"No, not cancer. It was a—an allergy. We just discovered it last night, pumped out his system, and put him on an alternate treatment. He's responding as well as can be expected right now, but he should show signs of improvement within days."

Julia frowned. Why was he making up stories?

Michael glanced at Derrick and Melchizedek, and it was obvious that respect for the Shepherd of his soul fought with duty. "I'd like to talk to the family privately but I know how close you are. Please keep what we say in this room confidential."

Derrick looked uncertainly from the doctor to Julia and nodded. He moved to stand behind Julia's couch.

Was he staking out ownership? Or just offering support? Either way, she could do without it. Julia eyed a chair against the wall with sudden longing, but she didn't dare move and draw attention to herself.

Her dad moved restlessly at the delay. "Michael, is there something wrong? Something about my grandson's condition that only the family should know? And where is Madeleine?"

Michael shook his head. "Ryan will be fine. He has round-the-clock care." He closed his eyes for a moment, and his lips moved in prayer. When he looked at Mark, his face was full of pain. "Now, about Madeleine."

Owen took a step forward, his fists clenched. "What about her? Why wasn't she in Ryan's room this morning? Is she all right?"

"She's fine. But she—she—" He paused. "She's going to need your support over the next several weeks."

"Of course she is. She's been through hell lately. Why would you think we wouldn't give—"

"What I'm trying to say is that she—well, she isn't herself right now." His fingers made parallel dents in the vinyl covering of the back of the couch. "We have evidence that she may be suffering from a disorder. Of the mind. And in the grip of that disorder she may have behaved in a way that wasn't normal."

Owen stared at the doctor incredulously. "What are you saying?"

"We have reason to believe that she may have been, ah, adding something to Ryan's medication in um, the mistaken belief that she was helping him, but in reality..."

Michael stopped in the face of Owen's and the McNeills' identical expressions of horror and hostility.

"What?" Elizabeth snapped. "Are you saying Madeleine was causing Ryan's illness? Our Madeleine? Are you crazy?"

"No, Elizabeth, I'm not. The police are involved."

Owen seemed to understand what Michael meant several beats ahead of Julia's parents. Julia stared out the window. She couldn't bear to look at her brother-in-law's face.

"The police? Why? There hasn't been any crime committed here. I want to see my wife. Maybe she can make more sense than you are, Michael."

Dr. Archer gathered his resources. "I'm afraid that's not possible, Owen. You see, she's been arrested on a charge of attempted murder."

Everyone shouted at once. Julia got up and went to the window, wishing herself anywhere but here. Dimly, in the pandemonium, she was aware that Derrick hovered in the background, uncertain of his welcome should he attempt to speak to her. She leaned her forehead against the glass, longing for Ross, longing to be told she'd done the right thing.

After long moments, the noise died down and she realized Melchizedek had taken control of the situation. "Michael, this is untenable. What are we going to tell the church? That our Elder's wife has been arrested on grounds so unbelievable I can hardly bring myself to name them? Impossible!"

"I will not let you vilify my wife!" Owen cried. "This is a horrible mistake, brought on by a misdiagnosis on your part!"

"Owen, please calm down," Melchizedek said in the voice he used to condemn the flesh and the Devil. "We need to put the church ahead of our own emotion and horror."

Owen looked like a stranger to Julia. His shirt was wrinkled, his face bathed in sweat, and his eyes... She swallowed. His eyes were alight with condemnation of Michael Archer and fiery defense of his wife.

"All right." Owen controlled himself after a moment. "I'm listening."

"Michael, please tell us exactly what has happened," Melchizedek ordered.

"We believe Madeleine has been suffering from a disorder known as Munchausen's syndrome by proxy," Michael began, eyeing Owen and Elizabeth as if he feared they'd leap for his throat. "People who suffer from this disorder harm their children in order to—to—well, to increase others' opinion of them. A woman might do it to appear as a selfless and caring mother during her child's repeated visits to the hospital."

"My Madeleine *is* a selfless and caring mother!" Elizabeth hissed. Her eyes were narrowed to slits.

"We all know that," Owen said. "Go on, please, Michael."

"She has certainly been successful," Michael said. "But Ryan has paid the price. If not for the discovery of her disorder, Madeleine would surely have killed him. Last night she tried to tamper with the cardiac drip, after weakening his system over a period of years with isopropyl alcohol." His voice trailed away with unutterable disillusionment and weariness.

Melchizedek spoke over the babble of angry voices. "Folks, please! We must not let this discourage us. Remember, these are only accusations. Nothing has been proven."

Julia blinked. Nothing proven? Hadn't he heard what Michael had just said?

"The truth will set us free," Melchizedek declared. "We must be strong in the Spirit, and encourage our sister Madeleine to do the same. And in the meantime, we will hold fast to her shining example. She is our Elder's wife. We must protect her reputation as best we can, and in doing so protect the Elect from the arrows and slings of the wicked. We won't speak of this to anyone. We'll tell our brothers and sisters that she had a breakdown from stress and has gone somewhere quiet to recuperate. The joy of knowing Ryan has at last been diagnosed *correctly* was too much for her." He gave Dr. Archer a cutting glance. "And if we hear anything else, we will know its source, and know that the Devil is behind it."

Julia's stomach revolted, and she dashed out the door.

Chapter Twenty-Four

✤

By the time Julia reached the sanctuary of the stairs, she felt less like throwing up than punching a fist through the plate glass. With a shuddering sigh, she sank down on one of the steps and dropped her head on her crossed arms.

How could they? She had sacrificed everything she held dear—friends, family, future—to do what was right. She had helped to save Ryan's life. And now they were sacrificing the truth for Madeleine. And for the church.

The only way Julia could continue to live in her world was if the people she loved believed the truth. Then she could live with her own actions, even if no one ever found out how Ross had used her. But no one was going to reveal the truth, or even believe it. They were going to cover up, to deny, to keep Madeleine's example shiny and angelic, for the sake of how it would look.

"Julia?" She didn't lift her head at the uncertain sound of Derrick's footsteps. "Are you all right?"

"No."

"Please. Let me help you."

"I need to be alone right now."

"Don't worry," he said, lowering himself onto the step beside her as if he hadn't heard. He probably hadn't. "Madeleine will be all right. Melchizedek is talking to Owen. They're going to go over to the police station to get this straightened out. You'll see. It'll all work out in the end."

"Derrick, please go away."

Four floors above, a door slammed and someone descended a flight. The third floor door shut behind them, the sound booming eerily in the stairwell. Derrick didn't move.

"I know this is a terrible time to ask, but have you given any more thought to my proposal? What is it now, six times?"

His attempt at humor echoed in the silence. Julia sighed. Would this nightmare never end? Other than running away to the top of Mount Ayres, when was she going to get the time to think things through? She would just have to go by her gut instincts. They, at least, were screaming loud and clear.

"Yes." Her voice was flat.

"And?"

"No."

"No? You're not going to marry me?"

"No, I'm not. I'm sorry." From somewhere she marshaled the strength to lift her head and look him in the eye as she said it.

His face sagged, and his gaze dropped to the painted concrete step between his feet. "I'm willing, you know. Even after...everything. The Shepherd tells us that any two people filled with the spirit of God can live together in harmony. I'm willing to step out on that promise."

"You may be willing to settle for living together in harmony, my friend," she said gently, "but I'm not. I want the real thing."

"But I love you," he protested. "I always have. Otherwise how could I keep asking you, even after everything that's happened?"

Julia winced. "I believe you care, and I'm grateful for that. But I don't think it will be enough. Because I don't love *you,* you see."

He was silent for a moment. "It's him, isn't it?" he asked, his tone low and rough.

"Maybe. I don't know yet." She paused, surprised at the bubble of anger that came welling up out of nowhere. "It isn't a matter of you or him or anybody else. It's me, and how I'm going to spend the rest of my life."

"You'll be Silenced," he predicted gloomily.

"Not if I go Out." She gave the thought words for the first time. The reality of speaking the forbidden aloud frightened her. But what choice did she have? "Not if I make my own life, without people laying down the law and telling me how to do it. And whom to marry."

"Wha-a-a-t?" he said on an indrawn breath. "Go Out? Oh, Julia, you can't do that. Even being Silenced is better than that. Promise me you won't think about it anymore. You'd be committing suicide, spiritually. Losing your salvation. And for what? There's nothing for you Outside. The Devil is just using this hard experience to get to you. Please, dear, accept God's will and in time people will forget."

"Accept God's will, or Melchizedek's?" she asked bitterly.

"They're the same, Julia, you know that."

"God doesn't ask people to lie and cover up."

"Julia!"

"Don't *Julia* me. You don't know all the facts."

"Are you saying you believe your sister did this?"

"I saw her, Derrick. On the video. That's pretty hard to argue with."

He got to his feet. "And we all know video is a tool of the Devil, just like television and the Internet. I'm sorry you're deceived, dear. I'll pray for you."

She closed her eyes. "You do that." When she opened them again, she was alone in the echoing space. Alone with the betrayal of those she loved. Alone with an empty future that included neither friends nor family.

The light pouring through the windows splintered in the tears welling in her eyes, and she squeezed them shut against the brilliance and the pain.

Ross heard a woman crying softly as he mounted the stairs. It had taken a couple of hours to process Madeleine, whose immediate future was still up in the air. He felt drained and tired, so much so that all he could think of was finding his two girls and collapsing with them somewhere dark and quiet, and not coming out for a week.

He wondered when he'd begun thinking of Julia as his. He couldn't remember. They'd grown together gradually, and then his own stupidity had torn them apart. Sometimes it hurt more to heal something with the truth than it did to perpetuate a lie.

But God had promised that the truth would set them free. And despite the emotional wrenches they'd both suffered lately, he believed that both he and Julia would receive the benefit of that promise.

He just had to be patient.

Which was why his immediate future included finding Julia and then going home to Kailey. He wasn't going to think any further than that.

At the third floor, he turned the corner of the staircase and saw her, sitting on the top step.

"Hey," he called softly, and took the remaining stairs two at a time. He sat beside her and gazed into her face, where the evidence of her crisis was plain in her stricken eyes and white, tear-streaked cheeks.

"Are you all right? How did it go up here? Did Michael break it to them?"

Julia sighed and folded into his arms. "Yes. They're going to cover it all up and say Madeleine is away resting after breaking down from stress."

"It's what any group would do. Band together to protect one of their own." He dipped his head to breathe in the scent of her unruly hair, drawing strength from her as he offered what comfort he could.

"But what about me?" she murmured into his T-shirt. "I'm one of their own, and they're going to Silence me."

"I don't think you are, honey. Not anymore."

She went still under his soothing touch. "It's true, isn't it?"

"Yeah. And think about the kids. At least for now, if Ryan and Hannah don't have to know their mom is disturbed, then I'm all for it. Think how that's going to damage Ryan even more than he is now."

Too many damaged kids. *Dear Lord, help me to help Kailey deal with her recovery, too...*

"Will she get away with it?" Her question was soft, hesitant.

"I'm going to do my best to make sure she doesn't. Between Michael and me and Harry Everett, we'll lobby hard for a long treatment program rather than incarceration. Ninety days, to start. And regular monitoring when she gets out."

The road to recovery was going to be hard for all of them.

She closed her eyes. "It's not black and white, is it?" she asked softly. "It's not a matter of crime and punishment. Even though I want it to be."

He continued to stroke her back. "That's one of the hardest things I had to learn in this job. When you're dealing with people, you deal in compromises and half truths and injustice."

"Even with people who do wrong?"

"Even with them. Look at your situation. The Elect think you're the bad guy, when both of us know you were acting for the best."

She'd been brought up to look at everything in terms of good and evil. But Ross knew from experience that seeing life in black and white, without the lens of the love of God, led to harsh judgments and even harsher punishment.

"I was acting for the best," she agreed softly. "For a child I love."

God knew he loved his daughter. Everything he'd done in his life since she was born had been motivated by love for her. But could he remember that Annie had done what she'd done thinking it was best for Kailey? Could he learn to forgive? He would need all the strength God could give him to look past the barrier of anger in his heart and answer that question. He might doubt his own ability to do it. But he had no doubts whatsoever that enough help waited for him. All he had to do was ask.

That was the solution Julia was discovering, too, he had no doubt.

"So I have one more question."

"What's that?" Her voice was muffled in the front of his T-shirt.

"What kind of answer are you going to give old Derrick when all this is over?"

"I already gave it to him."

"Yeah? And that was?" His arms tightened around her.

"No."

"No, you won't tell me?"

"No, I said no."

The breath he had been holding fanned the hair over her ear. "So you'd rather take the punishment?"

"They can't punish me if I'm not Elect, can they?"

He looked down into her eyes. "You're sure you want to do that?"

She nodded, her eyes filling with the tears that hadn't been far from the surface. "I've spent my whole life looking for approval from the Elect because I couldn't get it from my parents. But looking for approval isn't going to work anymore. Not now."

"What will you do?"

She lifted her shoulders briefly in a shrug. "I don't know yet. Take stock of my life. Decide if I'm going to stay here or not. I'm still Ryan and Hannah's aunt. I don't want to fall out of their lives right when they're going to need me, whether I'm Elect or not."

"These are big decisions, honey. They take time and a lot of thought. I think you're doing the right thing." He hugged her, a slow squeeze that brought comfort to them both. "But meantime, know what I need?"

"What?"

"I need to get out of this hospital. I need to be with Kailey. And you. Alone. Just the three of us. I think that's a good start, don't you?"

When she looked up, she was smiling through her tears.

"Sounds like heaven to me."

Epilogue

Three months later

The pager beeped as Ross took the freeway exit to Hamilton Falls. He guided the pickup truck with one hand and pulled the unit off his belt to glance at the number.

"What does it say?" Kailey took it and studied the readout. "555-7212," she read slowly.

"Good job. Whose number is it?"

"Daddy, it's Julia."

"Should we call her back, or surprise her and just go to her house?"

"Go to her house." Kailey nodded firmly and gave it back to him.

It was crazy that an investigator who had been hardened by pretty much the worst human nature had to offer should feel such a lift of anticipation at the prospect of seeing one woman. Ridiculous it might be, but Ross was learning to savor the simple pleasures of life, such as looking forward to a weekend with Julia, or the feeling of accomplishment he'd shared with Kailey when she'd learned all the numbers up to one hundred and made it halfway through the first-grade reading list.

In a few minutes Ross wheeled the truck into the driveway at 1204 Gates Place and noted that Rebecca's car was gone. Not surprising. If he remembered correctly, she would be at the Elect prayer meeting. As they climbed the stairs to the top-floor apartment, they heard shrieks of laughter through the open windows. Was Julia baby-sitting? He turned the knob and he and Kailey went in without knocking.

Julia and two little kids, one of whom he recognized as Hannah Blanchard, were sprawled on the floor around a board game, laughing about something that probably had less to do with the game than the story Hannah was trying to tell. The little girl broke off in midsentence when she saw they weren't alone.

"Auntie Julia, it's the angel from hell." She giggled and poked the other child in the ribs.

"Hannah Nicole, how many times have I told you not to call him that? His name is Ross."

"Investigator Malcolm to you, shrimp." Ross pulled his best stern policeman face and sent Hannah off into another paroxysm.

Kailey couldn't take her eyes off the brightly colored board game. "Daddy, what's that?" she whispered.

"It's called Candy Land," he whispered back. "Want me to teach you?"

"I'll show her. We just learned." The blond boy rolled to a sitting position and waved her over.

"And who might you be?" Ross crossed the room to sit next to Julia, who had pulled herself onto the couch and sat with one leg draped over its arm. She leaned against his shoulder and smiled up at him.

"I'm Ryan," the boy said indignantly.

Ross sat up straight, dislodging Julia from her comfortably boneless position. "You are not."

"Am too."

He blinked. "So you are."

Ryan's cheeks had filled out, the skin no longer stretching over bone. While the flush of laughter had faded from them, leaving them pale, at least he looked like a kid instead of a skull. His hair was no longer lifeless and flat, matted to his head with sweat. It was blond and freshly cut, springing up from his scalp, practically bristling with life. His eyes were clear and very blue.

"Now, that's what I call a recovery," he murmured to Julia, when the kids were absorbed in the game.

"More like a miracle. Once he came home from the hospital it was like watching a video on fast-forward."

"Since when do you know anything about videos?"

"I went in the video shop," she said proudly. "And watched a whole movie on the display screen. I didn't rent anything because I don't have a VCR to play it on, but I went in there."

"It's a start," Ross allowed.

"It felt weird at first, but I got used to it. Next step is a movie. In an actual theater."

"Something appropriate for children, perhaps."

"That would be pushing it. The only reason I have the kids at all is because I insisted. Everyone has gone to Spokane for the hearing."

"So they'll still talk to you?"

"Oh, yes. Once I'm Out no punishments apply, you see. They treat me like any common acquaintance on the street. I just happen to be related. And even my mother could see that having the kids along today would be a bad thing."

"I notice you didn't take them to prayer meeting."

Julia gazed at the children. "I thought about going for the kids' sake, but I think moments of togetherness like this are more important than listening to Melchizedek thunder about the children of Israel hewing and slaying."

He squeezed her shoulders, then ran a soothing hand up and down her arm. "Do you miss it?"

After a moment in which he watched her struggle to find an answer, she said, "Yes. I do."

"What do you miss most? Not about your family. About the Elect."

"There's the whole social aspect. The phone doesn't ring as much as it used to."

"It works both ways."

"I know. But I don't have anything to say to Claire and Derrick anymore. They think I'm deceived, and any time I try to tell them about how flawed the Elect system is, they fade out and leave. Eventually I gave up."

"A person's relationship with God is something they have to discover on their own. The way you did."

"I know, but their relationship is more with the system of worship than with God."

"That's also something they have to see on their own. So what about yours?"

"My what?"

"Way of worship."

"I'm not ready yet, Ross."

"I know. But all worldly churches aren't deceived. You know that, right?"

"Hearing you say it is different from experiencing it myself. But God loves me whether I worship in a church building or not."

"Of course He does. But it's hard to love someone you don't know. And it's hard to learn about Him if you don't have teachers and fellowship with other believers."

"I have the Bible, and prayer. Isn't that enough?"

"Having the relationship is what matters."

She was silent, and he grieved that the woman he loved should have been so damaged by her family's devotion to a system of worship instead of the One who deserved their praise that she was avoiding religion altogether.

"You'd like my church," he said thoughtfully, settling her more closely under his arm.

"Ross. I need time. I need more than a few months to grow away from the Elect. It's like withdrawal. Or breaking up with someone. I need a period of mourning."

"But you can't spend the rest of your life mourning the death of the old without giving the new a chance to be born."

With a sardonic glance, she murmured, "Okay, let's call it a gestation period."

"I don't think there's a gestation period to be born again. Just an open heart."

At this she straightened, and her elbow dug against his hip. He felt a spurt of alarm. Maybe he'd gone too far. Maybe in his love for her soul as well as her self, he'd pushed her away.

"I do have an open heart," she said. "I pray every day that God will show me His will. Meantime—"

Both of them heard the footsteps on the stairs. Julia glanced at her watch. "That can't be any of the Elect. Prayer meeting isn't over yet."

Someone knocked on the door, and Julia got up to answer it.

"Mom," she said, and stood aside to let Elizabeth McNeill in.

Elizabeth took in the children and Ross in one glance. "Hannah and Ryan would have been better off in prayer meeting," she said.

"I didn't want to share them tonight," Julia replied. "We had a good time together."

"Hello, Mrs. McNeill." Ross held out a hand, and she took it after a second's pause. With one shake, she dropped it again.

"Hannah, Ryan, it's time to go home," their grandmother said.

"Aw, Nanna. We just started another game. Kailey's never played Candy Land before."

"She can learn another time. Come on. Pack up."

Julia stood beside her mother, and Ross moved closed behind her. "So how did it go?"

"I hardly think you're in a position to ask. Besides, Mr. Malcolm probably knows much more than I."

Did her mother think that Ross represented the entire legal establishment? That he was personally managing her elder daughter's incarceration? "Mother. She's my sister. I have a right to know, too."

"You should have thought of that before you acted the way you did."

Julia bit the inside of her lower lip and controlled the words she wanted to say. "Mother, please."

"Nothing happened," Elizabeth said shortly after a moment of drawing out the silence. "The doctor said she isn't ready to be released from the treatment program. But," she added, "her progress has been very good."

"I'm glad."

"I'm sure you are. Hannah, you don't need to bring the game home with you. Leave it here."

"Can we play it next time, Auntie Julia?" the little girl asked.

"Of course you can," Julia replied, and bent to give her a hug. The little girl felt solid in her arms. Healthy. Real. Amid the wreckage of her life, that was something to be thankful for. "Bye, sweetie. Go with Nanna, and give Daddy a kiss for me."

She hugged Ryan. No matter how many times she felt his thin little body, she couldn't get over the feeling he'd be snatched from them at any second. But as long as Madeleine was in treatment, she supposed, he had time to get his strength back. What would happen when her sister returned to her family, she just didn't know. That was up to the doctors and the judge.

And God.

The reminder whispered in her mind as the two children trooped down the steps after their grandmother and climbed into her car.

She'd taken God for granted, she realized. She'd seen Him merely as the wallpaper backing her life, and not built the kind of relationship that would sustain her faith through a time like this. If she had, would her family's withdrawal hurt so much?

Maybe. Maybe not.

She curled into a ball in the corner of the couch. "I hate that she treats me this way."

Ross pulled one of her bare feet toward him and began to rub it, his strong fingers sure on all the nerve endings. "From what I saw, she treated you that way before."

"What?" She frowned at him, and tried to take her foot back. He hung on to it. "That tickles."

"Give me the other one."

She gave in, and he continued his skillful ministrations.

"I mean her treatment of you hasn't changed. From what I saw, anyway. It's just that you've moved out of her shadow enough to be able to see it."

Julia fell silent. At least she was moving somewhere. Not that she liked the view very much.

Kailey put the game board on the coffee table. "Daddy. Julia. Play Candy Land with me."

Ross smiled at his daughter with such love that Julia felt her own heart swell. "I never saw such a kid for learning stuff."

"I have to learn stuff," Kailey said, as if this were the most obvious thing in the world. "I have to catch up."

"Catch up to whom, sweetie?" Julia asked. "You can go at your own pace. You don't need to catch up to anybody."

Kailey shook her head. "Hannah knows Candy Land and she's just a little kid. I want to learn what other kids do."

Could she learn from a seven-year-old? Julia wondered. Maybe the thing to do was to absorb as much as possible so she, too, could reach out and grab life the way Kailey was doing. Maybe she, too, needed to catch up so that she could walk through life with Ross without feeling as though her side of the path were a step lower than his.

Maybe she just had to stop talking about it and simply open her heart to the One who had the wisdom and love to lead her in the way she should go.

Ross and Kailey were already bent over the board. He glanced at her, and in his eyes she saw the kind of quiet love that wouldn't demand, that would only point the way. The kind of love she could trust to do the right thing for her, if she'd only let him.

"Your move," he said.

She reached for the game pieces. "Yes," she said. "I believe it is."

* * * * *

Love Inspired®

HIS SAVING GRACE

BY

LYN COTE

His right-hand woman had been silently in love with him for years, but computer system designer Jack Lassater was clueless. A sense of duty prevented Gracie Petrov from resigning when he needed her the most. Could her strong faith help Jack reconcile with the father who'd abandoned him? And show Jack their partnership could mix business…and marriage?

Don't miss

HIS SAVING GRACE
On sale April 2004

Available at your favorite retail outlet.

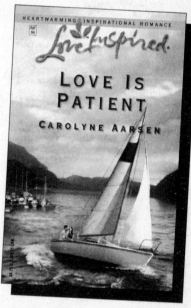

Love Inspired ®

HERO IN HER HEART

BY

MARTA PERRY

Nolie Lang's farm, a haven for abandoned animals
gave hope to the disabled. Working with the injure
firefighter Gabriel Flanaghan, who refused to
depend on anyone, including God, tested her faith
Could Nolie make Gabe see that, no matter his
injuries, he would always be a hero in her heart?

Don't miss

HERO IN HER HEART

On sale April 2004

Available at your favorite retail outlet.

LIHIHH-TR

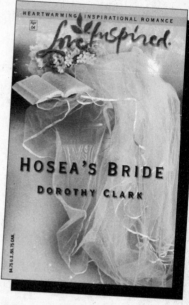

Love Inspired®

HOSEA'S
BRIDE

BY

DOROTHY
CLARK

Overcoming a traumatic past was easy once
Angela Warren found the Lord. But her reformed life
was threatened when a new pastor was appointed—
the man who'd saved her years ago. Trying to avoid
the persistent and romantic Hosea Stevens was difficult,
as was dealing with her own turbulent feelings. Could
Hosea bring her back to his church…as his bride?

Don't miss

HOSEA'S BRIDE
On sale April 2004

Available at your favorite retail outlet.

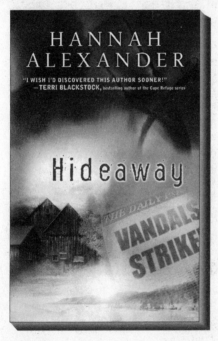

A captivating story of love, loss and faith regained,
by acclaimed author

LENORA WORTH

**"Lenora Worth orchestrates...romance in her classical,
emotionally rich style." —*Romantic Times***

Alisha Emerson is drawn to Dover Mountain, situated in the beautiful
north Georgia mountains where blue spruce trees reach up to heaven.
There, she feels a sense of healing and communion, and she hopes
she and her unborn child will thrive in this idyllic setting.

A man without hope and without God, Jared Murdoch is attempting to
flee his demons when unforeseen circumstances compel him to help
Alisha deliver her son safely, and he decides to stay in Dover Mountain.

But when they encounter the darker elements of village life,
Alisha and Jared begin to wonder—is Dover Mountain
really the sylvan sanctuary they thought initially,
or a much more sinister place?

Available May 2004.

Steeple
Hill®

www.steeplehill.com

SLW514-TR